Table of Contents

PROLOGUE 4
CHAPTER ONE 7
CHAPTER TWO 10
CHAPTER THREE 13
CHAPTER FOUR 16
CHAPTER FIVE 19
CHAPTER SIX 22
CHAPTER SEVEN 25
CHAPTER EIGHT 28
CHAPTER NINE 31
CHAPTER TEN 34
CHAPTER ELEVEN 37
CHAPTER TWELVE 40
CHAPTER THIRTEEN 43
CHAPTER FOURTEEN 46
CHAPTER FIFTEEN 49
CHAPTER SIXTEEN 52
CHAPTER SEVENTEEN 55
CHAPTER EIGHTEEN 58
CHAPTER NINETEEN 61
CHAPTER TWENTY 64
CHAPTER TWENTY-ONE 67
CHAPTER TWENTY-TWO 70
CHAPTER TWENTY-THREE 73
CHAPTER TWENTY-FOUR 76
CHAPTER TWENTY-FIVE 80
CHAPTER TWENTY-SIX 83
CHAPTER TWENTY-SEVEN 86
CHAPTER TWENTY-EIGHT 89

CHAPTER TWENTY-NINE	93
CHAPTER THIRTY	96
CHAPTER THIRTY-ONE	100
CHAPTER THIRTY-TWO	103
CHAPTER THIRTY-THREE	106
CHAPTER THIRTY-FOUR	110
CHAPTER THIRTY-FIVE	113
CHAPTER THIRTY-SIX	117
CHAPTER THIRTY-SEVEN	120
CHAPTER THIRTY-EIGHT	123
CHAPTER THIRTY-NINE	126
CHAPTER FORTY	129
CHAPTER FORTY-ONE	132
CHAPTER FORTY-TWO	135
CHAPTER FORTY-THREE	138
CHAPTER FORTY-FOUR	141
CHAPTER FORTY-FIVE	144
CHAPTER FORTY-SIX	147
CHAPTER FORTY-SEVEN	151
CHAPTER FORTY-EIGHT	154
CHAPTER FORTY-NINE	158
CHAPTER FIFTY	161
EPILOGUE	164

Dedicated to all my wonderful readers. This is for you as much as it is me.

HER LIFE

Chloe Pile

PROLOGUE

OLIVIA

I breathed out, my breath showing like puffs of smoke in the cold September air. It was still summer—according to British calendars, but there was a chill in the air that seemed to intertwine with my mood.

My eighteenth birthday is soon, and my parents couldn't decide which of them would buy me my first house. It's weird; they're acting as if I'm a college student going on taxpayer.

The constant arguments between my divorced parents had worn me down to a stump, and I'd soon cave inwards and collapse into myself. So I grabbed a jacket, slipped into my boots, took my phone and my keys, and left my mum's house—heading to the local park.

Originally, when they divorced, one of my parents would keep our original house and one would move out. But my parents couldn't deal with that; they sold the house and both moved out. My dad now lives a twenty-minute bus journey from my mum, who stayed in the same area. I didn't have to change schools; I stayed predominantly with my mother, leaving father-daughter time for the holidays and weekends.

I pulled my jacket tighter around my chest, walking towards a bench in the middle of the local park. I sat down on it and watched as the swings rattled in the wind.

My phone blared in my pocket; another incoming call from one of my parents. I sighed and declined it like I had done the other twenty times.

The argument today had been relentless. They'd been going at it since I got home from college on Friday. Problem is, they each want to be the starring role in my life, but there's two of them and there could only be one. My dad had started saying he would pay for the house since my mother hasn't had a stable job since their marriage ended three years ago. But my mother refused to take his 'charity work', screaming that all he ever did was look down on her. I don't understand why they just can't *both* put in money for a house.

Tears streamed down my cheeks and I wiped them away with the sleeve of my jacket. I had stupidly picked up the thinnest one. I sighed and slumped back against the back of the bench. My phone buzzed in my pocket, alerting me that I had a text. I wiped away a stray tear before fishing it out of my pocket.

From: Dylan.
Your mum has called me a thousand times, the hell are you, Clark?

I smiled and stifled a laugh. My freezing fingers composed a message back.
From: Olivia.
She's insane. Hope your mum still has a working ear. I'm out on a walk. Don't worry.

I put my phone down on the side of the bench and shifted around so that I was sitting cross-legged. I was going to be an adult in four months, and all I could do was sit in a children's park and wallow in the pities of life. It sounds like a typical Olivia Clark tragedy.

Neither of my parents had found love again after their divorce. At least, that's what *I* think. My mum thinks that my dad is off with some A-class supermodel. I told her to stop reading gossip magazines.

I watched the clouds above me inch forward in the wind, which would soon turn into strong gales; I would be caught in it if I didn't move. They covered the moon as if they were sheets of wool, strewn across the light, letting only tiny flickers through.

I pulled my legs up to my chest, resting my chin on my knees and huffing. I watched as a magpie perched on the railings of the children's park. It seemed to be pecking at something, but I couldn't tell what.

Since the divorce, my friends have been one of my main support systems. Not only this, but my friendship group seemed to span out infinitely when my parents divorced. Some would mistake me for the popular, perfect girl because of it. But really, I only had a few close friends who I knew I could trust. The rest were moral supporters, who smiled in the corridors, in the streets, liked my Instagram posts. Those kinds of things.

My phone buzzed again.

From: Dylan.

I'm being serious, Clark. Where are you? Before your parents call the police.

I rolled my eyes. Dylan had always been a close friend. I can't remember a time when he wasn't my friend. In primary school, there had been a massive scandal when a rumour broke out that Dylan had a crush on me, but he denied all accusations and told everyone we were just friends. It looked like a celebrity scandal from where I had stood in the playground, watching children circle around him like reporters. People always listened to Dylan, it was a fact. People talked to me, sure, but they didn't hear my words, just saw a friendly opportunity. Dylan had real charisma, the type that's hard to find today.

From: Olivia.

You're such a sap. I'm in Parky Park.

'Parky Park' was an endearing joke from when we were about five. I have no idea how it came about—either I couldn't pronounce the real name of the park, or Dylan couldn't, but he denies that he was ever inept.

Dylan and I were only two in our friendship group. There were five of us in total and we have been a close unit since year nine. Our friendship has a great dynamic; although we don't go to the same college, we see each other at least three times a week, since we all live close to each other. I was content within my friendship group. And then I had to go back home.

My phone buzzed yet again as the trees shook behind me as if they were trembling in the wind. The sun had set ages ago, and the streetlights in the park provided a dim light.

From: Dylan.

Stay right where you are. I'm getting an Uber round.

Dylan could be carefree sometimes, and then worrisome the other times. It stressed me out more than it stressed him out. I slipped my phone back into my jacket pocket and rose from the bench, walking towards the park entrance so that I could meet him there. It was a long walk since I had strayed so far from the entrance. When a drop of water hit my forehead and ran down the bridge of my nose, I knew that it was time to go—it was beginning to rain.

I was too busy shielding my face from the rest of the downpour to care about a twig snapping to the side of me. But when it happened again, I turned. I could see nothing for a metre out. I sighed, taking my blurred vision with me as I walked.

Suddenly, a shadow streamed across my vision, looking as if it had leapt out from the side. I peered out from under my hand, trying to understand what the shadow was. It was a person. Then I saw the sharp green eyes and the mess of curls that were matted onto her head.

"Aless-"

A sharp pain struck me in the chest. I fell to the floor and my vision became even more blurred than before.

Confusedly, I recalled the last few moments in my head. I had seen Alessia Trent. And she had stabbed me.

And then it all went black.

CHAPTER ONE

Beeping was heard beside me. My first instinct was to groan and flail around in my bed, trying to look for the source of the noise. My hand hit something and knocked it off the side—the beeping stopped. I smiled and relaxed into my bed. And then I felt a stabbing pain in my stomach.

Then it all came back. As a bad dream always does. Fast, and later than it should do. I shot up in my bed, pulling up my pyjama top, which I don't remember putting on, and looking for a stab wound. There was nothing there. I placed my palm over my racing heart and exhaled in relief.

But then I looked up. *This isn't my room.* A sudden thought jolted through my head, echoing in a voice that...wasn't mine.

Great, school again.

I frowned. *School?* I don't go to school. I finished school earlier this year with two C's, two B's, four A's and three A*'s. *Pretty sure I'm finished.*

Nonetheless, I swung my feet over the edge of the bed and pattered over to the window. I peered out of it. *Where on earth am I?* I had no idea what street I was on, but I vaguely recognised my surroundings.

Frowning, I turned around and found a mirror. I moved over to it, ready to relax my unruly brown hair. Then I froze. The girl looking back at me *wasn't me.* I fell backwards in shock and landed on the floor with a thud. Now closer to the mirror than before, I pushed myself off the reflection so fast that I nearly broke my hand. Or—*her* hand.

I swallowed. Staring back at me wasn't brown haired, brown eyes Olivia Clark; it was brown-haired, green-eyed Alessia Trent. The girl who had stabbed me in my nightmare.

I sat as far away from the mirror as I possibly could, just staring at the reflection in the mirror for what seemed like hours. Then, I took a deep breath and crawled back over to the mirror. At first, I stopped a metre away, but I needed to know—I need to know if this was real or if it was just a facade.

I got so close that, when I sat cross-legged, my knees touched the mirror. I tucked my legs underneath me and rose onto my knees, leaning into the mirror. Green eyes, light skin, brown hair, gorgeous lips, a button nose. I was Alessia Trent.

I held onto the chest of drawers beside me to stabilise myself as I pulled myself up off the floor. *What the hell is going on? Am I dead? Is this the afterlife?*

If that nightmare was real, I am inside my killer's body. A shiver ran down my—Alessia's—spine. I reached up and touched the porcelain skin that covered Alessia's face. It was soft and completely clear of any blemishes. *She's pretty, I'll give her that.*

But through Alessia's eyes, everything was dimmer. It was as if someone turned the contrast up, the brightness down, and the clarity up. Everything was so dark, and nothing around her held any beauty. It was all strikingly horrid. I blinked.

Okay. Fine. I'll play your game. You stab me; I die; now I live your life.

"I'm giving you one day, and then I'm either dead, or you put me back in my body." I had no idea who I was talking to, but I was more caught up in the fact that *Alessia's* voice spoke my thoughts.

I turned away from the mirror, wanting to see nothing more. I picked up the alarm clock that I had killed and grimaced as I saw that I had broken off some random plastic part. But it still ticked, so I guessed that it was fine. The time read 7:30 am. School started at 8:30 am. I had no idea where I was, and so no idea how to get to school; I was going to be late.

I closed my eyes, inhaled, and then exhaled. I am Alessia Trent, not Olivia Clark, and I *will* survive this school day.

I span around in her room in a daze for a few moments. I had never been in Alessia's room before—never mind her *house*; I had never really been close to her. I went straight to her wardrobe, but upon seeing an array of really extravagant frocks, I shut the doors.

Anticipation burning throughout me, I walked over to the drawers beside her vanity and rifled around in there, searching for her winter uniform. *Wait, is it still October?*

My heart hammered in my chest and I grew dizzy very quickly. I backed over to her bed and sat down, feeling as the springs complained under my weight. Alessia's phone buzzed on her bedside table. I picked it up hesitantly, seeing that it was just a reminder, which read '*wake Dad up at 7:40*'.

Instinctively, I placed my thumb over the home screen button, staring down at the phone with wide eyes when it opened. I mean, of course it would. But with Alessia's thumb—it was just a shock; I really *am* Alessia Trent.

The first thing that I noticed when it opened was the date on the calendar—Monday 11th. I did a double-take. It was Saturday when I died. And it was the 17th of September.

I hesitantly opened the calendar, and it showed me the date. The day, the month, and the year. All were different. It was Monday, the 10th of October 2016—a whole year ago. I think I almost passed out then and there.

Breathe in, breathe out. Okay, if it's last year then—

Exams are coming up.

Shoot, *do I really have to go through this again?*

I sighed, placing the phone down and plugging it into the charger I found on the floor. Now I had to wake up Alessia's dad, supposedly, and I had no idea where he was.

I left Alessia's room and looked around. Which room? I felt like an intruder.

I bet he's passed out downstairs.

It was another thought from Alessia, and one I greeted gratefully; I now knew the whereabouts of her dad.

I found the staircase and walked down the stairs, cringing as every step creaked. When I got to the bottom, I had to jump over a swarm of empty beer bottles. I walked past the front door and felt a slight breeze coming in. I frowned as I immediately found a large gap between the door and the wall. These aren't suitable living conditions.

I continued walking around her home and found her living room quickly; the loud blare of the television gave it away. I crept over to her dad, who reeked of beer and smoke. I switched the television off and shook his shoulder. It didn't work. So I did it more roughly. He woke up slightly and started swearing. He saw me and grunted.

"Move." He waved around at me and I dodged his hand, falling into the table as I backed up. He picked up his mobile from the side and switched it on. Then he swore.

"You brat!" He exclaimed, his eyes on fire as he jolted upwards. My eyes widened and I began to move backwards.

"You woke me up late!" He yelled, shoving the phone into my face, displaying the time as 7:46 am.

"It's only six minutes," I muttered. Then a fury broke out in him, and in one flash of a movement, he threw me against the door. The door handle caught my back and I yelped. But he wasn't done. I screeched and ran for my life, fleeing the way I came. I jumped over the beer bottles as his fingers scraped the fabric of my top. I squealed; my legs not moving fast enough as I sprinted up the stairs.

"I'll get you later, brat!" Alessia's dad yelled up the stairs and I flinched as I ran to Alessia's room, slamming the bedroom door behind me.

My heart was hammering against my chest as I slid down the wood of the door, leaning my head back against it. I can't do this. Alessia's life already looks horrid and it's only 8 am on a Monday morning. I closed my eyes and took deep breaths.

"I promised one day. And that's all you're getting. Then I want out." I spoke, as if to Alessia, or to whoever put me in this godforsaken body.

Then I pushed myself off the floor, and prepared to go to school as Alessia Trent, and not as Olivia Clark. One day.

CHAPTER TWO

There were various holes in Alessia's schoolbag, so I chucked it into the corner of the room and searched for another one. I found a pretty cute black backpack that looked and smelt as if it had never been used before. I checked Alessia's planner before rifling around on her shelf for the right school books.

Once the bag was done, I stood up from the floor and admired how Alessia looked in the school uniform. To be honest, she had never looked better. I had managed to get Alessia's unruly hair up into a half-up, half-down hairstyle that contained her hair but still let it frame her face. I had done my usual makeup on her. Not that she really needed it.

I found her school shoes by her bin and peered at them. They weren't bad, but they also didn't look clean. I sucked it up and pulled them on. I chucked deodorant, spare makeup and a hairbrush into Alessia's bag before I faced the door. I had heard the front door slam about ten minutes ago, but I was still absolutely terrified. I gripped Alessia's phone tightly, noting that I only had ten minutes to get to school.

And then I broke free.

I sprinted down the stairs, leapt over the beer bottles, ripped the door open and slammed it behind me. I breathed out a sigh of relief. Now, to school.

Having no idea where I was going, I decided to just walk whilst I searched up the school on Google Maps. I looked up to see where I was going briefly when I spotted a newsagent. *Score;* I could ask for directions in there. I slipped my phone into my pocket and opened the door, hearing the bell chime as I did so.

"Lessie, dear!" I jumped in shock but tried to make it look casual as I took to the first aisle I saw.

"Alessia, aren't you even going to say hi to your old Nells!" The woman laughed and my eyebrows shot up at Alessia's name. I slowly rose from where I had bent down to look at some prices and peered at the old woman at the till. She laughed at me so I waved awkwardly.

"Hi, Nells!" I grinned, hoping that I had the right name. When the woman chuckled, I figured that it was her name.

"What brings you here so early, Less?" She asked as I walked into another aisle. *Oh, you know, just trying to find directions to a school that I've been going to for over four years, nothing much.*

"Getting breakfast," I replied. "And lunch," I added, after remembering that I hadn't packed anything.

The woman laughed, "that's a little adventurous for you, eh?" She joked and I joined in with her laughter. I found a croissant for 79p, a sandwich for £1.50 and a drink for £1, then I realised that I didn't know if I even had money on me. I put the items down and rifled through Alessia's blazer.

I found an envelope, opening it with a frown. Seeing what was inside, I did a double-take and swore under my breath. Enclosed was eight £50 notes. *What the hell?*

Well I, couldn't bloody well use those in a newsagents.

So I put the envelope away and did some more searching, finding a crumpled up five pound note. *Score.* I picked up my items and carried them over to 'Nells'. She grinned at me and scanned the goods as I took my bag off my shoulders.

"That looks new." She commented, pointing at my bag.

I grinned. "Yeah, I picked it up in a sale over the weekend." I smiled and 'Nells' grinned at me.

"That's £3.29, dear." She said and I handed over the five pound note. She registered it before giving me back my change.

"Hey, Nells," I spoke hesitantly, and the woman rose an eyebrow as she handed me my change. "I heard some silly talk that the road on the way to school is closed, is that true?" I asked. I was placing a real bet here. I just hoped that if I got this whole thing completely wrong that I could lie myself out of the situation.

The woman laughed, the creases around her eyes reaching out as she did so. I put my change into my blazer pocket and undid my bag.

"Honey, even if the roads were closed, it wouldn't matter. You love your forest shortcut too much to ever use the roads." She joked and I breathed out a sigh of relief that she didn't pick up on my weirdness. Then I joined in with her laughter as I put my food away.

I slipped my bag back onto my back. "Well, I should get going, or I'll be late," I said with a grin.

"Like you'd care." The woman joked and I chuckled before waving and leaving. Once the door was shut behind me, I sprung into action.

Forest shortcut. Forest shortcut. Where the hell is the forest shortcut? Damn it. Damn it.

I crossed the road and took a right toward what looked like woodland. When I rounded the corner, there it was—'*Dearn Forest*'.

I held nothing back and pelted towards it, not changing my speed as I dashed through the forest. Alessia Trent will *not* be late. I don't care *who* controls her body.

I spotted a clearing and forced myself to go faster. I slowed down when I got there, jogging through the exit. Across the road, I spotted our school—here we are.

I checked the road three times before running across it, speeding down the school drive, arriving at the school entrance about five seconds before the first bell rang. I watched as a receptionist silently applauded me as I rushed in. I laughed in response but didn't have much time to banter.

I walked into Alessia's registration class as everyone was settling down. That's when I should have realised. Not only was this Alessia's registration class, but it was also mine. This was Olivia Clark's registration class.

Instinctively, I moved over to the far left of the room, where I usually sat during registration time. But when I saw that it was occupied, I realised that *I* was not Olivia Clark, freezing when I saw the *real* Olivia Clark.

Yes. I, Olivia Clark, in Alessia Trent's body, am seeing *myself. That's* when I realised that this was Olivia Clark's registration class, as well as Alessia Trent's.

I watched as the real Olivia Clark burst out into laughter suddenly, shoving Dylan's shoulder. A spark of jealousy shot through Alessia and I frowned. I couldn't understand

Alessia's emotions, or how I could possibly feel them, but I was suddenly staring at my group of friends.

Ked, one of my friends, soon caught me staring. "Earth to Alessia." He waved his hand around in front of me.

"Trent, sit down and look alive, please." The teacher hollered from the front of the room, and the whole class erupted into laughter. To me, it sounded like a joke, and I even found it funny. But to Alessia, it was an attack. Seeing all those people laugh at her made her feel inferior and silly. She hated being the centre of attention. She hated being belittled. And so her legs started working before I told them to. She found a spot at the very back on the right side and sat down. On her own.

I thought Alessia had some kind of friends, doesn't everyone? Or at least people that she can talk to. But as seconds turned to minutes and minutes turned to boredom, I realised that Alessia really *was* alone.

With my chin on my hand, I found myself gazing over at the real me and my friends. Whilst Alessia longed for Dylan, I longed for my old life back. I sighed. *One day.*

CHAPTER THREE

By the time that lunch rolled around, I realised that Alessia really didn't have any friends at all. 'Nells' seemed to be her only acquaintance, and maybe the receptionists. I was walking down the corridor to find a place to sit in my suddenly lonely life when the *real* Olivia Clark rounded the corner in front of me, nestled into Dylan's side as he held her close with his arm. She had her arm looped through Kiara's arm and was laughing yet again. Kiara was another close friend of mine, but that didn't matter now; I was not myself anymore.

To Alessia, it seemed that I never stopped laughing; there was never a time when I wasn't happy. Whilst the rest of the world was dim, in her vision, I seemed to radiate perfectness. To her ears, my laugh bounced off a million walls. It irritated her, but only because she noticed how much Dylan loved it. I had never noticed that.

She hated that I seemed to have Dylan sucked in and that he appeared happier when I was. I had no idea that she felt so jealous of me, and especially over Dylan.

"Guys, let me check my locker." Tommy, yet another one of my friends, announced and I frowned. I couldn't remember this day, suddenly. They stopped beside Tommy's locker, and I watched from afar as they all peered into it as he opened it. The real Olivia Clark's eyebrows shot up and she grinned.

"Score!" She yelled as Tommy pulled out his science textbook and held it up like a Grammy award. I stifled a laugh at his endearment.

I watched as the real Olivia Clark began to say something, leaning against a locker. What I saw through Alessia's eyes surprised me—everyone seemed to be paying attention to me. Everyone was so engrossed with me and what I was saying, to the extent that when I smiled, they smiled too.

Alessia hated that. Alessia hated that I seemed to absorb all the attention in the corridor. And she hated it even more that Dylan was giving all his attention to *me*. She noticed that he always seemed to be the closest to me, and her eyes couldn't help but trail down to Dylan's fingers, which were playing with my sleeve. She acknowledged that Dylan always seemed to find a way to touch me—and I had never acknowledged that. She was jealous. I hadn't known that before, but I do now.

I watched as the group started a new discussion whilst walking away from the lockers, and in my direction. Seeing my own face, my own life, through someone else's eyes was so surreal. I could notice everything in one second. The way Kiara blushed when Tommy winked at her, the way Ked smiled at everyone he saw, the way that Dylan was such a gentleman to, not only me, but to every girl he set eyes on. I could tell why Alessia fancied him. I also noticed how completely oblivious Olivia Clark is. She sees everyone but she just doesn't see enough.

The real Olivia Clark's eyes met mine, and her eyes sparkled with curiosity. I didn't see what happened next, but I was suddenly shoved back into the lockers, the real Olivia Clark being the only person who was in front of me at that moment. But...I would never—I wouldn't do that. I've never shoved anyone.

But Alessia believed that I had done; she was furious. Anger boiled up inside of her, and what she thought next scared me. It was something of pure hatred, but mostly revenge. She wanted revenge.

I found it hard to see anything as clear when Alessia was so intent in believing the worst about anything. But I did it. I almost felt her anger simmer down as my attention refocused, and I saw the real Olivia Clark slapping Tommy a million times over.

She was screaming, "Stop pushing me!" As she slapped him on the arm once more. Alessia Trent needed to stop jumping to conclusions based on what she couldn't see. I hadn't shoved her.

No matter how it happened, though, I *had* fallen into Alessia, and I didn't apologise. And in Alessia's mind, this was the beginning of the end.

With that, I walked off to eat. *Where does Alessia usually sit? Where do loners usually sit?* I sighed and pushed the door to the cafeteria open. I took a deep breath and looked around.

"Alessia-Lessia-Less," someone approached me, right in front of my face, until I had to back away for comfort. "Less friends by the day." I rolled my eyes at the joke, which was spoken by the school's biggest idiot, Leon Junior. Crap name for a crap person. *Yes, okay, you've caught me out. I hate him.*

In year nine, when he had arrived at the school, he had some kind of...infatuation with me. And I fell for it. We went on a few 'dates', and then he made a mockery of me in front of the whole cafeteria, denying that he ever felt anything for me since I was too "frigid and boring" for him. I had run out of the hall, tears streaming down my face. Dylan wanted to punch him; I told him that the action would probably *fix* his face.

So, from then onwards, he became a player and the biggest regret of my life. He was probably the only person in the school I hated. But it seemed that Alessia hated him too, as I soon heard profanities flitter around her skull.

"Go away, Leon, don't you have a girl that you need to keep occupied?" I waved my hand in his face as if to dismiss him before finding an empty table. Leon followed me over to it.

"Who said you could talk to me, huh?" I turned around to give him a disgusted look before putting my bag down on the table.

"I don't need permission to talk." I replied with anger.

"Oh, yes you do, Less-Less, aren't you aware of your position in society by now?" He asked, shoving my shoulder, sending me reeling back into a wall.

"It seems I've forgotten." I spat, "perhaps you'd like to remind me." I shoved his hand away.

"You're nothing. And you being in this cafeteria violates all those who *actually* mean something. So take your life's work," he picked up my bag and chucked it towards the exit of the cafeteria. "And get the hell out of here." He seethed, taking steps closer to me so that my back was pressed against the wall. Suddenly, the veins in Alessia's body closed up, and her lungs constricted. *She's claustrophobic.*

But I was not. I shoved Leon away from me, walked over to Alessia's bag, picked it up, dusted it off, and slung it over my shoulder. Then I did something that Alessia would never have done.

"Thank you for watching, everyone," I announced, and everyone who wasn't already looking at me stared. "I see how important your reputation is to you." I spat before I took my leave. Running out the doors, though, I bumped into someone. *Dylan.*

Suddenly, tears were pricking at my eyes. The whole group stood there, just staring. They hadn't helped. The real Olivia Clark didn't step in as she should've. Like I *thought* she would have. And Dylan the gentleman didn't even break a *sweat.*

I intended for my words to be spoken to all of them, but my eyes were only on Dylan. "I expected more from you." I hissed and Dylan's eyes became jaded by something had never seen in him before. He felt guilty, yet he couldn't say sorry. None of them could. I made sure that they all knew just how much today cost me, and how they had taken apart in it, before shoving past them and leaving the cafeteria.

Alessia Trent's life isn't what I expected it to be. She wakes up and gets beaten by her 'dad'; at school, she is bullied by the kids; when she cries, no one cares.

I guess now I know why she carries around a broken bag, she doesn't want to get her other ones ruined. Because that's what those cruel people did to that bag. And nobody stopped them.

CHAPTER FOUR

By the end of the day, I had been called more names than I had cares left to give. The truth is, Alessia Trent has a crap school life, and I never cared to notice. And *that* makes me a bad person; you don't need to make the rude comments to be the cause of someone's unhappiness, you could be a bystander who just didn't do anything at all. Doing nothing is the problem.

I crossed the road, pulling my bag up my shoulder, heading towards the same forest that got me here in the first place. During my walk, I spotted a huge grey rock, with many indentations and carvings on its skin. I walked closer and stood by it, just stopping to ponder on today's horrors. That's when I saw it. Carved onto the rock was.

'Alessia was here.'

I brushed my index finger over it and sighed. I wish Alessia could be here right now, too, so I wouldn't have to live this miserable life anymore. If she were here, her body and her life would be hers...and then maybe mine would be mine again. I can't do this again, not another day.

I left the rock and continued onwards through the forest, twigs snapping under my feet. Soon, I could hear the buzz of the street once more, cars whizzing past and oblivious people living in an oblivion of hatred. I shook my head, kicking a stone at my feet.

I walked down the pavement, with feet that weren't mine, and crossed the road, turning to the left. Alessia's miserable house came into view and fear suddenly crackled up within me. *What if her dad is home? What if he* isn't*? I don't even want to know.*

I trudged along what was left of the gravel path and rummaged around in Alessia's blazer for her keys. When I found them, I pushed them into the lock, then froze. Locked around the key was a photo, and I brought it closer to my face to get a better look. The photo was of a woman holding a young child. If I could take my guesses, I'd say that the picture was of her mother and Alessia. I guess her parents, like mine, are also complicated. Just more so.

I twisted the key and hesitantly pushed the door open. It got jammed so I shoved it, stumbling in as it flew open.

"Ay, Bill, the stripper hath arrived!" Some random man yelled and I looked up, seeing a man dressed raggedly. He held a can of what I guessed was beer and was bellowing at me as I stood up. Alessia's father leaned around the wall to see the commotion and I cowered back. *Oh, shoot.*

He laughed coldly. "Ah, no, that's just my dismal attempt of a daughter." He narrowed my eyes at me, so I yanked the keys out of the lock, closed the door, and started for the stairs.

"Perhaps for the after party, then." The man joked as I walked up the stairs as calmly as I could. I felt disgusted; is this what Alessia was subjected to in the comfort of her own home?

I got to Alessia's room and shut the bedroom door as I sighed. Her life was a disgrace—there were so many things wrong. Her life would never change, at least, not by *my* hands. I tried today, yet it didn't make the slightest bit of a difference. No, someone outside this damned body would have to help her.

Then I wondered, what *is* the problem? I stared in the mirror. There's no way that she's ugly, unlike what all the kids say at school; Alessia is *gorgeous*. From her pale green eyes to her pixie-like frame. She is not ugly.

What could she have done wrong? Is she just labelled as the school's punching bag because no one else signed up for it? That's disgusting.

I sighed. It was 4 pm. What the hell did Alessia do for dinner when her dad was home? I stared at her reflection in the mirror once more. Maybe there is a reason why Alessia is so slim. I shook away the thoughts and assured myself that I would eat dinner. Eventually.

I slipped off Alessia's bag, blazer and shoes. Then I pulled her phone out of her pocket and fell down onto her broken bed. There was absolutely nothing on her phone. I mean, she had all the important apps, the social networks. But nothing—no notifications. It was like a ghost town on her phone—like an entire population of a city wiped out and it was just...*silent*. I was so used to the buzzes, the ringing, and the growing numbers. The silence chilled me.

I roamed around on her phone for a while, trying to find out exactly who I had become. In her notes, I found a list of people, phone numbers and addresses. There wasn't a title to the list so I just assumed they were misplaced contacts or something. I left the note and started to read through the next note. It was another list. But this one had my blood freezing. They were names that I recognised.

Rosie Willis
Chad Young
Leon Junior
Thomas Gordon
Kiara Beckett
Hilary Dean
Kieron Hunter
Chelsey Williams
Olivia Clark
Dylan Evans

I froze. Tommy, Kiara, Ked, Dylan. Those were my friends. And worst of all, *I* was on the list too. Olivia Clark was on Alessia Trent's list. And now I inhabit her body.

Maybe all these people inhabited her body too? *No, that's the craziest idea yet, Olivia.*

Some had stars next to, and some had lines. Tommy and Kiara had stars, whereas the rest of my friendship group had lines—except for Dylan.

Confused, I sighed, dropping the phone onto the mattress beside me and placing a palm to my pounding head.

Trying to distract myself, I opened Alessia's planner and it immediately fell apart. I stared at it hopelessly for a few moments before sighing and getting up to find another notebook. After filing through her drawers for ten minutes, I finally found an A5 notebook and decided it would have to do, and then I fingered through the tatters of her old planner and copied every important and recent piece of information down.

She had a keyword test in Religious Studies the next day, and although I hoped it would never come to that, it was probable that I'd have to take that test. As Alessia.

Hearing the men downstairs still, I decided that now wouldn't be a good time for dinner, and so I would shower instead.

I walked into her bathroom and locked the door, then my search began. I pulled out shampoo after shampoo, trying to find one that I trusted. She didn't have many conditioners, but she did have a very lonely looking hair mask sitting at the back of her cupboard.

After exchanging an old sponge for a new one and putting a new bottle of shower gel into her shower, I pulled back the curtain and peered at it.

Her shower actually didn't look as bad as I expected, or as bad as the rest of the house looked.

I spotted her face-wash sitting on a shelf in the shower and added the items I had found to it.

Then I stripped. I didn't look into the mirror; it felt weird to. Then I stepped in, shut the curtain behind me, and prepared to shower as Alessia Trent.

CHAPTER FIVE

Washing her body was the hardest part, but I managed it without *too* much discomfort. 'Washing Alessia', the bestselling novel by Olivia Clark. *Dylan had always told me I had an author's mind.*

I shook off the thoughts of my life outside of this body as I shook off droplets of water. Finding a towel, I wrapped it around my body and stepped out of the shower. The room now misty, I leaned over to open the window, but was left confused when the handle came off. *Hey, at least the window* opened. Broken, but open.

I padded out of Alessia's bathroom and found a clean pair of pyjamas in her drawers. I hung up the towel and got dressed.

With no idea what to do to past the rest of the time this evening, I pulled my lip between my teeth—and then went snooping.

I found some of Alessia's old school books. The running theme seemed to be that she was appalling at English but thrived in Art, and wasn't too bad with Maths either. We were very dissimilar.

I guess Dylan is right; maybe I'm more of an English kind of girl. Whilst *he* was more of a Science guy—he didn't like to rub it in, but I knew that he got A's for all three sciences in the tests, whereas I barely skimmed a C grade.

I dropped Alessia's books and sighed. I missed Dylan. I missed that, if I were me right now, I could call him up and tell him about all my many problems. I used to do that all the time after school, but Dylan complained that all he could ever hear was my parents shouting at each other.

I pondered this for a few minutes, feeling my heartache. Exhaling, I jumped up from the floor, running over to Alessia's bed and pulling the charging lead out from Alessia's phone.

I searched through her phone for a while before I found Instagram. I opened the app, immediately a guest to her feed—which was covered in nature posts and depressing quotes. I frowned; this was a world away from Neptune, volcanic jewels and poetry—stuff that *I* liked.

I ignored it and opened up her account, frowning when there were only two posts. One was of a flower from 2014, and another of the side of her face from early 2015. Apart from that, she hadn't posted for a while now. I opened her most recent post—the picture of her and was shocked at the comments.

I followed Alessia, sure, but not when this picture was posted—I can't have been; I didn't remember it.

Reading all the comments, I was absolutely disgusted and horrified. I was so horrified, in fact, that I felt as though my heart was about crack open, that I'd have nightmares about this for nights.

Somewhere, in the back of my head, I just knew that Alessia *did* have nightmares.

Continuing to read the comments, I froze when I saw a comment from a username that I recognised.

It was a comment from Kiara. Knowing Kiara, I thought it would just be a throwaway comment about how she liked her earring. That's the Kiara I know, I'm *sure* of it.

But it wasn't.

I read it with a lump in my throat.

@olivia.cclark omg wtf look at her LOL she can't even post a whole photo of her face HAHA call your mum's surgeon ASAP hunny

I stared at the comment, reading it over and over again in shock. *What?* Kiara would never have written this. It must be her brother using her account again—he *always* did that; he even commented on a photo of me at my cousin's wedding using Kiara's account once, telling me that I looked like a spatula.

But this? She tagged me. *Why would she do that?*

I frowned down, reading the replies. Some were just from girls at school, agreeing or sending the skull emojis, some were from boys, only replying to get into Kiara's DMs, or her bed—depending on how desperate they were. There was also one next to *my* username.

I had replied.

I read it, fist clenched.

@urbabykia omg, stop! Lol

Not being able to stomach anymore, I threw the phone down onto the bed, watching it land face down. *I did that? Did I really contribute to the worst days of Alessia Trent's life?*

I took a breath, picking the phone back up, tears ready to spill as I squeezed my eyes shut, trying to return to the Instagram home screen with them shut so I didn't have to see the comments anymore.

When I opened my eyes, I took a deep breath and navigated my way to Dylan's page, smiling when I saw pictures of him, some with me in too. Still smiling, I started to message him through the DMs. But, I only got as far as 'hey'.

What do I say? '*Hi, this is your best friend living inside of Alessia Trent's body, hope you're enjoying your day*'?

I shook my head, deleting the message and swiping my finger so that our chat disappeared, but then a whole new world was unearthed before my eyes.

Alessia's DMs.

I bit my lip. I can't possibly look through these, it would be an invasion of privacy and I wouldn't like it if someone did it to me.

Instead, I let my eyes gaze down at the messages I *could* see. They were the opening to the messages, and I could read them without opening the chats.

'Aight Rat, calm your..'

I swallowed, tears coming back for a second try at escaping.

'Fix your nose before yo..'
'Stop breathing??? You h..'
'Pls just die rn LOL sto..'
'It's your fault he cheate..'
'Ugh, you pig face. Stop t..'
'Lose weight you buffal..'

I was suddenly shaking. I closed the app quickly, swearing at myself. I should not have looked at those stupid messages.

I plugged her phone back in and left it where I found it, before jumping up and looking in the mirror.

Her nose was small and cute.

Her face did not resemble a pig one bit.

And she did *not* need to lose weight.

Frustrated with people who used hate on others to get attention, I pulled up a chair and sat in front of the mirror.

Alessia did not need to change.

But maybe she could.

I sighed. "I know I told you one day," I began, "but maybe I could use another; I'm going to stop this. I know I can. There are people in the school that love Alessia or at least don't *hate* her. I'll use tomorrow as a trial run to prove it. I *know* I can do it. Those DMs won't be there tomorrow. I want to help you, Alessia."

Obviously, I got silence in response. And I'm sure that, if someone recorded me in this room, they *would* have something to bully Alessia about—this looked *insane*.

Nonetheless, there is nothing wrong with Alessia Trent, and she and everyone else should start seeing that.

I blew out a breath. I wanted to be out of this body, but not a minute before Alessia sees just how much she is loved.

With that, I tied up Alessia's hair and completed her homework to the best standards I could reach.

With everything prepared for the next school day, I slipped into bed at ten, setting her alarms with a definitive click of determination.

Alessia Trent, you will not be a victim of this anymore.

CHAPTER SIX

When Alessia's alarm blared the next morning, I was already up. I had crept downstairs at 6 am to fit breakfast into the day, though it was probably the scariest thing I'd ever done.

Now upstairs sipping a coffee, I was organising Alessia's bag, thinking about the day ahead. I would hand in all of Alessia's overdue homework, complete all her class-work, and fix this mess.

Finished with my coffee, I zipped the bag up, leaving it in the corner of Alessia's room before I took a deep breath, tip-toeing out of the room.

I silently made my way downstairs and into the kitchen, where I cleaned my mug quickly, before putting it back where I found it. Checking my watch, I saw that I had a minute before I hate to wake Alessia's dad up. I was standing over him for maybe thirty seconds and, when it was finally time, I shook him awake, letting him check the time and grunt. Then, I quickly disappeared back upstairs before he could use me as a punching bag again.

This is going to be a good day for Alessia. I've got it sorted.

Returning to Alessia's room, I got dressed into her school uniform, before starting on my usual makeup and hair. Alessia didn't seem to have much of a routine with her appearance when we were in school, but I did.

Since Alessia's hair was so curly, there were limited styles I could work it into, but I could pull it into some sort of half up, half down hairstyle. When it was up, I found a strand of ribbon and tied it around the hair-band—it was my signature look.

I kept my makeup similar to my usual, though I added a few other bits since I had time to spare.

Finished, I took a deep breath and rose from her vanity chair. I tied her shoelaces, pulled on her blazer and bag, before leaving her room with anticipation.

Reaching the bottom of the stairs, I heard Alessia's dad start to yell, but I took Alessia's mental advice and ignored him. I ran out of the front door, checking the time as I shut and locked the door behind me.

Seeing that I had just short of fifteen minutes until school started, I started for the corner shop, walking with a spring in my step.

I pushed the door open, the bell announcing my presence. "Hi, Nells!" I called, starting for the back of the shop once more, pulling a water bottle out from the fridge before walking down a few aisles and finding a sandwich and a snack.

I only had to wait in line for a few minutes before I reached the till, placing my items down as I beamed up at Nells.

She smiled in response, scanning the items, "You look happy, Lessie," she acknowledged, "does this have anything to do with that new job you had to complete yesterday?" She asked as I was rifling through my blazer for money.

I frowned, pausing, "...Job?" I asked, pulling out a five-pound note and handing it to her.

She smiled, "Don't be so modest, Lessie, you told me yourself that there's always business to handle on Thursdays. It's good, though, becoming independent; maybe one day you can get out of this place." She said, suddenly becoming grave.

I opened my bag, shoving my items in. "Right," I said, "maybe."

She smiled, handing me my change and receipt. I thanked her before heading for the door.

"Bye, Lessie!" She called out to me as I pushed the door.

"Bye, Nells!" I yelled back, "Have a good day!"

With that, I pushed the door open, frowning over what was just discussed. Alessia has a job? Well, I guess it would explain the wad of cash in her blazer pocket. But why weren't there any reminders about it on her phone? Or any shifts in the calendar?

I shook it off, checking the time on the watch I had found in a box under Alessia's bed. I had just less than ten minutes to get to school.

I smiled, before making a run for it across the forest. I slowed as I made it to the end, sorting out my hair and trying to appear casual as I emerged from the forest. I checked the time, seeing that I had more than enough time to get to registration.

I crossed the road safely, walked across the school drive and through the entrance to the school.

I rushed to the toilets to freshen up and watched as a group of girls who had been loitering by the mirrors immediately left. I frowned, not understanding what the rush was, but disappeared into the cubicle nonetheless.

When I was done, I walked round to the sinks and washed my hands before I neatened up my hair before spraying myself with perfume. I had found a similar scent to the one I usually wore—though as myself, Olivia Clark.

"I know what you did," someone said suddenly, and I looked up into the mirror to see Katy Oswalt standing behind me, arms crossed as she leaned against the wall.

"What do you mean?" I asked, turning around to face her, ignoring the fear that trembled Alessia's body. I knew Katy from German; she was loud, but no harm.

She scoffed, "I know you're the girl Shawn cheated on Lizzie with,"

I pulled a face, "*what?*" I asked. I knew that Shawn and Lizzie had broken up in Year 11, but I had no idea that this was the reason why. And with *Alessia*, too?

"You're going to pay for this, you whore." She spat, taking steps towards me.

"I didn't do it!" I yelled suddenly, but I didn't know why.

Katy gritted her teeth, "I almost believe you—but I know you're about to do the same with Dylan." She said.

I froze, "Dylan?" I asked.

"Yes," Katy said, eyes narrowing at me, "Dylan Evans." She said.

I stared at her, speechless.

"You know, *Olivia Clark's* best friend?" She asked, filling the silence as I gaped at her. She rolled her eyes, "I may not be best friends with Olivia, but you have my word that I'll warn her about this." She said, voice threatening.

I shook my head, "I have no idea what you're talking about."

Katy pulled a sour expression, "Dylan loves Olivia," she said, making my heart stop. *What? What on earth is she talking about?* "I mean, he's never said it but it's kind of obvious. If you mess this up, I'll mess *you* up."

She took more steps towards me, making me tremble on my spot. She ripped my bag from off my arm, making me stumble slightly.

"What are you doing?" I asked her as she rifled through my bag.

She smirked, "Taking compensation." She told me, pulling out my day folder and taking one of the projects out.

When I saw the sheet, I recognised it.

"Katy, please don't, that's my French homework; it took me all of yesterday to get that done," I told her, watching her smug face as I tried to snatch it out of her hands.

"Uh, down, slag, you should feel lucky that I'm not doing worse to you." She opened up the papers, peering at the work.

She laughed, "This was due in weeks ago, why are you still holding on to it?" She asked.

"I never handed it in, so, please, Katy, just give-" it was then that Katy ran the tap from the sink I had washed my hands in, throwing my work into the sink, keeping the tap on as she drenched my work.

"Katy!" I screamed, trying to push her away from the sink. She shoved me away from her, sending me flying into the sink opposite. I fell to the ground with a thud after my back had smashed into the sink.

She laughed, snapping a picture of me before she stalked out of the bathroom, "Enjoy your day!" She called over her shoulder before she left.

Silence overcame the room as I felt tears emerge from my eyes. Sniffing, I pushed myself up from the floor and pulled what was left of my homework out of the sink.

I was thinking about drying it under the dryer, but it was way too far gone, so I ended up just dumping it in the bin. I now saw why Alessia missed homework deadlines—it's not because she didn't do the homework, it's because she couldn't give it in.

I sighed, staring at myself in the mirror. I brushed my tears away, zipping my bag back up again and throwing it over my shoulder.

I wanted this day.

So I will use it wisely.

Olivia Clark is not giving up on Alessia Trent this easily.

CHAPTER SEVEN

I decided not to go to registration. Not because I was backing out, but because I now had to re-do Alessia's French homework. It was a good job I also took French for GCSE, otherwise, I really would be screwed.

I actually came out with an A in the final exam, so it wasn't exactly that I couldn't do the homework. I was just so angry. *How could someone be so rude and hateful?* It was all over something that wasn't even true.

I know I can't know that for sure, though, since I'm not Alessia, but she seemed pretty confident that she hadn't done what Katy accused her of when I was talking to Katy, so I believed her.

I managed to sign in for the morning at reception, and also find a copy of the worksheet I needed for the French homework.

I was now in the library, slaving away over a French textbook and a notebook, writing 'mon cher' and 'sourir' so many times that I almost lost my mind.

When it was almost time for lesson one, I packed my stuff away, though was not done with my French homework, and checked what lesson I had. Just as I was doing so, I heard a voice that I recognised.

Dylan's.

"..Did you get the invite to Matt's party?" He asked someone, and I turned to see that it was Olivia. A pang of jealousy hit me suddenly; most of it didn't come from me, but from Alessia.

I frowned, confused at her feelings.

The real Olivia Clark smiled, nodding as she pulled out a textbook from the shelf.

"So, mon amour, are you going?" He asked, leaning against the bookshelf. I furrowed my eyebrows, suddenly seeing a new side to Dylan—and not because I was watching him from behind him.

Olivia laughed, turning around, textbook in hand. "Just because I was helping you with that coursework, it doesn't mean you have to carry on speaking it." She said, hitting him with the book and walking away.

She went to get the book stamped, and Dylan ran after her.

"You never told me if you were going," he said.

She smiled, slipping the book into her bag, "I am," she said, patting him on the chest, "now go to biology; you'll be late." With that, she spun around and left.

Wow, I kind of look ditsy with those ribbons.

I watched as Dylan ran a hand through his hair, a smile on his face. I frowned at him for a while, trying to figure out what he was feeling now that the real Olivia had left.

I didn't have enough time for it, though, since I suddenly realised that I was about to be late to biology.

With Dylan, apparently.

In school, Dylan and I were in different classes for science, and he didn't like to boast, but he was pretty good at it. I was in the set below. But Alessia, seemingly, wasn't.

With a smile on my face, I left the library, brushing past Dylan as I did so. I headed for biology, walking into a class of commotion.

I frowned. *Is this what higher sets are like?*

Watching everyone take their seats, I soon realised I had no idea which was mine. But it wasn't hard to spot which one it was—the one with the chair pushed over and a pile of rubbish on the desk.

I sighed, grabbing the bin, sweeping the rubbish into it, before picking my chair up off the floor and brushing it down.

Just as I sat down, Dylan walked in. He smiled at the teacher, having a private word with him before he greeted all his friends.

It was weird seeing him through Alessia's eyes. Whereas I calmed whenever I saw him, Alessia seemed to dig herself a hole and lie in it, heart beating wildly.

The lesson began, and the teacher introduced a new project and group work. The class seemed excited—until the teacher explained that *he* would be choosing the pairs.

The teacher began to read out the pairings, and few complaints were made across the room.

"Alessia with Dylan," the teacher said. I shot up suddenly, frowning. *Dylan?*

As Olivia, I was desperate for a chance to connect with Dylan after two days as Alessia and no human contact with anyone.

As Alessia, I was overjoyed but also very, very nervous. I was suddenly patting my hair down and brushing the pads of my fingers under my eyes to remove any makeup lines.

"I'm sorry," someone called out suddenly, and I watched as a hand went up. It was Mia Souse. Mia was in my history class and was a really nice girl, though could definitely be less distracted in class.

I frowned at her as she started to speak, confused. "I don't think that's a good idea, Sir." She said sweetly, shrugging.

"And why would that be?" The teacher asked, lowering his notebook and raising an eyebrow at Mia.

"Well," Mia began, but it was not her that finished, it was Matt, the guy whose party it was on Friday night. Aka, *tomorrow.*

"Because Dylan shouldn't have to be around someone like Alessia."

"That is enough," the teacher said, "Mia, I'm sending you to the library, where you'll do your half of the project alone. Matt, just go to the Head Teacher's office—*now.*" The pair scrambled to their feet immediately, but not before they threw me the most disgusted of looks.

I suddenly felt ugly, an atrocity. I just wanted to bury myself into the ground. *Why was Alessia treated like this?*

When the teacher was finished reading out the pairs, he made us move into our places. Since Dylan was staring down at the project, reading over it and not moving, I packed up my stuff and moved to him.

Trying to hide my smile, I joined Dylan's side.

He looked up at me, and I relaxed into those chocolate brown eyes.

"Hi," he said, "I would've moved; I'm sorry." He said sheepishly.

"It's okay." I told him in response, smiling. When the awkward silence and staring became too much, I looked away and over at the project in front of us. Being in a lower set than Dylan, I was thoroughly confused.

"Did you want to take part A or part B?" He asked, gesturing to the worksheet. "I'll do whichever one you don't want to do." He assured me.

I pulled a face at the worksheet, glancing between it and all the equipment beside us.

"What's wrong?" He asked suddenly, laughing.

I frowned up at him, confused, "why are you laughing?" I asked him, smiling.

He shrugged, "This is going to sound weird, but I know that face."

My heart, due to Alessia's reaction, melted. "This face..?" I asked, watching him nod, "What do you mean?" I asked him.

He shook his head, "You know my friend Olivia, right?" He asked.

My heart stopped. "Uh," I said, trying to unfreeze myself, "yeah I do," I responded. In fact, I *am* her.

"Yeah, well, not to embarrass her, but she doesn't really understand science, and that's the kind of face she pulls whenever someone talks about it." He explained, making me laugh. And want to cry. I wanted to be that girl again—I wanted to be Dylan's friend, the one that cries internally when she sees maths, or teaches him all about French when we go to cute bakeries after school.

I want to be Olivia Clark again.

But, I promised this day, so I'll give Alessia this day.

"Oh," I said, grinning, "yeah, I'm slightly confused." I told him, feeling embarrassed. But he only nodded, telling me it was fine.

He then began to explain everything that Alessia knew, but I didn't. Where I was so confused that my head hurt as I listened to him, Alessia found him cute and smart. With both of those feelings, I found myself thinking that Dylan was confusing me, though that he was also cute.

When Biology ended, I was sad to let Dylan go. For a second, our conversations and jokes mirrored that of the ones we'd have when I was Olivia Clark, and I felt detached when I walked away from him.

I handed in my overdue work to the science teacher—which fried my brain last night, and I probably failed—explaining that I had lost the work and that I was very sorry.

I left the class unscathed, checking for my next lesson, which I found to be English Literature, with myself—Olivia Clark—and Kiara.

Let's do this, Alessia Trent.

CHAPTER EIGHT

I was pretty good at English Literature, in fact, almost top of my class. But as I got Alessia's homework back—which she had completed as Alessia Trent—I realised that *she* wasn't. A grade D+ was not something that I would like to receive as Olivia Clark. And so, as the teacher set another mock question for next Tuesday, I vowed that—if I still had to be Alessia for this mock—that a D+ would not be a grade she would see again.

For me, Olivia Clark in the future, GCSE's were gone, and I was already in college, a few days in. I therefore hadn't been around anything GCSE for eleven weeks. That meant I would have to focus even more, spend more hours in the library pouring myself over work and textbooks.

Alessia's social life may be in tatters, but I won't let her future become the same.

I spent the lesson in silence, refraining from saying anything since I'm sure I'd say all the wrong things. Instead, every time Olivia Clark raised her hand to say something, I jotted it down. As I knew I was pretty secure in my English work, I knew that anything I said couldn't be *too* wrong. In no time, I was pretty up to date and in the right mindset.

That was until the teacher called on me to answer a question. I froze, everyone's eyes suddenly on me, sharing sniggers and looks across the room.

"Number three, please, Alessia." Miss McKinnon requested, waiting for my response.

I swallowed, glancing down at my copy of the book before I began to speak.

"Well it's metaphorical," I started uncertainly, "she can't *actually* reach the top of the mountains, and even if she could, she probably wouldn't do it for him—so I guess there's a bit of comedy there. She also speaks in hyperbolic language when she mentions the maid, which is when I think she finds the link between the two." I explained.

The class fell into silence suddenly, and even Miss McKinnon took a while to respond.

"Yes," she said, frowning, "well done, Alessia, you seem to have done some extra work." I nodded, smiling. Or, *maybe*, I'm Olivia Clark in Alessia Trent's body 7 months in the past? *That gets more complicated every time.*

The lesson continued after that, but I couldn't help but drag my eyes over to the *real* Olivia, and Kiara. I watched as Olivia shrugged, Kiara turning around. When she saw me, she glared at me.

Confused, I quickly looked away. *Does Kiara hate Alessia? What could Alessia have done for her to hate her so much?*

Submerged in these new thoughts, I blanked for the rest of the lesson, and it wasn't long until the lesson finished and everyone began packing up.

I quickly joined them and shoved all of my things into my bag. When I was done, I let everyone else leave the classroom before I approached Miss McKinnon.

"Hi, Alessia," she greeted me, smiling up at me.

I smiled back, "Hi," I began, "I have some work that somehow never made it to you—I have a feeling maybe I messed them up the first time so I wanted to re-do them, who knows," I said, making her laugh, "but here they are." I said, handing them over to her.

"Thanks, Alessia, and well done for today." I grinned at her, thanking her before I left the classroom.

"Teacher's pet." Someone spat as I left the classroom. I turned to see Kiara on the other side of the door, arms crossed over her chest.

"What?" I asked.

She shook her head, shrugging. Confused to why she was still standing there, I turned around to see the real Olivia talking to Miss McKinnon, holding out her notebook and pointing at things.

I scoffed. *So Alessia got called the teacher's pet but Olivia was* fine *to spend extra time with teachers?*

I rolled my eyes but left nonetheless, taking the outside route to the library so that I could eat a quick snack before I dipped into building.

I tucked my food away as I reached the library, opening the door and stepping in. I surveyed the library for a spare seat—since GCSE and A Level mocks were fast approaching, the library was pretty booked out these days.

I managed to find a seat in a corner on the second floor of the library, and set my bag down on the table. I took a seat, pulling out my French homework and beginning.

"No, no, this is the part you always mess up, Dylan," I heard laughing, and tried to ignore it, but after hearing Dylan's name, I glanced up. It was the real Olivia and Dylan sitting in a corner in the non-quiet area of the library. *How did they get here that fast?*

"It's bonjour, mon cher—we cut cheri out after your teacher crossed out the 'i', remember?" I heard Olivia say as Dylan played with the ribbon attached to my-*her* bag.

"Okay," Dylan began, "bonjour, mon cher." He said. I smiled at that; his accent was good, but he didn't sound anywhere near fluent. It was kind of funny. The real Olivia thought so too as she laughed.

"What?" Dylan asked, frowning.

"Nothing," Olivia said, shaking her head, "it was perfect." They stopped talking suddenly, and just sat there staring at each other. From an outsider's point of view, it looked kind of weird, but nothing was weird between Dylan and me.

I shook my head, returning to my French homework.

I got the majority done, but I'd still have to do some at lunch. I still had a bit of break left but I liked to get ready for next lesson early so that I wasn't late. I, therefore, began to pack up, *almost* surprised when the real Olivia started doing the same.

With a sigh, I flicked Alessia's hair off her shoulder, placed her bag on her shoulder and started walking. I breezed past Olivia and Dylan, trying not to look back as I started for the stairs.

I found the toilets nearest to my next lesson—P.E. I was actually quite good at sport as Olivia Clark, but I had no idea how Alessia would fare.

After going to the toilet, I made my way to the sports hall and found a cubicle to change in. As I pulled the shorts over Alessia's legs, I noticed a massive dark blue bruise on the side of her leg. Staring it at, I had a sudden flashback to when Alessia's dad had sent her body pummelling to the floor yesterday morning.

I took a deep breath and fished around in her kit bag for the leggings I knew I had washed last night, before ripping the shorts off and replacing them with the leggings. I sighed, leaning against the cubicle wall and taking a deep breath.

"Alright, girls, two more minutes!" I heard the P.E teacher yell.

I rolled back my shoulders and sighed, reaching into my bag to grab the trainers I had also cleaned up last night, slipping them on Alessia's feet and tying them up.

When I was done, I whipped my hair up into a ponytail, which was harder with Alessia's wild hair.

I left the cubicle, seeing that I was one of the last girls to leave the changing room. Just as I was about to find a locker for my belongings, the P.E teacher approached me.

"Did you want me to take your bags into my office again, Alessia?" She asked, making me frown. I fumbled slightly, but then turned to face her, plastering a smile on my face.

"Yes, thank you, Miss," I said, letting her take my bags. I frowned after her as she walked out of the changing rooms. Alessia kept her bags locked away in the PE teachers' office? *Wow, things must be bad.*

Just as I was about to head out of the room too, I bumped right into someone.

I apologised profoundly, trying to catch the person by the arm. When I did, I realised who it was. *Myself.*

I stared at her-myself. She stared back, a frown on her face relaxing slightly.

"I'm sorry," I said once more, just staring at her.

The real Olivia smiled, "It's okay, don't worry." She said. As Olivia brushed past me and left, I stared after her, confused. *Why did Alessia dislike me-the real Olivia?*

When Alessia sees Olivia, she doesn't feel scared, she doesn't feel relaxed or happy, but nor does she feel hatred. Just...detached and annoyed.

Why does Alessia feel that way about me?

CHAPTER NINE

P.E was horrible. I should've known that the bullying would've only gotten worse when tennis rackets and hard tennis balls were involved.

Alessia only made it worse for herself by feeling jealous every time the *real* Olivia Clark swung her racket and hit a tennis ball that was incoming from Dylan. They had paired up for the games.

I didn't get it. *Did Alessia hate me or envy me? And what's the reason for both?* I wasn't exactly popular, or pretty, or have all the guys around me. I was just like her...which is why I'll never understand why she gets bullied and I don't. Dark hair, same build, okay, different eye colours—but there was nothing stellar. I don't get it, and I never will.

I helped pack up the gym equipment, so that I wouldn't look so weird loitering around outside the P.E office to get Alessia's bags. The P.E teacher and I made small conversation as we packed up; it seems that Alessia and the P.E teacher spend a lot of time together. I couldn't help but feel that leaving her bags in the office wasn't something that Alessia had just started doing last week.

I jumped when someone else joined us, "That's all the cones, Miss," the person said, and the voice made a chill run down my spine.

Because the person who spoke was *me*—the real Olivia Clark.

"Thank you, Olivia." The teacher said, taking the cones from Olivia and smiling at her.

"No problem," she said, "I'll see you next Tuesday." With that, she turned and left.

The teacher didn't say anything else after that, and I soon had my bags back in my hands.

In the cubicle, I changed with much relief. Although, I now only had three minutes to get to R.E, in which we were being given a keyword test.

When I was dressed, I sprinted out of the sports hall and across the school grounds to my class, slowing and trying to act casual as I reached the corridor. When I walked in, everyone was just getting seated, so sought out Alessia's seat.

I had R.S with Alessia when I was Olivia Clark, so I knew that she sat at the back of the class somewhere.

"Alessia, fifth row, next to Renton, I'm sure you can't have forgotten it after two terms in Year 11."

I cringed as everyone laughed. Mr Laughton had always been known for being harsh. As Olivia Clark, I had worked my way into being someone he didn't hate *as much*, of course by putting in the work and getting good grades. But I didn't know how he felt about Alessia.

Still flushing, I took my seat next to Mark Renton, ignoring him as he sniggered at me before shifting his chair over slightly.

When Mr Laughton gave out the keyword list, though, I couldn't help but feel a little excited to put my A* grade knowledge on paper—which I had gotten on results day for RS.

I had the keywords done five minutes before the end, and five minutes before most people. But when I looked up, the real Olivia Clark was already finished, her answers face down and her pen lying on top.

Where I was feeling wistful, Alessia was suddenly feeling angry. She had put effort into this. Yet, I still beat her. Every single time, and at *everything*.

I put a lid on Alessia's emotions and simply checked over the keywords before burying them under my arm to keep them safe until it was time to give them in.

When Mr Laughton announced that the time was up, I double-checked the words once more and that my name was printed clearly at the top before I handed it in.

After that, the lesson went pretty fast, and Mr Laughton ended it by running into lunch by five minutes. As Olivia, I was only slightly annoyed; I didn't mind being in class the extra time but, as Alessia, I couldn't be more pleased—*I have no friends.*

It was a deafening thought, one that bounced off all the sides of my skull, giving me a headache. But it was true—the longer I spent here, the less longer I had to spend being alone at lunch.

When the lesson was finally over, everyone ran out of the class, and I watched as Olivia packed up quickly before she pulled Mr Laughton over for a private word. I packed up slowly, giving her time for her conversation so that I could hand in my work in private.

I watched as Dylan slung his bag over his shoulder, not even noticing me at the back as he picked up the real Olivia Clark's blazer from the back of her chair.

When Olivia was finished, Dylan handed her blazer to her and she grinned, thanking him. They left in a discussion, and it took me a while to drag my eyes away from them.

When I did, I saw Mr Laughton staring at me expectantly.

I smiled, "I have a few pieces of homework that seemed to have gotten lost in transit." I said sheepishly, handing them to him.

He shook his head, "well, the deadlines have all passed, but I can mark them for you."

I thanked him a couple times before I turned and left the classroom, wringing my hands in and out as I navigated my way to a door that would lead me outside. I hid in a mass of trees, eating my lunch, before I left for the library.

Getting inside, I smiled over at the librarian before I found a spare seat. Again, I fished out my French homework and spent almost the entire lunchtime working on it.

When I was done, I had ten minutes left of lunch, and so rushed to the nearest toilets so that I wouldn't be late to French.

Walking into the ladies room, I was welcomed by a group of girls. The group of girls that made Alessia want to bolt out of the room every time she saw them.

When the girls turned around, I recognised them all, but there was also Kiara. I tried to ignore them, pushing doors to see if any were vacant.

"They're all in use," someone said, tauntingly. I turned to see Kiara heading straight for me.

"Look, Kiara, I just want to-"

"I know you followed me last night," she said suddenly, "on Instagram. At first I was just going to leave it alone, but after talking to Johnny, I realise that it's creepy as heck. Tell me, what cult are you planning on selling me to?" She finished, and I watched as girls that had come out from cubicles quickly left.

I swallowed, backing away, "Kiara, I have no idea what you're talking about."

She huffed, digging her hand into her pocket and pulling out her phone. "I had a feeling you'd deny it, so I got the evidence ready." She shoved her phone in my face, and I read the notification she was pointing at.

@alestrent started following you.

I frowned, shaking my head, defeated. "I'm sorry, Kiara, it must've happened by accident." I told her.

She scoffed, and the girls behind her laughed. "Unfollow me, or I'll undo your bag and rip whatever you've been working on all day." She threatened, and I nodded quickly.

"Well, do it then!" She exclaimed, making me jump. I had never seen Kiara so angry; so *scary*.

"Kiara," I said, acting as Olivia Clark, "please, I just-"

"Oh for God's sake," she said, lunging for my bag. I yelped, stumbling back and trying to push her off.

She grabbed hold of me, slamming my back into the farthest away wall so that no one else could hear or see what was going on between us.

"I've tried to hold back, but you're-"

"I'll tell Olivia who you really are." I blabbed suddenly. I was confused myself, before realising that even hosts of bodies are blocked sometimes. Alessia's impulses are always here, and they just made an appearance. Alessia had spoken that sentence, my control suddenly breaking. It was back within a second but it scared me that it could happen; I thought I was in control, not a viewer.

Kiara retreated suddenly, "what are you talking about?" She asked.

I had no idea myself—I was so confused. I mean, I could tell that Kiara acted differently around Alessia to how she used to act around me. I can see that now, and so clearly. But it seemed like there was more—more that I didn't know. I stayed quiet for a moment, listening out for Alessia—but she chose to remain silent.

I put on a brave face, "I'll tell her if you don't leave me alone." I threatened.

She scoffed, taking her hands off me. "Unfollow me, rat!" She yelled, backing away before she disappeared through the door. All the other girls left suddenly, and so I dashed into a cubicle, locking myself in.

It was there that I broke down. Alessia Trent, I am so sorry; I had no idea that you're life was like this in school. I get it now, and I'm sorry.

CHAPTER TEN

I was five minutes late to French, and when my teacher pulled me aside, I just calmly explained that I had forgotten which lesson I had next. As Olivia Clark, the teacher would have smiled and dismissed me, but I think I've come to notice that things with Alessia Trent rolled slightly differently.

She dismissed me, but without a smile, and with a heavier workload than the rest of the class.

I couldn't concentrate in French. I didn't need to, since I was the top of my class in school, but it would've been a good idea to dodge the wrath of an already angry teacher.

Alessia was upset, angry, and distracted all at once. The latter was the only emotion not caused by Kiara, and why? Because Dylan was sat in front of her. I had learnt over the past two days that Alessia either had a fascination with Dylan and wanted to be his friend, or just had a very secret crush on him. I sure hadn't suspected it when I was in school.

As Olivia, I had become detached, saddened by the fact that I couldn't just walk up to Dylan and ask him to repeat his French speaking to me, or let Kiara braid my hair in English literature, or laugh along to Johnny's jokes in the corridors, or get Ked to help me pick between plaid and stripes.

I missed my friends.

I missed my *life*.

I sighed, shaking the thoughts away and speeding through the work that the teacher had given me. I only had ten minutes left of our double lesson, and a lot of work to do. I also noticed that she had given Alessia D grade and C grade work to do. I didn't know how good or bad Alessia was at her subjects, but I thought maybe that that was aiming too low. I had convinced Dylan to ask for higher grade work in school, so maybe I just had to do the same for Alessia.

When the end-of-school bell rang, I packed up my stuff with satisfaction, having completed *all* of the work. I fished my French homework out from Alessia's bag for the last time today, since it was now all done.

I piled up all the work I had to give into the teacher and approached her when most of the class had gone. She rose an eyebrow at me when she noticed that I was there. I swallowed, handing over my class work first.

"Um," I began, "I also have the homework that appears to have never left my bag. It was due a while back, I'm sorry." I told her, expecting her to lash out on me.

She didn't, instead, she sighed. "Thank you, Alessia," she said, frowning when I remained in front of her. "Was there something else?" She asked.

"Is there a possibility that you could give me higher grade work to do?" I asked her, watching as her eyebrows shot up. "I know that it's sudden but I'm really trying to get my head down for GCSEs now, and I think I'm ready." I told her, smiling.

"Well," she said, discarding my work on her desk, "it's a bit late for that now, isn't it?" She asked. I suddenly felt my cheeks flush—I wouldn't have been as embarrassed if I didn't know that there were still students in the room, but I could feel them lurking behind me.

"But you said that it's never too late." I said, frowning as I remembered all the things she had said when I was at school.

She shook her head, "it is for you, enjoy your evening, Alessia."

With that, she turned around and slipped the work from today into a folder. Still in shock, it took me a while to register what had just happened. I guess Alessia doesn't have a good bond with her teachers.

I span around, completely embarrassed and angry. Angry at myself, for putting myself on the spot like that; there's no way I could've done those high grade papers. She's right.

I ran out of the room, letting Alessia's thoughts get the best of me. I bumped into someone suddenly, sending their folders falling to the floor.

"Oh my god, I'm so sorry—" but I didn't have time to hear the rest; I kept walking, ignoring the fact that I knew exactly who that voice belonged to. I knew exactly who I had bumped into.

Myself, the *real* Olivia Clark. Again.

I ran past everyone and to the most out of the way toilets I could think of, before locking myself in the toilets and breaking down again.

I was so angry. Angry that, even though I had tried so hard today, I still couldn't do it. I couldn't help Alessia feel happier at school. And it also made me feel like crap too.

When I was finished sobbing, I brushed through my hair, reapplied my face powder and tried to get rid of the redness in my eyes. I took a deep breath as I stared at my reflection, before I pushed open the door to the toilets and left, running down the stairs and out of the exit to school.

Sometimes when I'm in a flurry of emotions, I'm walking and I suddenly end up home. Or I get two buses and I suddenly end up in town.

That happened now, except, I ended up most of the way through the forest, which is when I bumped into someone. However, it was when they didn't let me go that I realised that I hadn't bumped into them. They'd taken me by my arms and pulled me to the side.

"Trent, where's my stuff?" Someone asked gruffly and I refocused to see a woman in a hoodie staring down at me.

"Sorry?" I asked, confused.

She huffed, "Look," she said, inching closer, "I want my drugs, okay? The ones you were supposed to get me yesterday?" She asked.

I stared at her, very confused.

I masked it though, smiling apologetically, "I'm so sorry, I'll meet you back here in twenty minutes and I'll get them to you then."

She shook her head, exhaling through pursed lips. "You almost cost me my party. It's a good job I booked to collect it ahead of the date, huh?" With that, she shoved me, and then sped away into the distance.

Still very confused, I watched her disappear before I turned around and kept walking. *Alessia is a drug dealer?*

I guess it would explain the stash of notes in her pocket. It makes sense; it doesn't seem that her father does a whole lot for her, so she got a job—or, whatever this is—to cover it all.

When I got home, I hurried to Alessia's room and past her dad's pity party on the sofa, closing the door behind me and locking it.

I searched the room for a while, trying to look for Alessia's secret stash.

When I got onto the floor to look under the bed, I found a large wooden box. I pulled it out, unlocking the lid and pushing up. I gasped when I saw what was in it.

The box was separated into lots of compartments, and each contained a few bags of the same thing, but different to the other assigned spaces. I could only guess that Alessia had multiple customers, and each space is for a different one and their 'usual'.

Without having a clue which customer had confronted me in the forest, I picked up a random bag and stuffed it into my pocket. I checked the time on my watch before I shut the lid of the box, shoving it back under Alessia's bed.

I tiptoed out of the room and down the stairs, listening out for Alessia's dad. When I heard nothing, I dashed down the stairs as quickly as I could, opening the front door and closing it as soon as I was out.

I headed to the forest quickly, only having five minutes to get there. I really should've allowed myself more time.

I waited by the large rock that I had seen yesterday, the one with Alessia's writing and name carved into it.

The woman suddenly appeared in front of me, looking at me expectantly. I shoved my hand in my pocket, but she stopped me, eyes wide.

"Hey, hey," she said, looking around us nervously.

"There aren't cameras here." I told her, confused.

She rolled her eyes, "No, but there are people. Just, do it slowly."

As I slipped my bag of drugs out of my pocket, she produced an envelope, gave me a quick look of the three hundred pound notes that were in there, before shoving it in my pocket.

She hummed when she saw the packet of the drugs, "I like the extra stuff you added, nice touch since you stood me up yesterday." After that, she hugged me, grinning.

"Okay," she said, walking off, "see you later!" She yelled.

I watched her go in silence. Alessia Trent, who *are* you?

CHAPTER ELEVEN

When I woke up the next morning and my ceiling wasn't covered in stars and planets, like my ceiling back home, I started to cry. In fact, I *sobbed*.

I tried two days as Alessia Trent, and I didn't like them. I don't know why I've suddenly switched bodies, or how. But it isn't funny anymore.

I'm still Alessia Trent.

I screamed into my pillow, squeezing my eyes shut so tightly that I thought they'd burst. I clenched my fists, burying myself so far into my pillow that I hoped I'd fall back into my own bed.

But when I turned back over, unclenched my fists and opened my eyes, that same horrible ceiling was there. I sat up in the bed, taking deep breaths, trying to relax myself before I passed out.

I whipped the covers off and stumbled over to Alessia's vanity, reaching over it and opening her window before slumping down on her vanity chair. I turned around on it, facing the mirror. I stared at my reflection, my heart aching. I had never wanted to feel or to look like myself, like Olivia Clark, more than in this moment.

This day just clarified it all. The first day was a shock, the second a trial-run, the third was always a certainty. Three times is always a curse. I'm stuck, and this day is proof.

I sighed, turning away from the mirror so that I wouldn't have to face the fact that I was Alessia Trent for much longer.

Since I had spent so much time sobbing, I had to sprint down the stairs to make it in time to wake Alessia's dad up. I shook him awake, watching him roll over, grunting.

He threw his arm all across the place, knocking over beer cans and vodka bottles. I had no idea how someone could live like this.

Alessia's dad picked up his phone, which I'm guessing he had been looking for the entire time. When he saw it, he roared, shoving the screen in my face.

"What do you call this?" He yelled at me.

I shrugged, though my heart was beating faster than it ever had done before. "Your phone..?" I answered, watching him raise from the sofa slowly. Then, suddenly, he punched me right in the chest. I fell to the floor, feeling as though my ribs had collapsed.

"Not only did you wake me up late, but you also had the decency to get cocky with me!" He screamed, kicking my body as it lay limp on the ground. I tried to cradle my head in my arms to protect it, but it only meant the rest of my body was at risk.

He stopped suddenly, and I felt him get dangerously close to my body. "I have some friends coming over after dinner tomorrow, and if you're not gone, I'll sell you to them." With that, he kicked me once more in my stomach before he stomped away.

I didn't move for quite a while. I didn't know if I could, but I was also too frightened to. When I finally shifted, even just by a fraction, I felt my entire body ache. I rose to my feet with my fists clenched and the insides of my cheeks between my teeth.

I barely made it up the stairs before I crumpled to the floor in Alessia's room. I had never felt a pain like this before. It felt like every bone in my body had been broken, like every breath left in my lungs had been taken, and like ever beat of my heart no longer exists.

I dragged myself over to Alessia's floor length mirror, curling up in front of it, breaking out into sobs once more as I looked into the reflection.

I couldn't go to school in this state.

I breathed in and out slowly, trying to calm myself. As Alessia Trent, I was numb and vacant from my body, as Olivia Clark, I was losing my mind. I was notorious for losing my cool and even having mini-anxiety attacks or panic attacks sometimes.

This was one of those times.

I squeezed my eyes shut, trying to calm myself. When I was calmer, I got up from the floor and ran myself a very cold bath, rummaging through Alessia's cupboards and finding painkillers. I took two and stuffed the rest in her school bag.

As the tub was filling up, I sorted out my folders and books, before grabbing a towel and my school uniform.

Back in the bathroom, I turned the taps off and stripped in front of the mirror, seeing red marks, already forming bruises, and scratches along Alessia's skin. Most would be hidden by her clothes, but some were still in plain sight.

I dipped my toe into Alessia's bath, shivering as I slipped into the ice water. I entered the bath as I had left Alessia's dad—fists and jaw clenched, and biting on my tongue and cheeks.

I thought maybe a cold bath would relax my muscles, calm any swelling and keep the bruises away. Now shivering, I wasn't certain it would do all that, but I still laid in the cold bath anyway. I dipped under for as long as my breath would last, before I emerged for air, breathing fast and gulping oxygen down.

I knew I'd be late today. I'd probably miss first lesson at the most; it wouldn't be detrimental.

When I was done in the bath, I climbed out and stood dripping in the centre of the bathroom for a while before I finally grabbed a towel, wrapping it around my damaged body.

I drained the bath before I began to dress myself. I looked into the mirror again after washing my face and brushing my teeth, seeing the bruises that I needed to cover up.

I sighed, leaving the bathroom so that I could get to work on covering up the marks. The ones on my face disappeared when I finished my daily makeup routine, but I had to apply heavy makeup on my arms and neck to make the rest go away.

When I was finished, I left the house without my ribbons—my Olivia Clark statement.

I was feeling less and less like Olivia Clark every single day, hour, minute, and second that I spent trapped in this body. In this life. In *her* life.

I slipped into Nell's shop, not greeting her, not responding at the till, and not saying goodbye when I left.

I walked slowly across the forest walk, dragging my feet and my will to live along with me.

When I got to school, I was ten minutes early to second lesson, and told the receptionists that I had an appointment this morning. They dismissed me, as if this was a usual occurrence.

I had biology next, with Dylan as my partner. I slipped into the class, the teacher murmuring something about sitting with our partners. I didn't respond, and instead sat on the stool next to Dylan's, watching as people filed in.

"Hey," someone said suddenly. I jumped, looking up and seeing Dylan smiling down at me. As always in Dylan's presence, I was instantly calm.

I smiled up at him, though the smile didn't quite reach my eyes. "Hey," I responded, watching him unpack his bag and sit down.

We had to pay attention to the teacher for a while, but we were soon set off on our own.

"I can't actually get into the library at lunch," Dylan said, "I have a hot date with a tutor." He said, grinning.

I smiled, frowning. "Tutor?" I asked, copying down the notes that Dylan had made for homework, pretending that I understood what they all meant.

He nodded, "AFrench tutor." He said, making me freeze. We *both* froze—Olivia Clark and Alessia Trent. I froze as Dylan referred to revision with the *real* Olivia Clark as a 'hot date', and Alessia froze at the idea that Dylan was unattainable.

How had I never known that Alessia felt this way about Dylan? It was so blatantly obvious.

Noticing me frozen, Dylan frowned, "Are you okay?" He asked.

I nodded quickly, "Absolutely fine." I told him.

I spent the lesson getting closer and closer to him. And not just bonding; I needed to be *near* Dylan. He was the only one who wasn't different around me when I was Alessia—well, not *majorly* different. Kiara and Johnny seem to hate Alessia, and Ked just appears too scared to approach her.

But Dylan doesn't hate Alessia, and he isn't scared of her. Alessia loves being around Dylan, even though it kills her heart to be. She gets cold and hot flashes and palpitations.

Alessia Trent has a crush on Dylan.

CHAPTER TWELVE

At lunch, I hid myself in a corner in the library, eating my lunch and working on my part of the project with Dylan. Finished eating, I logged onto a computer—using Olivia Clark's ID, of course, since I didn't know Alessia's—and did the research we needed.

When lunch drew to an end, I felt my stomach flip. I hated school as Alessia Trent. Nothing was how it used to be, and I was no longer happy to roam the corridors, ask teachers for help, approach any soul in the school, attend my dance lunchtime class, and talk to my friends—talk to *anyone*. I was no longer happy.

Alessia really didn't have the secondary school experience that I had.

When the last lesson of the day ended, I felt like being sick. I remembered the threat that Alessia's dad had given me this morning. I had to be out of the house by dinner, otherwise, I feared for my life.

As I left school, everyone was cheering and shouting loudly about Matt's party. It was not unusual that Matt would throw a party, even Alessia knew that, but as Olivia, I was usually invited. Truth be told, no one is really 'invited', you just turn up. But don't let that fool you—we've had people turn up before and be rejected. They all said the same thing. *Everyone's invited.* Apparently, that rule didn't quite matter for *all* people.

I was afraid that Alessia would be one of those people.

Crossing the road, I was startled when my body was grabbed and yanked backwards. Then, looking as a car full of angry people zoomed past, I realised what had happened. I wasn't paying attention as I crossed the road.

I turned round to see who was holding me, looking up to see Dylan. My heart stopped.

"Dylan?" I asked, though in a whisper.

He smiled, though looked confused, "Are you okay?" He asked, "you just walked into the road as if you were sleep-walking," I followed his hand as he gestured to the side, supposedly to where he had just been, seeing his friends waiting for him. *My* friends. I watched as Olivia watched me. She seemed to smile, but that's not what Alessia saw.

I turned back to Dylan, my breathing suddenly laboured.

"Dylan I need help," I said, watching him frown.

"What is it?" He asked as I grabbed hold of his arm.

I smiled at his immediate concern, "I just need somewhere to stay overnight, somewhere to be, apart from at my house." He raked his hand through his hair, glancing around him, something he did when he ran into a problem.

"I'm going to a party tonight," he told me, "but if you meet me here at twelve, I can sneak you into my house." I nodded. It was as good as I could get. But it still wouldn't be enough. Regretfully, I let him leave, thanking him.

I watched him approach Olivia, who grinned at him. I sighed, turning away and crossing the road after looking both ways this time, before I disappeared into the forest in front of the school, walking fast. On my way to Alessia's house, I checked Instagram for details of the party; it said it would run from '8 till late'. That was good enough for me.

When I got home from school, I prepared myself a ready meal whilst I thought over what I could wear. I didn't know if Alessia had any party clothes, and I didn't really shy away from dressing up as Olivia Clark, so it could be tricky if her dress collection is non-existent.

Dylan would always tell me that I looked good in any colour, any outfit. I had no idea what Alessia usually wore, or what suited her.

I ate my dinner up in my room, switching between doing that and rifling through Alessia's wardrobe. I found multiple skirts and dresses that were good, yet not good enough. I sorted through her drawers, finding a black sequinned top. *Score*; I can work with this.

I eventually found a pair of black heels that were abandoned in a very dusty, wine red shoe box, and checked to see if they would fit before smiling. *They did.* Maybe Cinderella would go to the ball after all.

I returned to the clothes that were hung up, trying again to see if I missed a hidden gem. My fingers found a silk black skirt, paper bag style. I paired the whole thing together on the floor, and then smiled with victory. Alessia Trent is going to her first party.

It was probably the first thing I had been happy about in her body. As Olivia Clark, parties weren't my saviour and light, but they sure played a big part in my social life. They were also, admittedly, kind of fun.

I finished my dinner, chucked away the rubbish and slipped into the bathroom to get changed. When I was dressed, I ran out of the bathroom to check myself in Alessia's floor length mirror.

"Not too bad, Clark." I cleared my throat, suddenly noticing how my voice was very alike to Dylan's. I suppose that, if I'm to be a host in someone else's body, it wouldn't be too crazy to start hearing my friend's voices in my head.

Finishing my makeup, which was heavy on the eyes and light on the lips, I began my hair. Alessia's hair was naturally quite curly, and I decided that it was a great look. Except, maybe not *this* curly.

I dug around in Alessia's room, finding her dusty straighteners, cleaning them off and plugging them in. As I waited for them to heat up, I prepped Alessia's hair, and then ran the straighteners through her hair so that the kinks became gorgeous waves.

When I was done, I finished with the signature Olivia Clark touch. Half-up, half-down and a ribbon. I used a gold ribbon, having found a gold clutch earlier.

Finished, I decided to waste time by packing my bag and checking everyone's social medias, already seeing pictures emerging from the scene. With that, I decided to make my exit. I grabbed the most party-attire coat that Alessia had, before leaving her room and her house.

When I got to the party, I was glad that I had waited—if I had walked in any earlier, I would've stuck out like a sore thumb amongst the elitist popular group.

I slipped around the corners of each room for a while, until I finally made it to Matt's kitchen. Having eaten a small meal two hours ago, I was quite hungry. I opened Matt's snack cupboard, being familiar with the layout of his kitchen, and pulled out a bag of crisps. Probably getting *too* relaxed, I sat atop Matt's countertop and munched on my snack of choice.

"Aren't you *Alessia Trent*?" Someone asked suddenly. I jumped, looking around to see Lucas Roon. I nodded slowly, seeing him smile.

He leaned against the countertop, arms crossed over his chest.

"The hell are you doing here?" He asked, "you've never been to one before." He said, opening the fridge and pulling out a can of beer.

I shrugged, "it's never too late." I said. He laughed, nodding.

"Is that your mantra with Dylan?" He asked suddenly, making me choke on a crisp.

"Sorry?" I asked.

He smiled, and it seemed to appear wistful. "Well, it's obvious he fancies Olivia but, like you said, it's never too late. Right?"

I stared at him. As Olivia Clark, I was thoroughly confused; Dylan and I are, or were, friends. As Alessia Trent, I was embarrassed, suddenly cornered.

"That doesn't apply to that." I said in defence, though the reaction mainly came from Alessia. As Olivia, I was still in the dark about this, and so I let her decide how things panned out.

Lucas laughed, "Whatever, I'm not concerned," he said flippantly, "just avoid Kiara, especially when she's with Johnny. I love the girl but she really gives into him, *and* she's a very protective best friend. Those are two factors that are not good mixed together." He said, finishing his beer.

I frowned, "What are you saying?" I asked, suddenly Olivia again. I feel like Alessia knew the answer to that, but I didn't.

Lucas smiled and winked at me, "That you should come out of the kitchen and join the party." With that, he threw his empty can in the bin, before escaping to the party through a door.

I sighed, shaking my head and trying to ignore what he said about Kiara. I shoved the empty crisp packet in the bin, wiping my hands on a towel.

Lucas had actually been nice to Alessia. I couldn't tell if he perhaps wasn't caught up on everything, or he was just drunk. Since there's simply no other reason why someone wouldn't treat Alessia Trent badly.

She was a magnet for it, and I still didn't know why. Then, maybe there *is* no definitive reason. Maybe some things just are the way they are, and that's all.

CHAPTER THIRTEEN

When I entered the party again, I got swept up into a storm of drunken, dancing people. Nobody knew who I was, and even if they did, they didn't ask any questions.

I knew that it was only because they were drunk but it meant something to me, and I could feel that it meant something to Alessia too.

Suddenly, a face appeared in front of me, and I nearly lost my footing when I saw that it was myself. Nothing could ever prepare someone for seeing their own face looking back at them, and not in a mirror or an image.

"Hey," the real Olivia said. I smiled in response, not remembering this interaction from when I was Olivia Clark. "I noticed you over here and I..." she trailed off suddenly, glancing behind her. It was then that I saw her—*my* friends watching us. Alessia was suddenly angry, feeling as though this was a set-up. But I planted my feet in the ground and I didn't move; I knew that I wasn't bad person, and it's time Alessia sees that too.

"I recognised you from earlier, when you almost died." My eyes widened, before I smiled, nodding. She laughed, "I also actually *do* know who you are," she said, avoiding eye contact suddenly. "You're Alessia Trent," she said. I held my breath, anticipating the moment that she would turn on me.

"I've never really seen you at one of these things so I wanted to say hi," she smiled at me, and I returned the smile. *I knew it*; I didn't remember bullying anyone in school, and it was true—I really hadn't.

But Alessia didn't seem to think so. I was suddenly shoved backwards in terms of control of Alessia's body. I often allowed her control when I was stunned or confused, or if she knew something important. But, I was beginning to learn that if she was feeling particularly impulsive, or a certain type of rage or passion, I had no say.

"Yeah, well, 'hi' doesn't really cut it. I don't want to talk to you or your friends, Olivia. So cut it out and stop being so fake." With that, Alessia pushed her out of the way, storming away. Alessia got to the doorway before I regained control and turned around, seeing that Olivia had stumbled farther back than Alessia had expected her to. Alessia felt bad, and then Dylan caught her, held her, and smiled at her. She was so overwhelmed with jealously that she screamed, but no one heard her.

She marched away and up the stairs, where I knew, as Olivia Clark, that only couples went. They found a bed and they did the deed. Alessia obviously wasn't aware of this and, as Olivia Clark, I wasn't keen on being hunted down by myself and my friends for shoving myself when it wasn't even my fault.

My problems get weirder and weirder every moment I spend in this body.

Instead of finding a room, I headed straight towards one of Matt's bathrooms. Looking in the mirror, I sighed.

"Well, we're here now, aren't we?" I asked to the reflection in the mirror, sounding insane to even *myself. Yes, I'm talking to myself.*

"And I wasn't the one that attacked the queen of your problems, that was you, so you can't blame me for anything that happens after this very moment." I huffed, going to the toilet before washing my hands and returning to the mirror once more.

"I'm doing everything I can to help you, Alessia, and you just mess it up every single damn-"
The bathroom door suddenly opened. I jumped away, seeing Matt appear.

"Oh," he said, also surprised, "I'm sorry," he said, before he narrowed his eyes, probably noticing who I was. I gulped, looking down and away, trying to doge around him.

"No, hang on, you're that Alessia girl, right?" He asked.

I cleared my throat, "maybe."

He laughed, shutting the door, "Well, let's see." Suddenly, his hands were up my skirt. I squealed, jumping away.

"Oh come on, first Liv, now you," he whispered, getting too close.

Then I suddenly realised why everything had been a blur for me. Why I couldn't remember being here as Olivia Clark.

This is the party that Matt sexually assaulted me at.

He tried to get me down, tried to get on top of me, but I put too much of a fight up that he stopped. As one of Dylan's closest friends, he didn't want it all to get back to him, so he just left me alone, stalking off.

I guess this is where he had come next. Matt shoved me towards the marble countertop, where I fell into it, hitting my already damaged body.

When I tried to turn around, he gripped onto my waist, holding me into place. And then he smashed my front down on top of the countertop. Suddenly realising what was about to happen, I started to scream.

Matt ignored my screams, and pulled up my skirt. I was pushed up and along the countertop so that only my lower legs hung off. Matt pulled my legs apart, and then I heard the sound of a picture being taken. I started to scream again, trying to escape his hold.

And then he pulled off my underwear. I heard more pictures being taken, and then I was pulled backwards along the counter top.

I thought that would be it. This would be the moment that it would happen.

Olivia froze, falling limp. Alessia didn't, Alessia screeched, and kicked out. I heard Matt grunt and collapse onto the floor. Alessia jumped off the side, slipped her underwear on and pulled her skirt down before smashing Matt's phone just with her heel.

With that, I suddenly regained control of Alessia's body, taking over from her shaking self and running across the hall, remembering a nook at the end. I crawled into it, body trembling. I pulled my legs into my chest, holding onto myself as gigantic sobs began to leave my body. I was having a panic attack.

When I heard the bathroom door slam shut and footsteps down the stairs, I slowly emerged from my hiding place. After surveying the area, I made a break for it towards the stairs.

Reaching the bottom, I was shoved into countless amounts of people. I started screaming at some of them, telling them I had to leave and now.

I then overheard a conversation. "What did you *do*, Matt?" I recognised the voice. It was *mine.*

I suddenly knew how this story ended. After Matt had left me, as Olivia Clark, I soon came to the realisation that he'd probably just do what he wanted to do with me to another girl. And he was angry, too.

Now in Alessia's body, I sprinted past them, shoving past people and heading for the door. I ignored the shouts that came from the real Olivia Clark. The real Olivia Clark was shouting out to Alessia, trying to get her to stop.

Because this was the moment she realised that the girl in black who sprinted past her was Matt's latest victim.

I ran out into the night, running across a forest much alike to the one near school. When I was too tired to carry on, I stopped to sit on a log, burying my face in my hands and sobbing once more.

I stayed there for a while, listening to nothing but my own cries.

Then suddenly, "Hey."

I jumped up, backing into a tree.

"I'm not going to hurt you," it was myself, the real me. The thing is, back when this happened and I was Olivia Clark, I didn't recognise Alessia. Her makeup was streamed across her face and her hair dishevelled.

But now I knew; Alessia Trent was the girl that Matt attacked after me. After I fought off Matt and he left, knowing he'd be killed if he harmed me, he went to Alessia. He knew who she was, and knew no one would care. He knew she was an easy target. After protecting myself, I let Matt harm another girl.

It was my fault that Alessia was attacked that day.

CHAPTER FOURTEEN

After running away from the real Olivia Clark once more, trying to ignore her screams, I ran out into the town centre.

I checked the time on my phone. It was 11:50. Dylan said he'd meet me at twelve outside the school. I knew if Olivia was still at the party, that he would be too, but I counted on him anyway.

At the bus stop, I brushed through my hair and cleared up my makeup, returning to a saner look. I fixed my top and adjusted my coat before reapplying my lip stick. When the bus came, I appeared only as a partygoer, and not someone who was just sexually assaulted.

Sitting on the back of the bus, I could do nothing but play and replay what had just happened over and over. I squeezed my eyes shut. Alessia just wanted to get away from the party, but as Olivia, I was suddenly full of rage. Fair enough Matt did this to me, but at least I'm a part of his friendship group. I could've written it off as playful fun, but not this. This is *too* far.

When the bus called for the bus stop near the police station, I pressed the bell, and readied myself to get off.

I jumped off the bus, hurrying towards the police station. When I was inside, I headed straight for the desk.

The person there looked up, "Hi, how can-"

"I need to report a sexual assault." I said, making them freeze.

He nodded slowly, "Okay, just take a seat and someone will be right out." He told me. I turned around, finding the closest seat and sitting down. I was restless the entire time, fidgeting as I waited. I had never been in a police station before, never mind been here to report a crime.

Soon, a female police officer appeared before me.

She smiled, "Hello," she said, holding her hand out for me to take, "what's your name?" She asked.

I opened my mouth, ready to say Olivia Clark, but then I paused. "Alessia Trent." I told her, taking her hand and letting me take her hand.

"Nice to meet you, Alessia." With that, she guided me to a secluded room, letting me sit on the comfy chair as she took the office one.

"Okay," she said, sitting down, "I've been informed that you'd like to report a sexual assault," she said, pulling out a notebook and pen. I nodded, and so she continued to speak, "would you like to tell me what happened?" She asked.

I took a deep breath, recalling what had happened to her.

After I had told Alessia's half, I began to speak again, "This happened to me after this guy sexually assaulted another girl." I told the officer.

She frowned, "How do you know this?" She asked.

I froze. *How do I explain that I've lived* both *sides of this story?*

I shook my head, "She's a really close friend of mine; she'd never lie and so I trust that she's telling the truth."

"Well," The officer began, "we can't put credit to that unless she comes forward herself, but your account, Alessia, is definitely an explanation of a serious crime," the woman said. I smiled, feeling victory. "Could you give me a name? Or perhaps appearance or–"

"Matt Reeley," I told her, surprising her, "he goes to my school," I told her.

"Right," she said, jotting this down. "And did you know Mr Reeley personally?" She asked me next.

I shook my head, "No, but he's popular so I know a bit about him." I told her, watching her nod.

"Okay," she said, after asking for a few of my personal details. When she was finished, she stood up, smiling at me.

"Did you need me to call someone to pick you up?" She asked, leading me out into the hallway once more.

I shook my head, "Oh, no that's fine, but thanks." With that, I smiled and left. I walked out of the police station just in time to catch the next bus, and when I was seated, I checked the time. It was twenty past twelve. I hoped Dylan hadn't left.

When the school appeared in my vision, I pressed the bell with anticipation. Knowing Alessia's luck, Dylan would already be gone.

But, when I got off the bus and looked down the street and towards the school, I saw a figure. It was pacing, and I saw his car parked on the side of the road beside him.

I smiled, walking over to him quickly. When I was close enough, he heard me approaching and turned to me.

"Alessia," he said, sounding relieved. I didn't give him a chance to say much else as I ran into him, wrapping my arms around him, just needing a hug from my best friend. Of course, he didn't know me as his best friend, he knew me as Alessia Trent.

"Are you okay?" He asked once I had pulled away, looking both confused and concerned.

"Yeah," I said, grinning, "I'm sorry for making you wait so long—but thanks for doing this for me." I said, making him shake his head.

"It's fine," he said, "I'm here if you need me."

I had no idea Dylan was promising things like this to a girl I barely knew in school. But I should've seen it coming. Dylan is probably the most compassionate boy I knew, and somewhere along the way, his parents had taught him right—women are to be respected. Dylan, of course, respected everyone, but it wasn't just something he extended to friends and family—for, here he was, lending his services to a girl he barely knew at midnight on a Friday night.

With that in mind, I slipped into his car feeling comfortable. Dylan is a really good guy.

Alessia knew that, and I think she has for a while, and being in this close of a proximity to Dylan as he drove along dark streets made her warm and fuzzy inside. If she didn't adore Dylan enough as it was, she worshipped him even more now—he was saving her, not only from her wicked dad but from the darkness, from the pain and from the memories of what had happened at that party.

At least Alessia and I had something in common—we were both attacked by Matt Reeley at the same party. We were both in pain because of that. And neither of us told Dylan.

Dylan doesn't know what happened to me that night.

When Dylan was pulling up into his drive, he was telling me that his dad was away overseas for work and that his mum had a night shift that she just left for. We had more than enough time together before I'd have to leave and go back to this monstrosity of a reality.

I stepped into Dylan's house, closing my eyes and breathing in the familiar smell. I opened them when I felt Dylan helping me take my coat off. I thanked him, letting him take my coat when it was finally off. I took a seat on the last step of his stairs to take off my heels also, like I always had done. And then we went upstairs.

Alessia was nervous and, although she knew that Dylan would never harm her, she was a little shaky and apprehensive after what just happened.

When we got to his room, he left the door ajar. When I was at his house, I always used to close his door, but I guess this was his way of trying to make Alessia feel safe.

"Where do you want to sleep?" He asked.

I smiled, sitting on his bed, "I don't mind." I told him.

He laughed, "Well you seem pretty comfortable there; I'll get the blow-up bed for me to sleep on."

I jumped up, not as Olivia, but as Alessia, "You don't need to do that," Alessia said, "I can sleep on the blow-up bed," she told him.

He smiled, shaking his head, "Take the bed—I like blow-up beds anyway."

I knew, as Olivia Clark, that Dylan couldn't *stand* blow-up beds. In fact, whenever I stayed over his house, I often woke up to find him in his bed—beside me.

When Dylan left, I didn't sit back down on his bed, but instead ventured around his room. I smiled, feeling like myself again—like Olivia Clark. Despite the fact that Alessia's life obviously wasn't anything but pain and darkness, it also hurt that I couldn't be in my own body. I didn't know which of those, though, hurt the most.

I missed all of my friends, my family, waking up and seeing myself in the mirror, not someone else.

I just wish that I was Olivia Clark again. I don't know how much longer I can do this for.

CHAPTER FIFTEEN

When Dylan came back in, I was holding a picture frame, one that held a picture of Dylan, Ked, Kiara, Johnny and me—Olivia Clark. It had been taken in the Christmas of 2016, and we all looked indescribably happy. That's the way it should've stayed.

I turned around, hearing Dylan drop a box on the floor. When he saw me holding the frame, he smiled.

"Sorry," Alessia said, making me put the photo back.

Dylan shook his head, walking over to where I stood. He looked down at his photos and I glanced over at them once more.

"I think this is my favourite," he said, picking up one that displayed a picture of Dylan and I—Olivia Clark. It was a selfie taken by me, with Dylan looking over at me as I grinned into the lense.

Suddenly, Alessia began to feel jealous, though slightly curious too.

"That girl," she began, "Olivia, right?" She asked and I mentally sat back, watching as she took control.

Dylan grinned, gazing down at the picture. "Yeah," he replied.

Alessia picked up another photo, one that was also of Dylan and I. "You guys seem close," she acknowledged.

He nodded, "We've been friends for eight years." He told her, putting the picture down before glancing over at the one she was holding.

"Are you going to ask her to Prom?" She asked suddenly, making him look up at her, a frown etched onto his face.

"I don't know," he confessed, shrugging, "it's still a while away," he said, leaning over to his curtains to draw them.

"Yeah," Alessia said, before pausing to take a breath, as if to ready herself for something. "But you don't want to leave it too long; someone else might ask her."

From where I stood in a metaphorical backstage of Alessia's life, I froze. This was it. Dylan asked if I had plans for Prom five months before it happened, and I thought that he was just filling a silence, or maybe just thinking ahead. I had no idea that it was an idea influenced by *Alessia Trent*.

Dylan did, in fact, end up asking me to Prom, but as a friend and just after our mocks in April. It was still early but at least it wasn't *five months* early.

"Did you want anything?" Dylan asked and Alessia thought that maybe he was avoiding the subject, "A drink? Some food? A relaxing bath?"

I laughed, suddenly coming forth in the mind of Alessia Trent. "All of the above." I said, making him laugh too.

"Okay, drink?" He asked.

I thought for a moment, "Hot chocolate," I told him, "with loads of marshmallows and frothed milk,"

He smiled, "Food?" He prompted next.

"I'm craving olives, yeah, I know, weird combination. But maybe some Oreos too? The ones with the white insides?" Dylan nodded at my request, laughing.

"I'll have to double-check on the olives, but yes, and...the bath?" He asked, making my smile grow.

"Not too many bubbles, but maybe a bath bomb and something to make your skin soft. Warm—not too hot and not too cold. And I want to shower beforehand; I hate just laying in a bath full of my grime." I said, grimacing, listening to Dylan hum in response.

"What is it?" I asked, confused.

"Nothing," Dylan said, looking away suddenly. When he looked back up at me, he looked confused. "It's just...you sounded awfully like Olivia then."

I froze, "With the shower before the bath?" I asked, trying to sway Dylan.

He laughed, "Not just that, everything else too. I mean, if you're trying to imitate her, you'd got her down to a T."

I shook my head quickly, "No, I'm not trying to copy Olivia. We just probably have similar interests and stuff," I said, trying to convince him.

He nodded, smiling up at me, before gesturing to his en suite behind me.

"This is the bathroom; did you want me to show you how the shower and bath work?" He asked, pulling a clean towel out from a rack on the door.

I shook my head, grabbing the towel from his hands, "I think I'll survive." I told him, making him laugh again.

"Okay," he said, "and all the bath stuff is in the cabinets under the sink. It's all stuff Olivia has accumulated over the years and she always seems to notice when something has been used, so take it easy." He told me, before he patted me on the shoulder and left.

I closed and locked the door as I smiled, placing my towel on the side of the sink. But when I looked up into the mirror and it wasn't Olivia Clark who looked back at me, my smile fell.

I sighed; no matter how hard I tried, I couldn't just be best friends with Dylan. I couldn't just be Olivia Clark again. Dylan said it himself—I sounded like Olivia. And whilst it's nice that Dylan knows me so well, and that I still hang onto little things from my real self, it's just not going to work. I'm Alessia Trent, at least for the time being, and I need to start acting like it.

When I was in the shower, my mind was completely open for Alessia to unearth herself in. And she did. Thoughts trickled. Stuff about her liking Dylan even more and that, perhaps, if Dylan liked me—Olivia—as much as she had just seen, she should act more like me.

Well then. So much for not copying myself—Alessia probably already dug herself that hole when we were at school.

I guess now I don't have to stop being myself to exist in this body, since being Olivia Clark all the time is probably what Alessia did last year at school to get Dylan's attention. There won't be much difference now.

After my shower, I dipped my body into the bath I had prepared before my shower began. I relaxed into the tub, closing my eyes and pretending that I was Olivia Clark again.

I'm Olivia Clark. And I'm at my best friend, Dylan's, house. It's just another sleepover. His parents, after all, trust us. And so they should; Dylan and I never do anything that isn't friendly—we don't go further than hugs. We've just come back from Matt's latest party and we're going to watch a film after I've washed away all of the drunken fun that we had tonight. If my back aches from all of today's standing and dancing, Dylan might give me a massage, and I'll comb through his hair—because he secretly loves his hair being played with; it relaxes him.

When I opened my eyes, I was still Alessia Trent.

I drained the bath, not sad, but not happy. I was in some transit between worlds I couldn't control—*forces* I couldn't control.

I threw my wet towel into Dylan's dirty washing bin before picking up a fresh dressing gown from Dylan's rack.

I unlocked the door, opening it slightly so that I could peak into Dylan's room. He looked up at me from where he laid on his bed on his phone, smiling over at me.

I smiled back, "Is there any chance that you have something I could wear? I didn't bring anything—sorry."

Dylan jumped off his bed, "No, it's fine, don't worry." He said as he pulled his drawers open. I walked over to him, watching him search his drawers.

"Okay," he said, "here are your choices," when he turned to see me standing beside him, he froze. "Um," he said, walking over to his bed and placing clothing items down. "We have an old short-sleeved top from H&M, very comfortable," he said, making me laugh, "or this, a long sleeved top from Hollister, old also," I smiled, taking the Hollister top from his hands.

He smiled, "And for bottoms, we have joggers from a store that I can't remember, these are also comfortable," I laughed, making him chuckle also. "And these black tracksuit bottoms, nice but kind of short," I smiled, picking the first option before thanking him.

I disappeared back into the bathroom to change and then, five minutes later, I reappeared.

"Oh," Dylan said, holding a bunch of DVDs in his hands. "I love those clothes. I think Olivia has actually worn that top a couple times."

I smiled and shook my head; eyeing the DVDs he was holding.

When he saw me staring, he smiled, "I thought we could watch a film," he said.

"Well," I said, "I want to dry my hair, but choose something relaxing, maybe funny—I trust your opinion,"

With that, I backed back into his bathroom, leaning down to the cabinet, opening the left door.

"Left side of the cabinet and bottom shelf!" I heard Dylan call.

I smiled, "Thanks!" With that, I began to blow-dry my hair, using my compact brush that I had brought to the party with me.

When Alessia's hair was almost dry, I stopped, sighing into the mirror.

"I'm thinking 'The Incredibles'," Dylan called out to me suddenly, pulling me away from my reflection.

I tucked the hairdryer back into the cabinet before walking out into Dylan's room. When I did, Dylan held up the DVD case, before I noticed that it was already playing on his TV.

I smiled, settling down on his bed, seeing the food I had asked for ready in front of me. "It's perfect." I told him.

He smiled, "I'll just get the drinks now." With that, he left.

I relaxed into his bed. I just want to stay here forever—even as Alessia Trent if I have to. I just want to be with Dylan.

CHAPTER SIXTEEN

When I woke up as Alessia Trent in Dylan's bed, I felt a bittersweet kind of emotion seep into my body. Looking beside me, I saw that Dylan was not there; not under the covers, his warm body close to mine. I frowned, sitting up to see him still sleeping on his blow-up bed. Maybe he doesn't hate blow-up beds as much as I thought.

I reached over to where I left my phone to charge on Dylan's bedside table, switching it on and seeing the time as ten to twelve. My eyes widened; his mum is sure to be home by now.

I slipped off Dylan's bed, quietly making my way to his bathroom so that I could go to the toilet and freshen up slightly. When I was looking for some deodorant, I found a bottle of my favourite perfume. *So that's where that half full bottle disappeared to.* I had forced my dad to buy the very rare perfume, which was my favourite scent, when he next went on holiday to Cuba since it had gone missing. He had first brought it back a year before my parents had divorced and I had been in love with it ever since.

If I ever wake from this body, I will march round Dylan's house and steal my bottle back. Maybe Dylan didn't know it was here but, if he did, I'm confused to why he wouldn't give it back.

I shrugged, reaching out for the bottle and spraying it a few times across Dylan's top, and also once on my neck.

When I was finished in the bathroom, I unlocked the door and walked out, which is what woke Dylan up.

"Afternoon," I said as I sat down on the end of Dylan's bed, unplugging my phone.

He grunted, "What?" He asked, rubbing at his face. I smiled, extending my arm out to show him the time displayed on Alessia's phone. His eyes widened, as mine had done, and he scrambled out of his bed and into the bathroom.

I laughed, getting up and folding up his sheets and leaving them on the end of his bed before leaving his bed to deflate.

When he came out of the bathroom, he was brushing his hair back with his fingers, something that Alessia found cute.

"My mum should be asleep by now," he told her, which was something I already knew but nodded along to anyway. "And she's a pretty deep sleeper, so we just have to be quiet as we walk downstairs, and I can make you something to eat." He said, before he blitzed around the room, collecting any rubbish from last night.

As he did that, I stripped his bed of the sheets I had used last night, throwing them in the laundry bin before getting some fresh ones from out of under his bed.

As I was dressing the pillows, Dylan appeared on the other side of the bed, straightening out the duvet.

"How did you know where to find the new sheets?" Dylan asked, frowning over to me as he picked up another pillow.

I swallowed, ignoring his eyes. "I just guessed...my bed has the same feature." It was a lie of course, from both ends; neither I—Olivia Clark—nor Alessia keep fresh sheets under our beds. I just knew it, as Olivia Clark, from being friends with Dylan for so long. I had been at his house and slept in his bed many times.

When his bed was freshly made, we made our way downstairs. I sat at the kitchen island as Dylan made bacon sandwiches—his favourite.

"This is my favourite," he told me, throwing another rasher into the pan.

I grinned, "Well I love bacon, so." He smiled, unwrapping a new loaf of bread.

"*Finally*, someone else apart from me and Olivia who understands the bacon phenomenon." He said, making me laugh.

"Have you ever noticed how many times you reference Olivia?" It wasn't me that had asked the question, it was Alessia. Dylan, who had been taking two glasses out of the cupboard that I could never reach, froze.

He slowly spun into action again after a few moments, closing the cupboard door and bringing the glasses over to me.

"I guess," he admitted honestly, "but she is my best friend, after all."

Alessia nodded, "That's true, but then so is Kiara, and Johnny, and Ked, and you rarely mention them."

Dylan nodded, checking on the bacon, "Well Olivia and I have been friends for longer than I've been friends with Kiara, Johnny and Ked." He told her, and she nodded, humming. I then decided to kick her out, though it wasn't exactly hard.

"Okay," Dylan said, "we have orange juice, apple juice, pineapple juice, or water."

I peered at Dylan suspiciously, "The pineapple juice is out of date," I told him.

He frowned, picking up the bottle and checking the date. "How did you know?" He asked as he emptied the contents of the bottle into the sink.

I shrugged, making him smile. "Could I have orange juice, though, please?" I asked, and he nodded, still smiling.

Truth is, Dylan wasn't a massive fan of pineapple juice—*I* was. I'm a believer that orange juice is the morning drink, but if it's not the morning, I'll take a water or pineapple juice. Hence why it would be out of date; only I drink it in this household, and I don't exactly live here.

"I'll have to order more," he said absentmindedly, pouring me a glass of orange juice and himself a glass of apple.

I smiled, "You don't seem to like it all that much,"

He shook his head, putting the juices away, "I do," he defended, "but we mostly keep it for Olivia."

He turned to me then, seeing me raise an eyebrow at him. I had caught onto what Alessia had said and it seemed plausible. Dylan *did* mention me an awful lot.

He turned around, after smiling sheepishly.

"Why don't you tell her you like her?" *Okay, woah, I did* not *say that.* That, as ever, was the doing of Alessia Trent. And I thought this girl was supposed to be in love with Dylan, why doesn't she try not talking about *me*, and more about herself?

"What?" Dylan asked, having being frozen for a few moments.

Alessia smiled, "Dylan, you never stop talking about her, you keep her favourite perfume in your bathroom, which, sorry, I used, *and* the entire school already knows."

On that note, I guess she has a point.

Dylan shook his head, cutting four slices of bread, "One, I explained the talking about her, two, she left that here once, and three, the school will ship anyone to get some gossip."

With that, he placed two plates on the counter, with ketchup between them.

"Fine," Alessia said, "I won't mention it again."

Sneaky. She runs Dylan into a corner so that she gets me out of his head when they're together. *Well, I guess it's smart.* Score for her.

Dylan nodded, sitting opposite her on the island, gesturing for her to begin eating.

When Alessia was almost finished, Dylan spoke up. "Did you want me to drive you home after this?" He asked.

Both Alessia and I felt as bile ran up our throat.

"Or," she began, "maybe I could go get changed, grab our project stuff which I completed yesterday, and then we come back here so we can work on it?" She proposed, taking a sip from her drink when she was finished.

Dylan considered this, before nodding, "I guess we could use the extra time, we *are* behind."

I nodded, watching him check his phone, before he confirmed to me that it was a good idea.

Soon enough, we were in the car on the way to Alessia's house. I didn't *exactly* know the way, but I hoped that Dylan wouldn't notice.

When we got there, I ran in quickly, seeing the place in an absolute mess. It reeked of alcohol and smoke. Alessia somehow knew that her dad wasn't here and so I trusted her, making my way up to her room.

I had a quick wash, brushed my teeth and got changed before I packed a bag of our project stuff, throwing in my toothbrush in case I stayed for another night. I hoped I would. I didn't want to come back here and neither did Alessia.

I just wanted to live in denial, that this wasn't my life now. But three days don't lie—I'm trapped in Alessia's body. And I'm not sure I'll ever get out.

CHAPTER SEVENTEEN

"Okay," Dylan announced, sitting the books down on his floor, despite the fact that he had a desk. "Where should we start?" He asked.

I got down on the floor, leaning against his bed. It was the side of the bed opposite the door, facing his window. If we sat like this, no one could ever find us—I knew because Dylan and I used to hide here when my mum came to collect me from his house. I never wanted to leave him, and him me.

"Maybe with you going through my work and either helping me understand what the hell I've written or telling me that I've done it all wrong?" I suggested, making him laugh. He joined me on the floor and picked up my work, spending a few minutes reading it. Whilst he was occupied, I spent the time spreading out the work so that it was easy to spot what we have and haven't done.

When he was finished, he hummed, "No, it's all right," he said, glancing over at me, raising an eyebrow, "but I guess now I'll have to explain it." He said.

I smiled, "Yes, yes please." I responded, making him laugh. He then began to explain it, and as ever when Dylan was explaining something science related to me, my brain hurt but I understood it.

"Do you get it?" He asked once he had finished explaining the entirety of my homework.

I took the documents from his hands slowly, "I actually do." I said, surprising myself.

He laughed, "Okay, should I explain my work now?" He asked. I'm not sure if it was meant to be a joke or not, but I nodded eagerly, shoving his work into his hands.

Again, he began to explain, but was interrupted by the sound of his doorbell. He paused, frowning.

"I wasn't expecting anyone." He said absentmindedly, standing up and looking out his window.

When he turned around, he did so in a rush. "I'll be back." He promised, before he escaped down the stairs.

I frowned, pushing myself up off the floor. Who could possibly be here that made Dylan bolt so quickly?

I leaned over Dylan's window sill to see who exactly interrupted our revision. Do you want to know who I saw?

Myself.

Yes, the real Olivia Clark is here.

I swore. I don't ever remember seeing Alessia here at Dylan's house but that doesn't mean that the real Olivia Clark won't see me now.

Despite my urge to stay hidden, Alessia had different urges. And, suddenly, I was tiptoeing over to the staircase, where Alessia sat, eavesdropping on Dylan and I. *That sneaky bi-*

"What do you mean, you're busy, Dylan?" I heard Olivia ask. I remember this day. Dylan, suspiciously, made me stand behind the door frame; he wouldn't even let me into his porch. I thought maybe that he was just really busy, or he found out what Matt did, or maybe he was finally having a fling, like all of the other boys in his friendship group. Dylan was the only one who remained a virgin—he never had a one nightstand, never forced himself on a girl, never seduced an innocent just to make his popularity soar. He was a good guy. But when I remember this day, I remember feeling disappointed because I thought maybe that was what he was hiding in the house. A girl he was about to have sex with.

I wasn't too far off. I mean, Alessia *is* a girl, who *does* like Dylan. Except, I don't think that feeling is, or was, reciprocated. So, I was actually wrong and, as Olivia Clark, I felt glad about that revelation.

"But this day is for us Dylan. Fair enough maybe I can't convince you with Biology revision, but can't we at least go to the cinema? See that Maze Runner sequel, or the last Hunger Games film?" Alessia knew it was selfish but she wanted Dylan to stay. She felt bad for keeping him away from Olivia—me—but she felt like she deserved this time with Dylan, since I, or Olivia, was always around Dylan. Like I was selfishly keeping him to myself. And now it was her turn to be selfish.

Alessia Trent, your life is very, very dark and I wouldn't wish the pain you experience on anyone, but you really are a bi-

"I'm really sorry, Olivia, maybe we can still catch a film later, or maybe I can clear some time for you tomorrow, but I'm actually really busy right now." Alessia grinned, falling more in love with Dylan after every sacrifice he made for her. Alessia had experienced firsthand Dylan's devotion to me—she thought he was obsessed. But to choose her over me proved a lot to her.

"Okay," Olivia said, "but why can't I help you? I'm sure it's only schoolwork, and-"

"Olivia, really, if I needed your help, I would've asked you in by now."

I closed my eyes, not as Alessia, but as myself. It was on this day that I had finally taken a deep breath, and decided to come to Dylan's house after what Matt did. I didn't want to tell Dylan what Matt had done, and I don't think I ever wanted to, I just wanted to be around him; as I've noted many times, Dylan makes me feel calm. And when Dylan turned me away like he did, it caused a storm. I was angry and upset, and I remember whirling around and storming away, tears spilling from my eyes.

If I was correct with my memory, there'd be a divide on Monday. This was the time of our worst argument ever. I couldn't believe how hard he had come down on me after what had happened, and he was confused to why I was 'over-exaggerating', since he didn't know what happened.

When the front door closed, I rushed back into Dylan's room and sat down in my spot, brushing my tears away.

"Sorry," Dylan said, coming in and shutting the door behind him.

I glanced up at him as he joined me once more, "It's okay," I said, "who was it?" I asked.

Dylan shook his head, "A parcel for our neighbours; they're never in these days yet they still make online deliveries."

I stifled a laugh, watching as Dylan turned to smile at me.

He was distant for a while, but Alessia didn't care; he had turned down Olivia for her. *Olivia.* That meant so much to her.

Dylan and Alessia worked through their project together for hours, until they were finally all caught up. Halfway through, Dylan's mum left for another night shift, and Dylan left for only few moments to say goodbye.

"Thank you for this," I told Dylan as I packed up the stuff I had brought. "And I don't just mean for teaching me the entire syllabus of biology in one hour," he laughed, turning to face me. "Thank you for last night—I really needed it." I whispered, suddenly curling up.

He frowned, concern appearing suddenly in his eyes.

"Alessia," he began and, suddenly, she came forth, assuming control. It was fine by me, I wanted to see how this would play out as an audience member.

"If you ever need someone, you have me, I promise." It was only a few words, but it was a very big promise.

Alessia smiled, ducking her head. "Dylan, you are way too nice, but thank you so, so much." She said, looking back up at his, what Alessia thought, beautiful face.

"It's okay," Dylan said, voice quiet. Alessia scooted closer, seeming to go in for a hug.

But, at the last second, something changed in her.

That's when I found Alessia Trent's lips on Dylan's.

Alessia was kissing my best friend.

And Dylan was kissing back.

CHAPTER EIGHTEEN

As Olivia Clark, I was in absolute shock.

I knew that Alessia had a crush on Dylan, something I had no idea about when we were in school. But now I learn that she had *acted* on her crush. She had *kissed* him.

I sat back, watching the kiss continue. Despite everyone's constant nagging at us about our apparent crushes, it seems that they were all wrong.

And then, Dylan pulled back. It wasn't to embarrass her; he didn't do it in a rude way. He pulled away slowly, eyes shut as he took deep breaths.

"Alessia," he whispered.

"I'm sorry," she whispered back, swallowing up anything he would've said.

"I'm going to call Olivia, see if she wants to come round and revise for her biology test on Wednesday, and I think that you..." he couldn't say it out loud. And Alessia and I knew why. Dylan was too nice. He had helped Alessia last night and today and he didn't want to be rude about anything.

"I'll go." Alessia said, swallowing the lump in her throat, picking up her bag and stuffing her clothes from the night before inside. She took one last look at Dylan as she sniffed. Then, she slipped on her shoes and left.

She ran down the stairs and out of the door, finding her bus pass in her pocket as she checked the time.

I was too shocked to resume my role in Alessia's body after that. I was still there, regretfully, but I let her make her way home on her own.

She felt regretful and a little embarrassed despite Dylan's efforts to remain respectful to her feelings. But, overall, she was happy. She had kissed the boy she liked and, although she then lost him to the girl *he* liked, she was still victorious.

School—it was a ridiculous few years of my life.

When Alessia got home, her dad still wasn't there and she wasn't surprised. I thought perhaps that he had a job that required him to work afar most of the time—and party with prostitutes on Friday nights, of course.

She ran up to her room, where she shut her door, leaning against it. And then she grinned, before throwing her body into some sort of happy dance.

This was the first time she had felt joy and success in a very, very long time. Though, I hope she knew that her cure to her long-term depression and lack of friends was harder than she thought to procure.

Alessia passed the rest of her Saturday by sketching Dylan in her sketchbook—which I had never seen in her room before—and she used a picture on his Instagram to do so. When it got late, she ordered a Chinese, becoming happier when she heard the doorbell ring. Well, at least we can both agree that food is emotionally enlightening.

As Alessia turned up the volume on her speakers, eating her noodles and smudging lines on Dylan's jaw, I felt betrayed. Alessia and I didn't really know each other, and so if I had known that Dylan kissed her when we were in school, I wouldn't have minded. In fact, I probably would've pushed him to take her on a few dates, maybe ask her to prom.

But tomorrow morning, I would've spent four days in her body. I just thought that maybe...

I don't know. We're not friends. She doesn't even know me. But I know her. I know every inch of her mind and body. I know that she has a mole on her upper hip, and no one else would've seen that. I know that there's a picture of her mum that she picks up every morning and kisses. No one else would've known that.

I know that Alessia owes me nothing.

But we're now bonded in the strangest of ways, and I feel like she crossed an invisible line.

When it was time for Alessia to go to sleep, she fell asleep with her phone in her hand, her pencil in the other and her sketchbook laid out in front of her. And when she woke up, the sketch of Dylan was still there and, even though she was starving, she couldn't wait to continue drawing him. She waited ten minutes for her phone to recharge, before she got straight to work again.

I was done helping Alessia. If what happened at Matt's party wasn't enough to convince me, Alessia definitely dug herself a hole when she kissed Dylan.

I won't dig her out.

She can stay buried until, and if, I want to come out to play again.

When Alessia knew that the coast was clear, she ran down the stairs and grabbed herself a quick breakfast, before sprinting back up the stairs again, locking herself in her room. She ate her late breakfast whilst watching Snapchat stories, and paused when she saw that, on Dylan's story, there was a video of me and Dylan. I was still very much asleep, cuddled up into Dylan's side and there was a film playing. Alessia would've been more annoyed if it hadn't been for Johnny's voice in the background. She was happy knowing that he wasn't spending time with just me alone.

What Alessia didn't know is that Dylan has been my best friend for eight years now. That's eight years of moments alone.

She can *shove it*.

When it seemed that Alessia was going to spend all day drawing Dylan, I shoved her out of the way, taking control again. I threw her rubbish in the bin, grabbing her sketchbook, deciding that she would have to watch as I burnt it. But, of course, there's only so much you can do as a visitor in someone else's body. I let out a frustrated yell, shoving her book under her bed before retrieving her homework from her bag.

I worked on her homework for two hours before I slammed all her books closed, packing her bag and zipping it up angrily. I stomped around in her room, getting her uniform ready and blitzing around her room so that it was actually tidy. When the rubbish bag was full, I tied it up and changed it, ready to take both Alessia's dirty clothes and her rubbish downstairs for a wash.

I let Alessia in for just a second, for her to let me know that her dad will be back in two hours, giving me enough time to put her clothes on a wash. I marched downstairs angrily, throwing her rubbish out the front; ready for collection. Her washing machine was in the corner, and I crept around the piles of rubbish and whatever the hell was stained onto the tiles, emptying the basket into the machine and starting a wash.

Since Alessia was too scared to leave her clothes, fearing that her dad would come back early and punish her for washing them here, I stayed downstairs. Her dad can go to hell. When they were washed, I threw them in the tumble dryer, increasing Alessia's fear.

I checked the kitchen clock—Alessia thought he'd be home soon. And if he was-

I jumped when tumble dryer beeped, opening the door quickly and throwing the clothes into the basket. I double-checked the tumble dryer and the washing machine for lost items and also did the same around the floor before I ran out of the kitchen, into the lounge and up the stairs. When I got to the top, I heard the front door open.

Slowly, and whilst holding my breath, I tip-toed over to Alessia's room, walking in and placing the basket on the floor. I turned around to shut the door—that's when I saw a singular sock lying on the stairs.

I swore internally, feeling Alessia's heart thump in her chest.

Okay.

I opened the door once more and listened out for Alessia's dad. I heard a click and, after waiting for a few moments on the landing, I smelt smoke. He was smoking. Inside the house.

I heard him grunt, and the sound of many things smashing and clanking around, before I heard the stove being lit. I remembered where the stove was, and if he was standing by it, his back would be to the stairs.

As I crept closer to the steps, I had to consider if they would creak. As I remembered, they would. The sock was close enough that I could reach it, yet Alessia's dad would see me if I took too long.

I took a breath, and placed my head in the corner of the banister, seeing her dad exactly where I thought he would be. With that, I quickly got down onto my stomach, reached out as quick as I could, latched onto the sock with only my index and my middle fingers before yanking it away.

I slowly rose, and used the same speed to get back into Alessia's room. I closed the door as quietly as I could before I locked it.

After throwing the sock in the laundry basket, I finally took a breath.

Alessia Trent, you don't even deserve my help; do anything like what you did to me today with Dylan again and I'll never help you ever again. I'll just sit here and watch your miserable life play out.

Don't cross me.

CHAPTER NINETEEN

When Monday morning came, I didn't even have to open my eyes to know that I was in Alessia's body still.

I kind of saw it coming—and then there was the eerie sense of joy, caused by the possibility of seeing Dylan again.

With a huff, I ripped the sheets off Alessia's body before jumping into the shower.

When I was clean, I brushed my teeth before drying my hair. I couldn't help but stomp around all over the place, and then I realised.

Alessia's dad.

I dropped all that I was holding and checked the time.

I had *one minute*.

I unlocked her door as fast I could, sprinting down the stairs so fast I almost slipped. When I got downstairs, I didn't even check the time before I shook him awake.

As always, he moaned and groaned, and then he checked the time.

He laughed, slapping my leg. "For once, my pathetic excuse of a daughter can tell the time," I ducked my head, seeing as Alessia thought that was best. "Then again, you always find some way to show me up," with that, he shoved me into the wall and walked straight past me.

Well, that wasn't too bad.

After checking that the coast was clear, I dashed back up to Alessia's room, leaving her hair as it was and starting her makeup.

When I was done, I quickly ran serum through Alessia's hair, turning her frizzy hair into beautiful curls. *You're welcome.* Like always, threw Alessia's hair into a half up-half down style, though turning the ponytail into a small bun on Alessia's head before tying a ribbon around the hair-band.

Slipping on Alessia's shoes, I sprayed her body with the perfume that smelt the most like my signature scent. I'm surprised Alessia didn't try to steal the actual bottle of my perfume from Dylan's house.

I almost forgot their project and so emptied the bag of everything I had worked on before shoving it into Alessia's school bag.

And that's when I saw it.

The t-shirt Alessia had borrowed from Dylan.

I hadn't let Alessia take control of her body for long at his house, and I don't recall her stealing his top when she did have control. Perhaps it was a mistake, perhaps I accidentally grabbed it. Or maybe she accidentally picked it up when he dismissed her after their kiss.

Whatever the reason was, I didn't care. I grabbed Alessia's bag and left her room, and then her house.

When I entered Nell's shop, I greeted her but kept the conversation short when I was paying since I was beginning to run late.

I got to school with ten minutes to spare and used the time to walk to toilets that wouldn't be occupied by the ghost of Olivia Clark's past. *Well, Kiara, but it's all the same these days.*

When I was finished in the toilets, I hurried to our registration class, taking my designated seat at the back in the corner. I spent most of the time putting the finishing touches on Alessia's homework, which I had deliberately left unfinished to make time throughout the day. My life was beginning to become very hard.

I was suddenly interrupted by the seat next to me being taken. I sighed, knowing that it would just be another bully coming to play. But, when I looked up, I recognised the boy as Lucas, the one person who had actually spoken to me at Matt's party.

"Hey," he said, holding out a packaged croissant, "whatcha working on?" Lucas annoyed Alessia, but *I* could actually use the friends.

So I smiled, saying, "French."

He frowned over at the sheet I was completing, "that's quite low grade stuff," he acknowledged. He wasn't mocking Alessia, but she thought that he was. After all this time of being bullied, she'd finally caved; her trust diminished. But I was not that way.

I nodded, "my French teacher doesn't think I can do the high grade stuff." I told him, watching as curiosity sparkled in his eyes.

"Say that in French," he said, eyes challenging me.

"What?" I asked, confused.

He smiled, leaning back in his chair, "I know you can do it; you used to be the top of my class before they made you drop a few sets." He said.

I frowned. As Olivia Clark, I was in Lucas' set, but I don't remember Alessia ever being in my class. Then again, I wasn't *always* in the top set; perhaps I got my spot in the class when she left it.

"So you want me to say what I just said in French?" I asked him, trying to recall what I had just said. He nodded, smiling.

"Okay," I began, starting a mental translation in my head. "mon professeur.." I began, seeing him nod, beaming at me. I grinned, and then continued, "..de français ne pense pas que je puisse faire les choses de haute qualité."

When I was finished, Lucas grinned at me, "C'est de la merde. J'ai un travail de qualité que vous pouvez emprunter?"

I paused, "Really?" I asked, overwhelmed at the first bit of kindness that I was experiencing in four days. And it felt warm and light. Lucas was going to give me some of his higher grade work. He beamed, nodding at me.

"I'll get it now," he said, raising from his seat and walking over to his friends. They watched as Lucas silently picked up his bag and placed it down on the table beside mine before he sat back down.

I glanced between him and his friends, "Are you sure?" I asked him, uncertain.

He nodded, smiling again, "Oh," he said, holding out the croissant he had been holding, "I brought this for you," I frowned down at it as I took it, "you told me you liked croissants when you were in my class for French." He said, shrugging.

I smiled up at him.

Well I'll be damned—I think Lucas has a crush on Alessia. Score for me.

It's too bad she's already pining for my best friend whilst I—out in my real body—remain oblivious to this fact.

I took the croissant gingerly, slipping it and the work Lucas had lent to me into my bag. We were soon dismissed, and I left the classroom for Biology, my first lesson.

When I arrived, Dylan and I were the last few people to get there; we quickly took our seats next to each other. That's when I metaphorically sat back, letting Alessia look at the mess she made.

She immediately shied away, hiding behind her hair. When the teacher set us off to do our projects, she doodled on the corner of her page for a few moments before Dylan finally tapped her on the shoulder.

"Alessia," he began, sighing when he got no response, "look, I know you're ignoring me because of what happened on Saturday..." he said, making Alessia pause drawing, "but I promise that it's fine; it happened and that's okay but, for now, we need to do this project."

Alessia squeezed her eyes shut, "I'm really sorry," she said.

"It's fine," Dylan replied. With that, Alessia tucked her curtain of hair behind her ear, smiling over at Dylan before she turned around in her seat to face him. Then they began to work on their project.

Since Alessia seemed to enjoy Dylan's company so much, and since I was kind of bitter over what happened, I let her have the reigns. But it was only because I was annoyed. I'll take them back as soon as she tries to do something else that's stupid.

When the lesson finally came to an end, Alessia was sad. In fact, she was already feeling the separation as Dylan began to pack up. She sighed, doing the same.

Spending time with Dylan made her light and happy, something I could relate to. Except, I know that she kissed him. She should probably tell him how she feels at some point—*what's holding her back*? If she's scared, I'll happily do it for her. I seem to be doing everything she needs for her these days.

Well, if this is hell, I'll have my own rules.

Whatever got me here, I have control of Alessia's life, and I'll play by my own rules.

As long as she stops getting herself into useless trouble.

CHAPTER TWENTY

By the time the lunch bell rang, I had no lunch to eat. Alessia's lunch and history work had been drowned at break time.

I wandered through the field uselessly, stopping at a random tree and slumping down. I didn't need a computer to re-do Alessia's history work, just immense inspiration; something I was just about out of. After Alessia's possessions took a bath, I decided to take my control back, shoving the girls away, grabbing what I could and getting the hell out of those toilets.

I kept finding Alessia incredibly useless. But once I had taken a breath and calmed down, I realised that she wasn't useless and just asking for what she got—she was indescribably terrified. It was just one look, one look from someone she didn't even know and she froze. I guess that's what happens when you're abused at home and bullied at school. And even if I hate being here, I've only been here for five days.

Alessia's had to deal with this for 16 years, and I'm stumped at *five days*.

I sighed and began Alessia's history work, finding a packet of crisps in Alessia's bag to snack on whilst I completed it.

I watched as the boys did cross-country across the field—something I used to do with Kiara in Year Nine. The girls and boys had their own separate sports at lunch times apart from on Fridays, which was when the sporty people could choose which sport they wanted to do altogether. It was usually netball or tennis.

I watched as Dylan ran past with a small smile on my face. Alessia was exaggerating my emotions, but I really was glad to see him. It also gave me nostalgia; back to Year Nine when Kiara and I would point out the hottest guy. Kiara always said that I should point out Dylan, but I didn't want to since he was my best friend. It was *weird*.

Alessia, however, didn't think it was. Then again, she wasn't best friends with Dylan.

I shoved her out of her own mind when she got too distracted, completing her history work before she wasted any more of my time.

"Hey," someone said, after a bag landed beside me.

I looked up to see Lucas joining me.

"I hope I'm not interrupting," he said, smiling down at me as he sat down beside me.

I grinned over at him, "No, I just-" I paused, "well, actually, you are," I told him, gesturing to Alessia's history homework.

Lucas nodded, seeming curious, "I didn't know you chose history." He said, pulling out lunch he did *not* find in school.

"Wow," I said, my eyes widening, "you're eating contraband for lunch." I retorted, pursing my lips.

He laughed, "My brother is in sixth form; he brought me back some." I nodded, before returning to my work once more.

"Where's your lunch?" He asked, opening a bottle of sprite.

I sighed, "Running along the drain pipes by now, I'd assume."

Lucas took a while to respond. "I've seen a few people picking on you, but I didn't know it was that bad."

I shrugged, "neither did I." I murmured, crossing out something that I had gotten wrong whilst being distracted.

"Well," he said, "I told my brother to buy extra," I turned to see him holding out another bag towards me.

I frowned, taking the bag and peering into it, seeing a KFC. I glanced between the bag and him, making him laugh.

"I hope you're not a vegetarian anymore," he said, taking a sip of his drink.

I smiled, shaking my head, "Even if I was, I wouldn't care." I ignored the look Lucas was giving me before I ditched my history work to lean over and give Lucas a hug.

"Thank you, Lucas." I said, pulling away to see him smiling.

"No problem, Lessie."

I had a feeling that Alessia and Lucas had some sort of history, perhaps they attended a summer camp together, or maybe they were just friends.

But, tuning into Alessia for a few seconds, I found that she in fact just wanted him to leave her alone.

I didn't understand their relationship that much but Lucas was a really nice boy; he has Alessia's best interests in mind. So I let him distract me from Alessia's work—which I only finished ten minutes before the end of lunch, thanks to Lucas and his ability to keep a conversation going.

When lunch came to an end, Lucas waited for me outside the girls toilets before walking me to my next class. Before he left me, he tapped his number into my phone, which I accepted gratefully.

You're welcome, Alessia.

The lesson went by pretty fast, and I spent a good majority thinking about Lucas. He was pretty sweet. My last lesson of the day was RE and so I made my way there, getting pushed around by Year Sevens—then again, there was nothing new there.

When we were all settled down, the teacher announced that we'd be doing paired work, before assigning us to each other. A light noise stretched across the room as people complained about having to split up. All Alessia kept thinking is how people could be so pathetic. She had no friends. Not just in this class, but in this *school*. Well, she didn't have any friends at all, really. They should find themselves lucky that, when the hour is up, they get to talk to their friends once more.

Alessia got paired up with Reece Brian, a really quiet guy whom I had never spoken to before. They sat at the back, but I was suddenly distracted.

I think I remember this lesson.

I took my eyes off the real Olivia Clark when I felt Alessia talking. It was so strange—hearing the voice you had been using for days but not intending for the words to be spoken.

After hearing some commotion in front of me, I glanced up, frowning around the room. Then my eyes landed on the back of Olivia Clark. She was sitting next to–

I froze. Alessia froze.

This was the day that the teacher had paired me up with Matt. But Alessia didn't know what Matt had done to me and rolled her eyes when she saw Olivia biting back at Matt.

The truth is, Matt had been putting his hand on my thigh under the table, saying things he shouldn't be saying to me. I remember growing more and more annoyed by the minute, and that's when my hand went up.

"Sir," Olivia called out, not afraid of attention, unlike Alessia. The teacher gestured for her to continue. "Can I please change partners?"

That's when everyone looked up, exchanging glances confusedly. The teacher gestured for Olivia to follow him out of the room, a frown between his brows.

The room grew louder when the teacher left the room and, when the door opened next, only the teacher returned.

Alessia frowned, confused. To her, I was perfect. Nothing could ever be wrong. My grades were pristine, my relationships with teachers and students were impeccable and, best of all, I had Dylan.

That's what Alessia thought of me.

The teacher had a private word with Matt, who nodded, throwing the teacher a smile. As Olivia, I pulled a face. Matt puts on a disguise, but he's really a disgusting mongrel.

He collected his work and I dragged my eyes along with him as he got up to move. He switched with Katy Moore, who took over from Matt, getting straight to work.

When Olivia returned, she thanked the teacher and, when she turned, she didn't look so perfect anymore. Alessia noted glassy eyes and frazzled hair—both of which were fixed almost instantly as Olivia seemingly realised.

She took a seat next to Katy, greeting her and thanking her. Alessia couldn't hear this, but I know that's what happened.

Olivia rose suddenly, attracting Alessia's attention once more. She frowned after her, not understanding what all the fuss was about. She noted that everything always had to be perfect with me—I was just a prissy princess in her eyes.

Alessia watched as I stood in front of Matt, arms crossed over my chest. She thought I was just asking for trouble.

What really happened is that Matt had 'accidentally' taken my work when he had moved, and I was simply asking for it back.

"You're such a frigid slut, Olivia." Alessia heard Matt say as he shoved her work into her hands.

Astounded, Alessia froze, though quickly ducked her head as the real Olivia Clark turned, not wanting to be seen.

But, when Olivia was seated, she dared to look up again at her. She watched the real Olivia through curious eyes. Still, she couldn't swallow the bitter taste that rose in her throat when she saw me.

CHAPTER TWENTY-ONE

When I got home, I was greeted by the stench of alcohol and cigarette smoke. Alessia's dad wasn't home, but the smell was thick enough that I could gather that he perhaps had been just recently.

I sighed, dragging my feet up every step until I got to the second floor, unlocking Alessia's door and slipping in, locking it again quickly. When you live with an abusive psychopath, it's kind of how you run things.

As I dumped my bag on the floor, Alessia's phone buzzed. I slipped her blazer and shoes off before checking it, frowning as I did so; Alessia didn't really *get* text messages.

I smiled when I saw that it was from Lucas. I had texted him between fifth and sixth period when I had his number, and now he had mine.

'*Wanna call later? We can talk about our day in French??*'

I smiled down at her phone, falling down on her bed on my stomach, beaming as I typed my response.

'*I've got nothing better to do x*'

I gnawed at my lip as I waited for Lucas' reply, feeling I had used the kiss inappropriately.

Eventually, though, after I'd changed and brushed through Alessia's hair three times, Lucas responded.

'*It's a date x*'

And then, suddenly, I had butterflies. I have had my fair share of boyfriends—well, *one*—but I'm a girl and it's common that a boy's interest in you makes you tingle slightly. And I was tingling. Alessia couldn't care less, *in fact*, she wanted to block Lucas' number. I mean, it wasn't exactly like she had mountains of friends to fall back onto—and I also just wanted to get to know Lucas; I hadn't really spoken to him when I was in school.

I passed the time waiting for Lucas' call by charging my phone and completing my homework. When it neared six, I dashed downstairs and prepared a ready meal, before running back up the stairs with it when I was done. As I was locking the door, I was suddenly aware of buzzing.

My eyes widened and I rushed over to my phone. Lucas was calling. I settled as much as I could, placing my meal down on the side and patting my hair. When I thought I was calm, I leaned back against Alessia's wall, seated on her bed, and picked up the call.

The screen loaded for a minute or two, and then Lucas appeared, sitting on an office chair, leaning across a desk.

"Bonjour, mon cher," he said, making me giggle.

"How long were you practising that for?" I asked, making him look away sheepishly.

"Well, you did take quite a while." He said, shrugging.

I smiled, leaning over to grab my dinner, "Well, I'm sorry, I was busy preparing my microwave food."

Lucas pulled a face, "*Microwave?*" He asked, and I nodded whilst taking a mouthful. "Can you not cook?" He asked.

I smiled, "If I couldn't would you hate me?" I asked.

He shook his head, mirroring my smile, "No," he told me.

"*Score,*" I said, making him laugh. When I settled, I said, "I just make microwave meals because I don't have that much time,"

I said, avoiding his eyes as I took more mouthfuls. "Interesting," he said, making me frown up at him, "you have a busy life."

I scoffed, shaking my head, "I wish; you're probably the first human being I've had this much communication with for a week now," I said.

"A week?" Lucas asked.

I peered up at him, suddenly realising what I had said. "Well, obviously my social suicide has been taking place for a while now, but I'm only just realising how bad it is."

Lucas laugh, "I'll save you from your annihilation." He said, making me smile.

Lucas and I continued to talk for hours, and when the time came for me to get in the bath, Lucas somehow convinced me to put him on voice call and leave the phone on the side of the bath. Lucas was so easy to talk to; conversation just appeared as and when we needed it. It reminded me, wistfully, of Dylan; a week is a long time to go without my closest friend. We've spent almost 9 years attached to each other; it was hard to accept that that just can't be when I'm Alessia.

Lucas completed his homework and had a quick shower whilst I was in the bath, returning as I got out of the bath and wrapped a towel around Alessia's body.

When it was time to go to sleep, Lucas told me he'd stay on the call until I was asleep, and promised he'd save me from my social suicide tomorrow after meeting me at the entrance to school so we could walk to registration together.

I fell asleep smiling. Lucas was a really good guy. I could tell that he really liked Alessia. Lucas and I had rarely had any interaction when I was in school, and so I know that Lucas isn't talking to me for me—then again, it is *my* personality in Alessia's body. *Maybe he fell for her looks and my talk?*

One can hope.

He's very sweet.

I woke up with the same thought, though also with a striking pain in my stomach. I knew it all too well by now—it was Alessia's period. *For God's sake—first her social life and now her bodily functions.*

I sighed, dragging myself out of bed and into the bathroom, getting ready sluggishly. My makeup had to be simple, what with the time I had left, and I left Alessia's hair as it was after brushing it.

And then I froze.

Alessia's dad.

I swore repeatedly, sweating profusely as I checked the time on her phone.

When I saw it, I'm pretty sure the colour drained from my face. Everything suddenly became dizzying, spinning around in front of me.

And then.

"*Alessia!*"

I dropped to the floor, frozen.

Oh my god.
Oh my god.
Oh my god.

I heard him stomping up the stairs and I began to shake, my body being seized by trembles.

Then, the door handle twisted. But the door was locked. I watched with wide eyes as the door handle continued to rattle.

"You *bitch*!" He yelled, "You've made me late to work!" And then the door was thrown open, "And your efforts to keep yourself safe are almost as pathetic as you." He spat before he marched over to me.

I jumped up from the ground, yelping. I tried to jump over Alessia's bed and out the door but he grabbed my leg, making my body freeze in the air and come crashing down to the floor. My chin hit the floor, and a striking pain soared through my head. It was then that I tasted blood in my mouth.

He picked up Alessia's wooden chair, hurling it at me. It came straight at my face, which I threw an arm in front of. The legs of the chair knocked my head back, skimming the top of my head, probably skinning it.

I cried out, trying to crawl over to the door. Suddenly, Alessia's body was yanked back by her ankle.

"I should do nothing but sell you off as a prostitute; maybe you'll do some good then!"

I started to sob, trying to get to my feet. Alessia's dad picked me up by the arm, twisting my body around before throwing his fist into her face. I fell to the floor, though not before the other side of Alessia's face hit the, very hard, end of her bed.

My body crashed into the floor, and I was in so much agony that I felt as though my body was a magnet and the floor was magnetic. Alessia's body was pushed over so that I lay on my back, and then Alessia's dad sent his foot pummelling down onto her stomach. I screamed, my already bad period pains becoming detrimentally bad.

And just when I thought Alessia's body would cease to be, Alessia's dad sent one lasting punch to Alessia's face. And it was his hardest one yet.

I think he left after that, but I couldn't see anything, feel anything, hear anything, taste anything.

That's when I blacked out.

CHAPTER TWENTY-TWO

When I awoke, I thought I was dead. Everything hurt so, so much. Every bone, every muscle, every stretch of skin. I felt broken.

A sudden buzzing made me refocus. Alessia's body was still in Alessia's room. But I had vacated her head. I didn't want to feel it, I didn't want to know it.

Alessia pulled herself across the carpet until she found her phone, identifying the caller, already crying when she picked up.

"Alessia?" He asked, making the tears fall faster, "Lucas has been worried about you all morning, and we have biology next—are you okay?" He asked.

She then let it out, letting her sobs become audible.

"Alessia?" He asked, sounding more and more concerned.

"Dylan," she responded, feeling every nerve in her body crack. "Dylan I really need help," she said, desperation replacing her pain momentarily.

"Okay," he said uncertainly, "what do you need me to do?"

"Do you remember where I live?" She asked suddenly, making his audio pause over the phone.

"Kind of, yeah," he replied.

She breathed out, eyes closed, "I really need you to get here. Like now. There's a key under the blue plant pot and I'm on the second floor, the room with the broken door panels." With that, she quickly hung up, not wanting to divulge any further details for fear that she might accidentally tell Dylan that she gets abused at home. It's been a long kept secret of hers that kept her sane at school; she did not want pity, but she also didn't want to be shamed for being the girl that no one loves. Not her dad, not anyone at school, and certainly not Dylan.

I could've poured ideas about Lucas into her brain; he loves her, cares about her. But I was numb and buried far too deep into Alessia's brain to be summoned so easily. I had retreated into the shadows and wanted to leave Alessia's broken body as soon as possible. I couldn't be here for any longer.

Alessia was lying limp on the ground for what seemed like hours—and then she heard the front door open.

"Alessia!" Dylan yelled, running up the stairs after slamming the front door shut.

When he got to her door, Alessia heard him curse. "Oh my god, Alessia?"

He rushed over to her side, leaning down and pushing her hair away from her face.

She smiled, though weakly, "Dylan." She whispered.

His eyes searched her, wide and fearful.

"What...what happened?" He asked, looking around the room before his eyes ran across Alessia's body, concern etched onto his face.

Alessia shook her head, "nothing important," she lied, "I just...I really need you to help me understand if anything's really badly damaged."

He nodded, thinking, "Olivia's dad is a doctor, I'm sure if we get her here-"

"No one else can know about this, Dylan, do you understand me? *No one.*" Alessia interrupted quickly, her heartbeat quickening.

"Well I can't.." Dylan trailed off, "I don't know about this stuff."

Alessia thought about this for a moment or two. "Call Olivia?" She suggested.

Dylan leaned back, pondering on this. "I guess so," he said, pulling out his phone and unlocking it, "she's in dance rehearsals so she can pick up."

Alessia nodded, watching him press his phone to his ear, noticing how quickly he was able to dial her number, as if it were a recent call or text message.

"Remember," she said, trying to forget about Olivia—*me*. "Don't tell her too much." Dylan nodded, though his eyebrows were furrowed as he did so.

"Olivia," he greeted her and Alessia noticed how his face lit up ever so slightly. "Yeah," he said, "yeah I know but something important came up," he said, eyes on Alessia's wounded body. Alessia's heart lifted as he referred to her as 'important'.

Dylan listened to whatever Olivia was saying for a while, before he nodded. "Are you free right now? I need your injury expertise."

Dylan smiled at whatever Olivia's response was, "Yeah, well I seem to think you're pretty good at it."

Dylan waited for her response, smiling and nodding at Alessia when he supposedly got it. "Thank you," he said, before putting his call on speakerphone, setting down his phone on the side and describing Alessia's injuries one by one, getting medical advice from Olivia in return.

I think I remember this. Dylan had made me so worried that day—going missing from school after lunch, then calling me up to talk me through serious injuries after I had been worriedly spamming his phone with texts and calls.

Soon, Dylan required bags upon bags of ice and a first aid kit, and so muted Olivia to ask Alessia where to get some. He then got up, leaving Alessia and taking his phone with him.

Alessia sighed, closing her eyes and resting her head against her carpet. She really liked Dylan, despite Lucas' attempts to get closer to her, and feared she'd never get as close as she wanted to Dylan because of me. She feared I'd stand in her way.

When Dylan came back in the room, he was slipping his phone back in his pocket with a smile on his face. Alessia was trying to sit upright, and Dylan quickly joined her to help her up.

"Maybe we should get you onto your bed instead." Dylan suggested and Alessia smiled, nodding at the idea. Dylan left the bags of peas, and the first aid kit he had found downstairs, on Alessia's carpet as he helped her up. He guided her over to her bed, helping her on and propping her up by placing pillows behind her back and her head.

Alessia smiled at Dylan, who passed her a bottle of water and two bags of crisps. Although it hurt, Alessia laughed, gulping down her water before opening her first bag of crisps.

Dylan placed the bags of peas where they needed to be, and Alessia watched Dylan care for her injured body with hearts in her eyes. She loved watching him, and watching Dylan actually care about her made her heart expand at a faster rate.

Dylan opened the first aid kit, attending to any gashes or deadly bruises. When he was done, he sat on the end of Alessia's bed, just watching her.

Alessia smiled, "Thank you so much Dylan—for everything."

Dylan nodded, "It's okay," he said, "maybe you should take tomorrow off." He said, pulling her duvet farther across her legs to cover them up completely.

Alessia frowned, shaking her head, "I'll be fine; I've had worse," she told him, finishing off the last of her crisps before opening the second one.

Dylan's gorgeous green eyes seemed to be clouded with concern—that's what Alessia thought. "What happened?" He asked quietly, as if he was scared that he'd break her if he spoke louder.

Alessia looked away, "Nothing," she said, "like I said, I didn't want to tell you details, you only know what you saw."

Dylan sighed, looking away before nodding.

"And you can't tell Olivia anymore than she knows—shut her down when she starts to question." Alessia told him, watching him appear uncomfortable.

"I can handle Olivia," he said, which made me pull a face from where I sat on the sidelines in Alessia's mind.

Alessia was more wistful, again reminded of the connection between Dylan and me. It was strange how everyone seemed to think we were some kind of couple, or that Dylan liked me, when Dylan has never said such words to me. People should stop assuming. Just because Dylan's a boy and I'm a girl, it doesn't mean we're going to be in love. *We're best friends.*

But that's what Alessia thought the strongest relationships were built on. She thought that if she could get as close to Dylan as I was, she'd stand a chance of him loving her. She thought friendship was the essential ingredient.

Well, at the rate I'm going at, it doesn't matter if Dylan and I love each other or not—I'll never get back to my real body.

I think I'm stuck here; for better or for worse, I am Alessia Trent now.

CHAPTER TWENTY-THREE

When morning came, Alessia dragged herself out of bed, lingering thoughts of Dylan on her mind. She remembered that, when he had left, he had grabbed her hand, reassuring her that nothing like this would ever happen to her again. Alessia, of course, couldn't and didn't believe him, but the kiss he pressed to her forehead silenced all those thoughts, and she was suddenly seeing rainbows and bright, blue skies.

She stepped into the shower smiling, refusing to wash away the remains of Dylan's lips on her forehead.

When she was finished, she pulled on her uniform, hitching up her skirt higher than usual, smoothing her collar down and smiling at herself in the mirror.

She threw her hair up into a towel before she left her room to wake her dad. Her blood boiled when she thought of him, yet even that couldn't dim her happiness. She shook him awake when it was time, let him call her a slut and shove her away from him, before she skipped up the stairs, twirling into her room and locking the door.

She began her makeup shortly after, putting more on than she usually did. When it was time for hair, she smiled, removing her towel from her hair and blow-drying her hair. She made it so that her curls were more relaxed, noting that that was what 'Olivia' usually did. I sat back, watching in shock as she attempted my signature half-up, half-down style. And with ribbons.

Although she couldn't quite pull it together like I could, she still did it. She had tried everything with Dylan—the only thing she knew was that he liked me. And so she would become Olivia Clark.

I almost laughed at the irony. *This girl thinks that becoming someone else will solve her problems?* Well I'm trying it, and trust me, it's making me go *insane*.

Of course, Alessia couldn't hear me. I was living out her life which has already happened, and so it seems that everything will take place as it did no matter what I do.

When Alessia was finished with copying everything about me, she slid on her blazer whilst she slipped into her shoes. Then, she made her way to her vanity, and I supposed it was to check her reflection one last time or to pick up something she left.

I was wrong.

Alessia opened the top drawer of her vanity, and then I saw it.

My perfume.

Alessia reached out and grabbed it, a smug smile on her face as she spritzed it all over her body.

I was desperately trying to figure out how she would've got her hands on my favourite perfume. Not even *Kiara* knew the name of this scent; she only knew that it was from Cuba and that my dad brought some back every time he went to work there. I had been given compliments for its silage ever since, hearing rumours that boys just wanted to hang around me to smell it. I, of course, knew that was a lie, or at least an exaggerated truth. But everyone knew it was my scent. A girl in the year below once told me she can distinguish Olivia Clark from the crowd because of the scent. During a game of hide and seek in the dark, a traditional game of our friendship group's, Dylan told me that he had only found me because of the scent.

And now Alessia had her hands on it.

Alessia was wearing my scent.

As Alessia locked up, a terrible feeling overcame me. I tried so desperately to deny it, believing Alessia was better than that. But I couldn't deny it.

Alessia must've stolen the bottle from Dylan's bathroom.

I never touched it. But that doesn't mean that Alessia didn't.

I was more angry than ever, and my strong emotions had me in and out of the spotlight. Sometimes I'd feel the wind against my face, my feet against the ground or smell the scent of my perfume as it lingered on Alessia's neck. Others, I'd feel only a gentle breeze, light sensations on the soles of Alessia's feet, and only a faint trace of my favourite perfume.

I tried to calm down, to give Alessia back her control, but that almost got me run over. Alessia cringed as the car beeped at her, and I instantly ducked back into the shadows, letting Alessia make her way to Nells' shop.

"Hi, Nells!" Alessia called as she skipped into the shop, darting straight for her favourite snacks and drinks, hearing Nells laugh from the tills.

When Alessia was paying, Nells noted that she looked different, saying that she liked her hair that way.

Alessia grinned, grabbing her stuff and shoving it into her bag, "I like it this way, too," she said, irritating me, "have a good day, Nells." She said, swinging her bag over her shoulder and leaving the shop grinning.

My distaste for Alessia growing, I was barely present when she was walking to school. Alessia immediately headed for most unpopular toilets of the school, and she used them in peace. I took a mental note of where the toilets were, just in case I ever end up controlling this body again. At this rate, I'll probably have to in order to avoid Alessia throwing herself at Dylan.

Alessia made her way to registration, drawing attention to herself with the grin on her face. Alessia thought that this was it—this was her happiest day, at least before she got to kiss Dylan again.

She calmed herself slightly, relaxing her smile before she slipped into the classroom. She sat down in her seat quickly to avoid drawing the attention of her classmates to her.

When Alessia was flicking through her planner to see if she had any homework she had to complete for today, someone joined her.

She looked to her left to see Lucas sitting there, beaming at her. She sighed, turning away, annoyed that he always seemed to be near her.

"Hey," he said, "I'm so glad you're okay, I thought something had happened to you yesterday," he said, sounding concerned. But Alessia didn't care; she just wanted him to leave.

"Are you okay?" Lucas said, making Alessia turn to look at him, seeing Lucas frowning at her.

"Just leave me alone, Lucas," she said, and I noticed his hand, which was holding a croissant out to her, retreat.

His frown deepened, "What? What's wrong?" He asked, making her roll her eyes and return to her work. It broke my heart to see her put him down like this. All Lucas had ever done was be nice to her. Just when she was about to say all kinds of profanities and shove him off his seat, I yanked her back and took control of her body once more.

I sighed, closing Alessia's planner before I turned to face him, smiling at him.

"I'm sorry," I told him, "I'm just a little irritable right now," Lucas nodded, eyes full of concern. *How could Alessia hate him?* He has so much compassion for her.

"You can stay," I told him, "in fact, I want you to stay," his smile returned, "and thank you for caring about me."

He beamed, "It's okay," he said, cheeks colouring slightly, "I brought you this," he said, holding his hand out again, the one that held the croissant.

I laughed, "Thanks, Lucas," I said, taking it and grinning at him.

So here I am, controlling Alessia's body once more. And not to stop her throwing herself at Dylan, but to stop her running away from Lucas. She deserved someone who always thought of no one else but her, and if she was right about Dylan, he isn't that person for her. Lucas is. And I won't let her throw this away.

CHAPTER TWENTY-FOUR

When I woke up the next morning, I didn't even ask if it was Alessia's body I was in or not. I just kind of knew. I expected that, if I wasn't, I'd feel different. Not more like myself, but more in tune...I don't know. These days I've forgotten what it's like it be myself, and not Alessia Trent.

Alessia's morning routine went by in a blur, and I was soon sitting in our registration class once more, feeling out of sorts as I watched one by one as people from my own friendship group joined the class, walking straight by me and towards the real Olivia Clark. She greeted them all the same, as though they were *all* her best of friends. Though, Alessia *did* notice that she was much more affectionate with Dylan, the hug lasting longer and a conversation sparking as soon as they sat down.

I think I almost cried then. Just watching Dylan and I interact, the way he took the seat next to me, the way he played with the sleeves of my jumper as I talked, the way he never took his eyes off me.

That hurt Alessia, especially after what Dylan had witnessed at her house the other day. I sighed, she sighed, though for different reasons.

When she felt a presence beside her, she was prepared to tell Lucas to go away but, upon looking up, she saw that it wasn't Lucas who stood beside her. It was Dylan.

Her eyes widened, and I decided to let her take control of this moment.

"Dylan," she breathed out, watching him join her.

"Hey," he said, softly, "how are you doing?"

She smiled, "And here I thought you were just going to ignore me and flirt with Olivia." She joked. Dylan smiled, ducking his head, as if embarrassed.

"But yeah, I'm fine," she said, making Dylan raised his head and nod.

"If you need anything," Dylan began.

Alessia smiled, "I know." She finished, leaning over to take his hand into hers. Dylan watched the action, eyes curious as they flickered between Alessia's face and her hands clasped around his.

"You'll forever be the kindest boy I know," she said, aware of someone lurking behind her, but not caring a single bit as she held Dylan's eyes for more than just a second.

The person behind her, however, apparently wanted to be noticed; they cleared their throat.

Alessia looked up.

It was Lucas who was standing behind Alessia, looking broken as he glanced between Alessia and Dylan.

Alessia didn't care too much about Lucas, and instead concentrated on the real Olivia and her friends as they glared at Alessia, whispering things to each other. Most of all, she noted Olivia's confusion, and it made Alessia happy to see Olivia upset.

I snapped out of it, and out of Alessia's control, to see Lucas running out of the door.

"*Shoot*," I said, pushing past Dylan, who had risen to leave, as I followed Lucas out. "Why, Alessia? For God's sake—I'm trying my hardest here-" I halted my speech as I broke out into a sprint, well, as fast as Alessia and I could manage.

"Lucas!" I called, finding him in an abandoned corridor. He slowed down, stopped and then turned around, seeming angry.

"Lucas, I'm so sorry," I told him, out of breath as I approached him.

"And why is that, huh? Because you know I like you and care about you, a goddamn lot, Alessia. And you're just here professing your love to Dylan Evans, of all people, Alessia!"

I gulped.

"Lucas," I said softly, reaching out and placing a hand on his bicep.

He breathed, closing his eyes. I raised my other arm, extending it and placing my palm against his face. His eyes fluttered open, and suddenly his lips were on mine.

I was shocked at first, but when his arms came around my waist, I melted into him, kissing him back.

And then Alessia came alive inside of me. I tried to push her back, but I was weak in the moment of bliss and she was angry.

She took hold, pushing Lucas back.

Lucas took note of Alessia's angry expression.

"Alessia..." he began.

She glared at him, "No. You don't get to kiss someone without their consent."

He stared at her, confused, "You kissed back." He said, though not angrily.

She scoffed, "Your morals are twisted."

With that, Alessia span around, stalking off.

"Alessia, wha-" he broke off as Alessia rounded the corner, and continued again when he caught up to her. "You chased after *me*," he said.

Alessia shook her head. "Why don't you get it? I like Dylan, Lucas, not you, so stop trying and leave me the hell alone." With that, Lucas fell behind and Alessia continued to march on, reaching her registration class as everyone left.

Alessia sighed, waiting with her arms crossed outside the room for a gap to sneak in.

Suddenly, she was thrown against the wall. When she looked up, it was Kiara that held her down, Johnny shadowing her.

Alessia wasn't in the mood for trouble, but she didn't want to say anything. She was afraid of the consequences if she did. That's all she knew—you speak, you suffer.

"This is from Olivia,"

Alessia swallowed, "so she actually asked something from you this time?"

Kiara held the neck of Alessia's jumper tighter, almost suffocating her.

She pushed herself closer to her, "Stay the hell away from Dylan." She hissed into Alessia's ear, before letting go, watching as her body fell to the floor.

"Oh," Kiara said, after taking her bag from Johnny's hands. "And I wouldn't expect your bag to be in a good condition when you get inside," she said, pulling a fake grimace before it quickly turned into a smirk.

As she walked away, both Johnny and Kiara started laughing, obnoxiously talking about Alessia.

Alessia was so angry and, as she saw the state of her bag when she entered the classroom, her angry grew to furiousness. Her blood boiled as she considered what Olivia had done to her this time. This time was different; usually Alessia could tell when Kiara was doing something just because Kiara wanted to, and that was often heavily influenced by Johnny, whom she always wanted to impress. But, this time, Kiara had even said it herself—it had come from *Olivia*.

I remembered this day quite well, actually—what Alessia had done in the morning had me conspiring all day. I didn't know why I was so annoyed—Dylan isn't exactly unpopular, and with his manners and his looks, he attracted a lot of girls. Perhaps it upset me to see him reciprocate this time. Then again, why *was* I upset? Dylan is my best friend and I should be happy for him if he gets a girlfriend.

Those are all the things I kept saying last year on this day, well, it actually lasted longer that. And the more I questioned what was going on between Alessia and Dylan, and why that meant so much to me, the more distance that grew between Dylan and me.

Alessia didn't know it yet, but a gap is about to open for her, and she'll be able to fall right through it and into Dylan's arms.

I shook off everything, reclaiming control of Alessia's body and absentmindedly unlocking my locker. Then I realised, it was *my* locker. Not Alessia's.

I was going to close it, and quickly too, but I was taken suddenly into Olivia Clark's world—into *my* world.

Whereas my feelings were nostalgic, Alessia felt detached as she looked at pictures of Dylan and I, stuck to the locker door.

After a few close calls with people walking past outside, I decided to close the door, but my arms froze.

Alessia had taken over.

She ripped the locker door open angrily, and then she tore through my pictures, throwing all of my stuff on the floor when she reached it.

Papers fell out of folders, folders fell apart, pens fell out of pencil cases. I watched with wide eyes as the culprit of the famous vandalism on my locker was revealed. This was the worst thing that I had ever experienced at school; I had been paranoid for months by who it could've been. I don't know why, but I had never been able to put my finger on it.

Alessia leaned into the locker, "you're the worst person I've ever met." She hissed at a school picture of me, before ripping it off the wall and throwing it on the floor. She found a spare bag folded into the corner, smiling when she saw it, taking it for her own.

Of course, *the bag*. That should've been the biggest indicator of who ruined all of my stuff, yet I had forgotten all about it in the frenzy.

Alessia didn't stop to care when something smashed behind her, loading all of her things into her bag, throwing her ruined one into the bin. When she turned around, slipping her bag onto her shoulder, she saw fragments of shattered glass lying on the floor.

She bent down, picking up a piece with curiosity—it was the glass head of some sort of figurine. She then found a wing.

Behind Alessia's eyes, I started to cry.

It was the glass guardian angel that Dylan had bought for me when I was 14; right after my nan had died.

But as Alessia rose from the ground and left, she showed that she didn't even care.

But I did. And, just like I had done when I had found out what happened to the angel last year, I cried. Yet, it didn't matter now—no one would ever hear my cries; buried beneath the life of Alessia Trent.

CHAPTER TWENTY-FIVE

Once she had found out, the whole school was called for an assembly. I never went to the assembly, and neither had Dylan, so he couldn't report back to me. That's because I was in the Head Teacher's office in tears and Dylan was right beside me, trying to calm me down.

I took a seat next to whoever was next to Alessia in the register. I looked up at the person who had joined me, seeing it to be Lucas.

I stared at him, open-mouthed. *Of course, R is close to T in the register.*

He cleared his throat, "You're sitting in my seat," he said, eyes in front of him.

"I'm sorry," I said, "I'll move if you want me to."

"It's okay," Lucas said, eyes flickering down to me for only a moment, "I'm sure no one will notice."

I nodded, looking forward, waiting for the assembly to begin.

When it did, the Head Teacher appeared. We all stood up but she quickly ushered us down.

"Now," she began, "I've called you all out of your classes to discuss a very, *very* serious matter," Alessia gulped; the Head Teacher was very angry.

"Just this morning, a violation of a pupil's property took place," she began, and whispers began to erupt, "we're discussing potential culprits at the moment, but if you know or saw anything, or you *are* the culprit, I would urge you to come forward." She said, doing laps across the stage.

"Not *only* is this misconduct, but this is a serious, *serious* offence. A lot of things were vandalised, including the destruction of items that held great personal value to the student. This is *unacceptable behaviour*, and it will *not* happen in my school." The students stared at her, faces ashen as her voice rose.

"So," she began, "if I do not get a culprit by the end of this week, we will be calling the police." Again, whispers erupted and shocked faces emerged.

"Until then," she said, "we are closing off the St. Andrews block, as it is now being treated as a crime scene. You'll now be dismissed to your third lesson." With that, we were dismissed and, as soon as the students left the hall, talk began.

Alessia snaked her way through the crowd and made her way to RE, her next lesson. She ignored all the talk, walking straight by people, the biggest piece of evidence to the crime sitting upon her shoulders.

When Alessia finally made it to RE, she walked in with her noisy and curious classmates, who were all trying to figure out what had happened, to whom and who was the culprit. Alessia felt almost *smug* at what she had done; she blamed Olivia mostly for her bullying, since Kiara was one of her main bullies and she worked for the interests of Olivia. Johnny was much the same, and then the rest of the school just joined in, blaming her for anything Kiara said she had done, whether she had actually done it or not. As well as this, Olivia had taken the only one who cared about Alessia—Dylan. She was also acutely jealous that Dylan fancied Olivia and not her.

I didn't know how to fight this one; Alessia's argument was valid, yet vandalism was a serious offence—and the guardian angel...

It still breaks my heart to this day, though Dylan said he'd look out for another one. It has been over a year, and he's not the kind to forget, so maybe there just *isn't* another one. There was only one. And Alessia destroyed it.

Alessia was stood up behind her seat, unpacking her bag, when someone joined her.

"I really hope, for the sake of my new manicure, that the vandalism wasn't you," a voice threatened behind me. I turned to see Kiara before swallowing, but it was Alessia who responded.

"Why would I mess with Olivia's stupid locker? I don't even know the code," she said, making Kiara's nostrils flare.

She took a step closer, and Alessia suddenly felt very claustrophobic. "*If* I find out that it was you, this will be the last time that you see this classroom—I'll have you *killed*,"

Alessia's eyes widened, "Even you can't go to those lengths, it's...it's too far, Kiara,"

"You say my name as if we are familiars," she spat, taking another step toward, "but make no mistake, if it *was* you, everyone in this school will hate you. And your life will become such a living hell that, one day, you'll just want it all to stop. I guess it would be a favour to us all if you were gone anyway." Kiara finished her death threat with a simple shrug, as if it were merely nothing to dangle someone's life before their eyes like a simple joke.

I was disgusted. I couldn't believe Kiara was this way. A simple warning would've been suffice, but to threaten Alessia this way...it was no wonder that she was so keen to hurt me.

Alessia was aware that this wasn't the first death threat she had received, which shocked me, but it was the first one she had received physically. The others were on social media, where the kids hid behind the blue screen internet, using names that couldn't be recognised, or saying what they needed to say before deleting it all, as if Alessia had only imagined the hate and abuse. They were sick in Alessia's view. And I agreed—but it doesn't disregard what she did to me.

Once it had begun, the RE lesson didn't go too smoothly and, with the teacher being closely acquainted with the Head Teacher in the ranks, it was easy to get distracted by pestering him for information. All he told us was what we could have already guessed—it took place in St. Andrews corridor, a student's possessions were vandalised and personal items destroyed.

Whispers spreads in the classroom about whether or not it could've taken in St. A3, which was our registration room, since that was the only registration room in the corridor that belonged to a Year 11 class. It made sense too, since there were lockers inside, which would describe the vandalism. They all thought the vandalism happened whilst opening the locker, and that expensive stuff was stolen.

The rumours carried out into the corridor, and as I made my way to Alessia's fourth lesson, they turned more imaginative. Word had got out to some pupils from other year groups, who seemed to believe that a teacher had gone rogue or someone had broken in.

Alessia was finally realising the magnitude of what she had done. She only meant to hurt Olivia; she didn't think about the consequences, or the fact that the whole school would be talking about it. She watched as Year Nine pupils got scolded for telling Year Seven pupils what they knew, before slipping into her next lesson. Biology.

When she got in, she was surprised to see Dylan there.

"Hey, Alessia," he greeted her as she sat down next to him. She noted that he already had everything for their project out and was already working. I knew for a fact that Dylan had left me fifteen minutes before the end of lesson three, and so he probably just went straight to Biology. Alessia guessed that much, though grew annoyed when she realised her crime had only brought us closer together.

"You okay?" Alessia greeted him as casually as she could, taking her books out from her bag.

He sighed, pinching the bridge of his nose, "Not really," he said, and Alessia stayed quiet, waiting for him to elaborate, "Olivia had a bad morning, and it's just hard to see," he said honestly, looking for Alessia's response.

She smiled, "We all have bad mornings sometimes," she said, shrugging, making me angry.

Dylan smiled, though shook his head gravely, "This is different," he said, yet said no more.

Alessia looked away awkwardly. "Is she okay now?" She asked him, watching him glance at her.

He sighed, "Not really, she might be taking tomorrow off, even though she really doesn't want to, and," he began, running his hand through his hair, "she doesn't know it yet, but I'm going to go 'round hers for the night with a Big Basket of Cheer Up."

Alessia laughed, though a bitter feeling crawled up her throat. *They were going to spend the night together?*

That's the thing, Alessia, Dylan and I are best friends, and nothing can stop that. I wish that I could scream that at her, but it's too late now.

CHAPTER TWENTY-SIX

At home, Alessia sat up in her bed for what felt like hours, just staring out into the distance. What she had done today let out most of anger, and all that was left now was regret and fear of what would happen if she was found out.

After gulping, she shot up and out of her bed, tipping out the contents of her school bag and putting them in another so that she wouldn't go to school tomorrow with flashing red evidence on her back.

When she was packing her new bag, though, she found what looked like a box of medication. When she turned it over and read it, she realised what it was.

An emergency contraceptive.

She stared at it, wide-eyed, wondering if Olivia really *had* had sex. Alessia refused to assume that this was with Dylan, though.

That contraceptive wasn't actually mine.

It was Kiara's; I had bought it for her so that she wouldn't have to get it herself, and simply passed her the pill in a public toilet. I was supposed to throw it out after, but I guess I never did.

Alessia stared at it, eyes wide as the hand that was holding it shook. Suddenly, she thought of a million things she could do with this information—tell Dylan, spread the rumours around school, send rumours around that it was Kiara's, forcing Kiara and me into an argument in which I lost all my friends. She wanted revenge—she wanted me to *pay*.

I watched, contemplating taking back control and just throwing the packet away. But I didn't, I sat back and watched her decide to do *all three* at once.

She'd start by pulling a younger year to the side—they didn't necessarily know of her unpopularity, and so they'd listen to her and spread the rumour. Soon, it would get to the Year Elevens and everyone would know that Olivia is the worst friend in the entire earth, and Kiara is as much of a working girl as she makes out to be.

It was a malevolent plan, one that only someone with pure hatred for me could concoct. It scared me that Alessia could really hate me that much, and right under my nose too.

Alessia went to sleep blissfully that night, dreaming of how her plan would work out.

She woke up much the same, and got ready with a spring in her step, checking her pockets for the packet before leaving her house.

What Alessia would never know is that, in the bin outside Nell's shop, is where I threw the empty packet after taking control for only a brief moment. She no longer had evidence.

Walking into school, she sped straight towards her usual bathroom—the ones that were out of the way, the ones she wouldn't be confronted in.

After freshening up and using the toilet, she rushed to her registration class, not wanting to be late. When she got there, though, she found the corridor sectioned off with police tape.

She stared. Alessia hadn't realised that it would've been this serious. But she didn't know the extent of what she had done.

After that day, I spent hours in tears, paranoid and afraid, holding the remains of my glass guardian angel. Because of Alessia Trent, I had to take the rest of the week off. It was, of course, supervised with the help of the school, sending me work and recommending that I sit down and talk about what I was feeling.

Yet, Alessia could not imagine why the school was making a big deal of everything.

She sighed, reading a list of room changes pinned to the wall. She eventually found that her registration class had been moved downstairs.

Alessia took one last look at the abandoned corridor before she span around and started for the stairs, running down them as fast as she could.

When she got to the class, everyone was there but the teacher wasn't. She took her seat at the back, pulling out books and trying to ignore the talk about what happened.

My friends were all present in school, though I was not, and Alessia stared at them, wondering if I had finally understood what she was going through. Alessia was constantly paranoid, looking over her shoulder. Her belongings were *always* ruined. She did not feel guilty at all. Not even a slither.

Alessia had to avert her eyes when Dylan looked up and caught her staring. He looked grave, face full of concern. Alessia hated that what she had done had also reaped some positives for me—she wanted me to suffer, not gain Dylan.

When our registration teacher arrived, he did so in an angry manner. He slammed things around, huffed and pinched the bridge of his nose.

He then proceeded to lose his patience with us.

"If I find out that *any* of you," he said, "were involved in this vandalism, there *will* be consequences."

He dismissed the class in silence when registration was over, whispers following us out into the corridor. Alessia didn't care for rumours, and I wouldn't suspect that she would since she knew the truth. She instead made her way to her first class, waiting for the rest of the class to turn up.

It was weird—that everyone seemed to ignore what had happened. Sure, few whispers made it across the class, but the teacher was as normal as ever, as if there wasn't a police investigation knocking on our doorstep.

By the time lunch had arrived, Alessia was sick of the zombie faces, and got bored enough during lunch that she actually decided to venture *inside*. She watched from a corner of the lunch hall as the dance team practised for the upcoming competitions. *I* was in that dance team—and I missed out on these vital practices because of Alessia's crimes.

That was when Alessia got an idea. She smirked, pushing herself off the wall and striding over to the stage. Few people watched, confused, as she climbed the stairs to the stage. When Alessia reached the top, the dance team stopped dancing, pausing the music.

Ashley Higgins, one of our front dancers, approached Alessia with her arms crossed and a frown etched on her face.

"What are you doing up here, Trent?" She asked, almost snidely.

Alessia shrugged it off though, smiling. "I want to try-out for the team," she said, making Ashley laugh, as if the idea was preposterous. It actually kind of was—Alessia hadn't been successful in any dance class I had seen her in, and this was the last year for our year group, so she had no experience and she suddenly wanted to join?

Alessia watched as the whole dance team mocked her for a few moments. "Look, Less," Ashley began sweetly, "the try-out period passed, and even if we're kind enough to give you a chance, Olivia isn't here." She said, shrugging.

Alessia huffed, "What's it to Olivia?" She asked, frowning as she became angry at the mention of me.

Ashley scoffed, "I don't know, maybe the fact that she's our dance captain and so is in charge of who we do and don't accept into our team?" She finished, rolling her eyes.

Alessia stared at her, mouth agape. "*She's* dance captain?" She asked, making Ashley exchange looks with her fellow dancers before bursting out into laughter once more.

"Sweetie, do you live under a rock?" She asked, mocking her once more.

Alessia's nostrils flared, "Just let me try-out, if Olivia really doesn't want me on the team, she can kick me off."

Ashley pursed her lips, but before she could say 'yes', like Alessia thought she would, another voice suddenly appeared.

"Over my dead body," it said, and Alessia turned to see Kiara stood beside Ashley. When Alessia looked at Kiara, she felt both furious and terrified.

Kiara turned to Ashley, "Run the dance through one more time with the girls, Ashley, let me deal with the delinquent."

Ashley glanced between Alessia and Kiara before huffing and nodding, spinning around and calling the girls back into another group circle.

Kiara took steps towards Alessia, backing her into the stairs, where she would fall if she wasn't careful. "Go back to where you crawled out from, and don't come back out." She said, voice low and threatening.

But Alessia persisted, crossing her arms over chest, "then let me try-out." She said, making Kiara scoff.

"Honey, if you tried out, you'd rework the definition of a failed attempt," she said, inching closer and closer.

Alessia gulped. "You *will* let me try-out," she said, making Kiara laugh, "or I'll tell everyone about those emergency contraceptives." She threatened. Kiara suddenly paled, staring at Alessia with her lips parted.

"What?" She asked, as if she hadn't heard Alessia.

Alessia smiled, "You know what I said, Kiara."

She averted her eyes, "How did you know?" She whispered.

Alessia smiled, "How do you think?" She asked, making Kiara meet her eyes again, "Who else knew about them?"

And that was it. As anger and betrayal flashed in Kiara's eyes, I realised that was the moment that Alessia had made Kiara hate me.

CHAPTER TWENTY-SEVEN

By the time the new school week arrived, Alessia's plan to absolutely and irreversibly ruin me was in play. And it was succeeding.

When I, Olivia Clark, walked into school in the morning, arm linked through Dylan's, I received a few looks, and whispers were passed right before me. I suspected that maybe they had figured out that the vandalism was on my belongings, or that they were curious to why I missed several days of school.

I never for one second anticipated what the real problem was. Alessia was standing beside a girl from the dance team as she was at locker, finding a spare CD full of all the songs we were using for the competition. Alessia watched, arms crossed as she leaned against the lockers, as Dylan and I walked through the corridor.

I didn't notice Alessia; she was unseen but saw everything. And she knew it.

She watched as I uncomfortably walked with Dylan past all the huddles of peoples, scowling as Dylan leaned down and whispered something to me.

I remembered what he had said.

"Don't worry, they're all staring at you because you look so pretty,"

Alessia watched as I beamed, Dylan pulling back and smiling down at me. She huffed, spinning around and facing the girl and away from Dylan and I. No matter what Alessia did, she noticed that I always remained content and happy. She feared that this would all blow over, and everyone would love me once more. After all, Alessia thought Olivia Clark was one of the most loved people in the school.

The girl from the dance team, Bailey, who Alessia hadn't cared to remember the name of, finally handed her the CD, smiling at her. Alessia pulled a fake smile before spinning around and striding away.

I honestly don't ponder for a minute how Alessia got in this state. She has absolutely no compassion in her body. Somebody finally stops, sees her and shows her kindness, and she can't even *thank* the girl.

There was also Lucas, the boy who cared most about Alessia. But she did not care even a fraction about him. She seemed to recoil at the presence of someone who showed her kindness. Maybe that's what bullying does to someone; she expects everyone to hate her, and so when they don't, she doesn't know what to do. So she hates them so that they'll hate her, and *then* she knows what to do. Then everything is normal again.

I couldn't help but also consider the possibility that her dad had something to do with her coldness. Alessia has obviously been abused, and for a while now. She bears scars both on her skin and in her mind. I can just tell. Maybe it has always happened, maybe he has never loved her, and maybe that's why she has never expected anything else from anyone else.

Dylan often tells me I'm so good and reading people, and that it's one of the most prevalent reasons why everyone is so kind to me. I can tell when someone is upset, and so I ask them if they're okay, I can tell when someone is happy, and so I ask them what they're happy about, I can tell when someone is annoyed at me, and so I confront them. It means I have hardly any enemies and many friends.

It may be a trait that Dylan loves about me, but it's Alessia's least favourite trait of mine. She thought she'd have to avoid my eyes for fear of being found out for vandalising my locker and possessions—as if I would ever be able to read someone that skilfully.

Alessia walked towards the library, seeking some quiet time. She sat down at one of the tables, pulling out all the many pieces of homework that were now overdue. I guess this is what happens when I leave Alessia to her own devices.

Alessia sighed, pushing it all to the side and pulling out her sketchbook. She flicked through the pages until she found her drawing of Dylan. She was *almost* finished. She just had to get the ears and the jaw-line right.

When it was finally complete, she beamed down at it, satisfied with her work.

"Nice work," someone said. She jumped, looking up to see Lucas hovering behind her. His eyes flicked between the drawing of Dylan and her face, appearing almost *hurt*. She, of course, though, didn't see this but only an annoyance.

She huffed, turning back in her chair. "Go away, Lucas, I'm busy."

But Lucas did not go away. He instead joined Alessia, taking a seat next to her.

"Busy drawing Olivia's best friend?" He asked, gesturing casually to her drawing. She gritted her teeth.

"You're just jealous I'm not drawing you." She said, making him freeze. He frowned, the confusion overtaking the hurt as it suddenly flashed in his eyes.

"I'm not." He told her.

She scoffed, "Sure," she said, packing up her belongings, noticing that lunch was almost over.

"Look, Alessia, I'm only going to tell you this because I don't want to see you hurt," he said as Alessia began to pack up. "But I don't think Dylan likes you in that way," Alessia tried to ignore the words coming out from Lucas' mouth as she slammed her bag on the table. "Word is he's obsessed with Olivia, and plans to ask her to prom," he told her, lurking behind her as she stuffed papers into her bag.

She shook her head, "You don't know Dylan; you can't be sure." She said, finally looking up at him.

He sighed, "neither do you Alessia; Olivia has eight years on you."

Alessia froze, hand in her bag. "You're right." She whispered, making Lucas frown.

"I am?" He asked, probably shocked that he had convinced her so quickly.

"Yes," she said, "I need to spend more time with Dylan, allow him to get to know me better, as much as he knows Olivia." She said, suddenly feeling inspired.

She pulled out her phone, composing a text to Dylan that proposed that they meet after school to go out.

"That's not quite what I meant," Lucas said, though Alessia ignored him as she waited for a response from Dylan. "What are you going to do, Alessia? Lock Dylan up for eight years and get to know him?" He asked, slowly making Alessia angry. "He's not right for you, Alessia-"

"And what?" Alessia burst out suddenly, disrupting a few people who were still working. "You are?" She asked, not lowering her voice. "Is that what this is, Lucas? A profession of love?" She asked, mocking him.

He swallowed, not saying anything.

She scoffed, "It's a little too late, Lucas." She said, just as her phone beeped. Triumphantly, she showed Lucas Dylan's response, which agreed that they should meet up after school.

"Bye, Lucas." She said, not even noticing or caring when Lucas' face broke as she pulled her bag onto her shoulder. But *I* noticed, and it upset me to see it. She lacked compassion.

She turned to leave, but was held back by Lucas as he grabbed onto her arm, forcing her to face him once more.

"You kissed back," he whispered, lips trembling.

Alessia rolled her eyes. "This again?" She asked, trying to wrench her arm from his hands.

"And all those hours we spent talking, at lunch, in registration, on the phone after school. Alessia, you can't just shut me down after that." He said, tears welling in his eyes.

She yanked her arm away. "Get over yourself, Lucas, I don't care about you, or your kiss or your talking, leave me the hell alone. I don't love you. I love Dylan."

With that, she spun around and strode out of the library, fists clenched. But when she got outside, she was no longer herself.

I was sick of her breaking hearts, breaking friendships and breaking every good opportunity she got.

I took control of Alessia's body, and I took her back into the library.

CHAPTER TWENTY-EIGHT

I found Lucas standing between rows of bookshelves, sighing against the section on criminology.

"Lucas," I whispered, grabbing his attention as I slowly walked over to him.

His eyes flashed when he saw me, and he quickly rubbed at his eyes, "What do you want, Alessia? To drive the knife in further?" He asked bitterly.

She really *had* broken his heart; I had never witnessed Lucas talk in this way to Alessia before.

"I'm really sorry," I began, nearing him and watching him try to avoid meeting my gaze. "I said all those things because I was scared—I meant none of them."

Lucas scoffed, "Alessia, you quite blatantly have a crush on Dylan, you didn't need to tell me for me to know."

I shook my head, "I know, and I do," I said, feeling as though I wasn't lying as much as I should've been. I was trying to play the role of Alessia Trent, who loved Dylan, but I suddenly felt as though *I* wasn't just drooling lies.

"But I care about you, too, Lucas; I was afraid of what that would look like. I-" I began, unsure of what to say. I had reached him, and was about ten centimetres away from him now. "I guess I'm very stubborn, and I'm scared to admit that you're right and I'm wrong." I said, making him frown.

"I can't love Dylan," I whispered, my breath hitching in my throat. "He loves Olivia," I said, almost believing it myself. "And I love you."

"Alessia, wha-"

It was then that I smashed my lips-*Alessia's* lips into his. It took a while for him to respond, but we were soon wrapped up in each other's embrace, kissing each other.

When we were finally done, Lucas pulled away and frowned at me. I shrugged, sharing a quick laugh with him.

"You're the most unpredictable person I know, Alessia Trent." He said, reaching out and tucking a strand of her hair behind her ear.

I smiled, "Isn't that a good thing, though?" I asked, making him consider this.

He shrugged, "Possibly, but not when you're breaking my heart." He teased, making me looking away.

"Hey," he said, placing a palm to the side of my face and bringing my eyes back to him, "I forgive you for that." He said, smiling down at me.

I beamed at him, watching as he pulled away to check the time. He pressed a kiss to Alessia's forehead.

"We're late." He said.

I jumped away from him, checking the time on Alessia's phone. "Oh my god," I said.

Lucas laughed, "What's the rush?" He asked, "You care the least about punctuality and attendance out of all the people I know." He said.

I grabbed onto his hand, pulling him along with me as I rushed through the library. "Yes, well, everyone changes." I said, pushing open the door and running through it.

When I reached my History class, Lucas pulled me in for another kiss, which I had to push away from in order to not be *severely* late.

I left Lucas feeling giddy, walking into the classroom to see chaos. It appeared that our teacher was absent, and so I quickly made my way to my seat, unpacking and making it look as though I hadn't been late.

A substitute teacher suddenly appeared as a paper plane flew across the room. She watched it, eyes pierced. Everyone fell silent.

"Whoever that was, pick it up," she said, hands on her hips as she waited for someone to stand up. That's when Johnny stood up, surprising no one but myself. I didn't take History, and I was in only one of Johnny's classes in my old life. I had only assumed that he was distracted in that class because Dylan and I sat behind him; I wasn't aware that he *actually* lacked studious abilities.

He picked up all his planes, placing them in the bin and muttering an apology to the teacher. She scowled at him, before she required silence to do the registration, before she wrote our tasks on the bored.

I immediately complied, needing to stay in tune with History since I didn't take it as a subject, and so basically needed to learn the stuff from scratch in order to even *begin* to compete with Alessia's classmates.

When the lesson was over, I skipped giddily to French, where Lucas wouldn't stop telling me, in French, how much he wanted to kiss me. How much he wanted to kiss *Alessia*. Only the teacher would be able to understand what he was saying, but she spent most of the lesson at the back of the class, lecturing those who continuously disrupted others.

"Que veux-tu faire après l'école?" He asked, making me laugh as I searched for a French word in the dictionary.

"You don't need to ask that in French," I told him, making him laugh too, "and who said we were doing anything after school?" I asked, making him shrug innocently.

I shook my head, smiling, "Maybe tomorrow," I told him, "I have a pile of overdue homework, and I still need to send Dylan on his merry way." I told him, making him laugh.

"Okay," he said, "mais je veux toujours t'embrasser." I smiled, shaking my head at him once more.

When the lesson was finished, Lucas and I found a small corner to kiss in, before I slipped into the toilets—despite his protests. He waited for me, grinning at me as I exited the toilets.

We walked down the corridor hand in hand, which wasn't much of a problem since no one was around this late after school.

"Okay," I said, pulling my hand away so that I could zip up my coat, "I'll see you tomorrow," I told him, reaching up to place a kiss on his cheek.

He smiled, lacing his fingers through mine, "Call me when you can." He said, making me beam. I nodded, before turning around to leave.

I found Dylan leaning against his car, thumbs tapping at his phone screen. I think I stopped for a moment and just smiled at him. I continued walking over to him slowly, exhaling as I prepared to say my goodbyes to him.

I was going to do that, before Alessia pushed me out of the way and took control once more.

It wasn't so much a conscious decision of hers; this was, after all, *her life*, and her mind and her body. I could choose to interact with it, but, ultimately, if Alessia's emotions are too strong, they overrule everything else and send me pummelling backwards.

She picked up the pace, and Dylan finally glanced up, smiling when he saw Alessia as he tucked his phone away. When Alessia reached him, she ran into his chest, wrapping her arms around him.

Dylan was hesitant, and I could tell he was also slightly confused. Pulling back, he said, "I cancelled on Olivia for you," he told her, "are you okay?" He asked.

"You cancelled on Olivia?" She asked, shocked.

He smiled, "Well, we didn't have a set plan, but we usually hang out after school." He said, shrugging.

"That's sweet," she said, leaning up to place a kiss on his cheek before walking around to the other side of the car. She got in, belting up and waiting for Dylan to unfreeze before joining her.

"Where to?" He asked, switching on the engine.

Alessia pondered this for a second or two, "How about the cinema?" She offered.

Dylan grinned, "The cinema it is." He said, before pulling out of the school.

Alessia enjoyed the car ride, laughing as Dylan attempted to sing along to the radio. Dylan made several jokes, to which Alessia responded eagerly to, enjoying the sound of his laughter.

After Dylan's most recent failed attempt at a high note, he said, "Olivia usually sings louder to drown me out." He said, laughing.

Alessia laughed, though feebly. "I can't sing, so I'd just make it worse." She admitted, making Dylan laugh.

When they were pulled up in the cinema car park, Dylan left Alessia to search for films to watch as he bought a parking ticket.

Dylan returned to the car and quickly slipped in, turning up the heat, "it's cold out there." He said, shutting the door hastily.

Alessia laughed, "it is a cold time of the year." She said.

"What did you find?" Dylan asked, rubbing his hands together to create warmth.

Alessia noticed this, putting her phone down, "Are you really that cold?" She asked, watching Dylan nod. She smiled, "I know something that'll warm you up." She said, a smirk overcoming her lips. She unbuckled her seatbelt, stared into Dylan's eyes for a few moments, and then threw herself at him.

I watched in shock as Alessia swung herself onto Dylan's lap, surprising him. She leant down and pressed her lips against his, forcing him to comply as she pressed her hands to either side of his face. She pulled away to breathe, tracing the lines of his, what she thought, perfectly sculpted face with her index finger.

"Alessia-"

But Alessia swallowed out the rest of what he would've said with another forceful kiss, of which Dylan broke away from.

"Alessia, I don't want to-"

"Shh." She said, starting to untie his school tie.

I watched with wide-eyes and little breath as Alessia Trent tried to make out with my best friend.

Chloe Pile

I watched with wide-eyes and little breath as Alessia Trent sexually assaulted Dylan.

CHAPTER TWENTY-NINE

Dylan was a gentleman. But sometimes that doesn't bode well for him. I could tell by the way that he was kissing Alessia that he didn't want to be doing it, but he did it anyway, trying to protect her pride.

When Alessia was finally finished, Dylan's shirt was unbuttoned and hers was slipping down her shoulders.

She smiled down at him. "I knew you didn't love Olivia as much as everyone said you did," she said, "you love her just as a friend, but there's still room for more." She said, brushing his hair back.

She pressed a kiss against his lips before pulling away and getting back into her seat, buttoning up her shirt. She paused when she saw Dylan staring out in front of him, eyes wide.

"What?" She asked him, confused.

He swallowed, quickly buttoning his shirt back up, "I'll be back," he said, leaving the car as he tucked his shirt in.

Alessia's eyes followed Dylan to where he paused a few metres away from the front of the car. I felt surprise as I saw who he began talking to. Ked.

Unbeknownst to Dylan, Alessia cracked her door open just enough to hear what they were saying. She had absolutely no idea of the meaning of privacy.

"-yeah, well here I was thinking you and Olivia were endgame; are you asking me to start shipping Alessan right now?" She heard Ked ask, making Alessia smile as she traced her lips with the pad of her index finger. She had enjoyed her kiss with Dylan, and it assured her that he was all for her and none for me. But *she* didn't know that it was all forced.

"I know, Ked and, trust me," he said, lowering his voice so that Alessia couldn't hear what he was saying.

"Yeah, but it still happened, and she's gonna expect you to kiss her a second time, and a third, and a fourth, and then it's bye-bye, Olivia." Ked said, shaking his head.

"I don't want to let Olivia go, Ked, that's not what this is," Dylan said, sounding upset. Alessia gritted her teeth at this, wondering if the only way she would be able to get rid of me would be to kill me.

Or, you know, have me be a prisoner of her life.

"Well you better sort this shit out, Dylan, otherwise *you'll* find Olivia kissing another boy—and I know that's not what you want." Alessia watched as Dylan ran his hand through his hair, tears springing to her eyes. She wouldn't let them spill, but she hoped Dylan wasn't just going to throw her away after what they just did.

Alessia, after what *you* just did. Dylan didn't reciprocate—even a *rock* would know that.

"Ked, I don't know what you want me to do." Dylan said, sounding exasperated.

Ked rolled his eyes, "Tell them both the truth—and you *know* which way round this should be." He said, before patting Dylan on the shoulder, murmuring something to him before he disappeared behind a wall.

It took a moment until Dylan finally turned around and walked back to the car.

He got into the car and sat there silently for a few moments before he sighed.

"Alessia I really like you, I do," he said, truthfully, showing as much as he gave her a sincere look. "And I don't think you deserve all the shit you get at school, but.." he said, making a crack run through Alessia's heart, "but what just happened can't happen again; I don't feel comfortable with it," he explained honestly, making a lump appear in Alessia's throat.

She cleared her throat, glancing away. "Okay," she said, "I'm really sorry," she said.

"It's fine," Dylan said, grabbing hold of Alessia's hand, "but maybe we should just be friends."

Alessia's heart broke.

But she forced a smile on her face and nodded. "Of course, whatever you want."

I was actually quite proud of her. She had spent the last few days bending things to her will, but she was finally sitting back and letting them shape themselves. I could feel that she did it for Dylan's sake, because she cared about him and wanted him to be happy. She also wanted him to be in love with her, but I wasn't too sure which desire was stronger yet.

Dylan smiled, "Let's see that film." He said, making Alessia's spirits lift.

She nodded eagerly, and so they got out of the car.

Alessia wanted to hold Dylan's hand as they walked to the cinema, but she couldn't. Instead, she just walked close to him, relishing in the heat his body brought to her.

When they got to the cinema, Dylan convinced Alessia to join the popcorn queue despite her protests about her not bringing money. When they got to front, he paid for two boxes and two drinks. Alessia watched Dylan adoringly, wondering perhaps if he was the last of his kind; she hadn't seen kindness like this from a boy—*ever*.

Food and drink provided, Dylan and Alessia showed their tickets to the girl at the door before walking in, making jokes about whatever came to their minds as they tried to find good seats.

Dylan pulled her to the very last seats at the cinema, guiding her into the centre. "*These* are the best seats," he claimed, making her laugh as he took her popcorn and drink from her hands as she sat down. "Scientifically proven by Olivia and I."

Alessia hummed, "There you go again," she said, trying to keep the bitterness from her voice.

Dylan shrugged, having taken his seat, "I can't help it; I've spent the majority of my life with the girl." He said, smiling as he took his items back from Alessia.

She nodded, "Guess that's hard to compete with," she whispered as the lights dimmed.

She thought she felt Dylan turn to glance at her, but she could see nothing whilst the screen was black. "Olivia isn't competition; she's a really nice girl, you'll see."

But Alessia wasn't too convinced by either statements and, as the film began, she pondered whether or not Dylan *really* knew Olivia. She assumed quite a lot since we're very close—but maybe I hid dark impulses from him, like when I asked Kiara to mess with her bag.

I knew that that wasn't exactly how it went; Kiara had seen my reaction to how Alessia and Dylan were in our registration class—inching closer, talking privately and holding hands. Dylan hadn't told me anything about Alessia, and so I guess I was a little confused to why he'd keep such a secret from me. I was also momentarily jealous. Kiara saw this and told me that she'd "break Alessia"—I just nodded and said "okay".

I guess I shouldn't have done that. I had never before known how cruel Kiara had been to Alessia, and so I didn't expect for a moment that she'd actually do it. But I shouldn't have been so naive. I should've turned to her, like the nice girl Dylan thinks me as, and told her that the idea was ludicrous, and that she shouldn't hurt Alessia.

But I didn't.

And that's what fired Alessia up, causing her to trash my locker...and apparently join the dance team whist I was gone.

The film was moderately scary, and so Dylan often reached out for Alessia's hand when she squealed, which made her feel light and joyous in her heart. At times, and it only happened once or twice, the build of tension was so intense that she buried her face in Dylan's shirt—who laughed, yet wrapped his arm around her. She felt safe and protected.

With Dylan, she felt safe and protected. And that's how I usually feel with him. That's how I feel with him when I am Olivia Clark.

But I am not.

I'm Alessia Trent, and with no hope of getting back to my life as Olivia Clark—if it ever even existed.

CHAPTER THIRTY

When the film was finished, Dylan drove Alessia back to her house, and left her with a sweet kiss to her cheek. It was nothing but a kind gesture to Dylan, but it was a heart-pounding moment for Alessia.

She entered her house smiling, closing the door and just standing there for a few moments to relish in what had happened.

"'Ere's a lovely lady, James." Someone said suddenly, a cold hand touching Alessia. She jerked away, gasping.

Her father appeared from behind the person who had touched her, stumbling through. "Ah, that's my daughter, but since we couldn't afford the hookers, just use 'er." He said, making Alessia's eyes widen.

The unknown man smiled, leaning in to place a sloppy kiss on her cheek.

Her dad grunted, stumbling back into the living room, yelling something about taking 'the other one'.

Alessia was soon dragged into the living room, where four other men awaited her. She stared at them, unmoving as they all drooled at her presence. As they tugged at her uniform, the doorbell rang.

Everyone froze.

"Oi, mate!" One of the men yelled, "That another hooker?" He called.

Unfreezing, Alessia said, "I'll get it," before excusing herself to the door.

When she opened it, Dylan was there.

"Alessia," he said, smiling, "sorry, you forgot your-"

Alessia threw herself into him, making him fall back in shock as she locked her front door behind her.

She grabbed hold of his hand. "We need to go, *now*." She said, running out into her drive and finding his car, watching him unlock it in confusion.

Getting in, she curled up in the passenger seat and began to cry. When Dylan joined her, he was confused, though pulled her in for an embrace.

"I think," she began, hiccupping, "I think that maybe I need somewhere else to stay for tonight." She said, sniffling.

Dylan drew back, brushing away Alessia's tears, "You've gotta tell me what's going on, Alessia." He said, eyes full of concern.

She shook her head quickly. "I can't." She said, staring deep into his eyes so that he understood.

Ruefully, he pulled back and sighed. "That's okay," he said, "my parents will be home tonight but I can sneak you through the window?" He suggested.

She laughed, though still sniffing. "That sounds perfect." She said, smiling, wishing that Dylan was always this kind.

Alessia noticed that in school, around his friends and around...me, Dylan was preoccupied, or just didn't want to look weird talking to her. For, what kind of reputation would precede him if he spoke to the most hated girl in school?

Alessia and Dylan sat in silence throughout the journey, the radio playing quietly in the background. Whilst Alessia was lost in her thoughts, she wondered what Dylan was thinking about. She couldn't gauge his feelings about her, and today's encounter with Ked made it all the more confusing. She didn't want to lose Dylan to me.

When Dylan had parked up on his drive, he shot Alessia a smile before shutting off the car.

"Right," he announced, leading her around to the back garden, which Dylan's bedroom faced onto. "I'll climb to the first floor and help guide you up, but you need to do the rest yourself. My window is open, and my door is closed, so you should be safe until I get up." Alessia nodded, apprehensive about scaling a wall.

Dylan smiled, "Okay, take notes." He instructed, before he began to climb up the wall. I knew the route to his room via the wall.

There were times where Dylan's mum would advise me to leave to catch up on sleep or homework, but Dylan and I had always wondered if she was just cautious of us spending...*intimate* time together. This was, of course, a crazy idea; Dylan and I are very close friends, and not in love.

I didn't want to get on the bad side of his mum, and so would pretend to leave, much to Dylan's dismay, but I always returned. After that, Dylan and I made a habit of scaling each other's walls. Nothing could keep us apart.

Alessia watched as Dylan scaled to the first floor with confusion, which Dylan laughed at when he reached the top. "Okay," he said, "put your right foot on the piping line." With a few more instructions and hauling up from Dylan, Alessia made it to the first floor.

Having helped her up, Dylan was quite close to her, and it made her heart flutter. But then he pulled away, flashing a smile.

"Now it's all you," he said, steadying her as she toppled slightly. She glanced uncertainly up at the window which she was supposed to reach.

"It's okay," he said, "here," she turned to see him standing over by the wall. "I'll give you a lift up to the ledge, and then you just have to push open the window and pull yourself in." He told her.

Alessia blew out a breath, before nodding. She accepted Dylan's step up, and was soon balancing upon the ledge.

"You can do it," Alessia heard Dylan whisper as she reached up to the window. She grinned, reaching up farther and pushing open the window. She grabbed onto the window sill, using it to pull herself in. When she was close enough, she grabbed onto Dylan's built in desk, hoisting herself through and landing with a thud on his bedroom floor.

She thought she could hear Dylan cheering, but she couldn't be too sure, and so quickly shut the window, getting up onto her feet. She exhaled, brushing back her hair with her fingers, grinning.

She switched Dylan's bedroom light on before moving over to his bed, placing her phone on charge before removing her shoes and tucking them into the corner. As she waited for Dylan, she sat atop his bed and investigated the drawers beside his bed.

She mainly found little trinkets, memories from the past. She found Christmas cards and birthday cards, some old photos and key-chains. Opening the second drawer, though, she found a pile of small notes.

She frowned, picking one up and reading it.

'Cute hair'

It read. She frowned, picking up the rest and reading them.

'You're so so funny'

'Thank you for my C in biology'

'Thank you for buying me food :) love you'

She frowned, heart stopping as she read the last one over and over. 'Love you'. She rummaged around some more, finding one that was signed off.

'Dylan, you're my most good looking friend,

O xx'

And that solved it. The notes were from me, Olivia Clark.

The notes were something Dylan and I began in primary school, back when he was too scared to ask me to be his friend, so he just wrote it down. Most of them these days were just *'buy me food'* or *'yours tonight?'* or, more famously, *'I'm tired.'* My ones from Dylan are stashed in many different places in my room, some long forgotten, but Dylan had made an actual place for mine. He'd kept all the good ones in pristine condition, tucking them away next to his bed.

I had never found these before, partly because I don't go snooping around my best friend's drawers for no apparent reason, but also because, when I stay at his house, Dylan tends to sleep on the side closer to these drawers. I leave the space vacant for him just in case he decides he wants to join me, since he hates blow-up beds so much.

It was sweet that he had kept them all, and it made me miss him even more.

When Alessia heard footsteps, she collected up all the notes, stuffing them back in the drawer and closing it gently. She turned as the door opened, revealing a smiling Dylan. She smiled back, trying to appear casual after she had found, what *she* thought were, love letters.

"Hey," Dylan said.

"Hey," Alessia responded with a smile, eyeing whatever he was holding.

Dylan noticed this, "I snuck out the back door and grabbed your school bag, and then stuffed this plastic bag with so much food I think you'll die."

Alessia laughed, but slapped a hand over her mouth to halt the sound.

He shook his head, smiling as he shut the door and set the bags down.

"Thank you," she said, watching as Dylan pulled out his phone.

"My mum said that Olivia called me by the house phone..." he said, trailing off as his eyes widened.

"What is it?" Alessia asked, watching as he stared at his phone screen.

"Olivia called me 43 times. Something's wrong," he said, suddenly very panicked, "I just need to ring her," he said apologetically, before dismissing himself and disappearing into his bathroom.

Alessia couldn't help herself—she listened in on the phone call.

"I know," she heard him say, "yeah," he paused for a few minutes. "Okay, Olivia, it's okay, calm down," he said, sounding soothing, with an underlying tone of deep concern.

"No, Olivia, not tonight," he said, "I know–no I know, I'm sorry, Olivia." Hearing the pain in his voice, Alessia squeezed her eyes shut, sighing.

She knocked on the door before walking in, making Dylan turn and raise an eyebrow.

"Give me a second, Liv,"

Alessia swallowed. "Did you need me to leave?" She asked.

He sighed, closing her eyes. "She's freaking out, Alessia, I don't know what to do." He said, sounding hopeless.

She nodded. "I can go, she can come 'round here."

Dylan ran a hand through his hair with frustration. Suddenly, he stood up straight.

"I have an idea," he said, "but I won't do it unless you feel comfortable with it." He said.

Alessia took a deep breath. She was *actually* sacrificing herself for me.

But, then again, I could feel that it wasn't on my account—she just hated to see Dylan so upset, *and* for it to be her fault.

"Okay," she said, "what's your plan?"

CHAPTER THIRTY-ONE

She sat down his bed, contemplating it for longer than I think Dylan was comfortable with.

He had ended the call with me, promising to call 'her' back in a short while, and had just finished explaining his plan to Alessia.

"Trust me," he said, "Ked doesn't hate you. Ked doesn't hate anyone." He assured her.

His plan was to send Alessia to Ked's apartment with his cousin, who gave him refuge after his parents kicked him out for coming out as homosexual in year ten. Ked had already agreed, and so it was now just down to Alessia.

With her eyes shut, she inhaled, and then exhaled. "Okay," she said, opening her eyes. Dylan frowned, eyes searching hers. "I'll do it."

Dylan appeared to sigh in relief, hauling Alessia to her feet and embracing her tightly. "I'm sorry Alessia, I know you wanted to spend the night here, but I'm too worried to let this go." He told her, pulling away.

She smiled up at him wistfully, "No, I get it; you care about her." Dylan smiled, averting his eyes and nodding.

I remembered this night vividly. Dylan hadn't necessarily stood me up after school, but there seemed to be some miscommunication, and so I ended up without a ride. Matt had assured me that he'd get me home safely. He did, and then he did the same thing Alessia had done to Dylan in the car. Except, *worse*.

When I didn't comply, he had locked the doors, preventing me from escaping as he tried to get my shirt off. When he realised that he wasn't going to get his way with me, he threw me out of the car and onto the floor, assuring me that the whole school would hear about how much 'of a slag' I was.

I was traumatised. And the only person I could think of was Dylan. And he suddenly wasn't there.

Alessia's sacrifice that night helped me massively, but her day out with Dylan also *cost* me massively.

Soon enough, Alessia was standing outside Ked's house, school bag in hand. Dylan rang the door bell and Ked opened the door shortly after. He invited them in, and Alessia stepped into Ked's house, noting that it had a particular 'home smell' as she eyed the interior.

Ked told Alessia to make herself at home; she started to take off her jacket after leaving her bag in the hallway. As she slipped her shoes off, she watched Ked pull Dylan over for a private word.

"Alessia," Dylan said suddenly, attracting the girl's attention. She smiled at him, and he returned the favour.

Her Life

"You don't have to say sorry again." She said, making him smile. He shook his head and walked over to her. Inches apart, he pressed a kiss to her forehead, stunning her, before turning to leave.

Dylan was, in my eyes, and it seemed in Alessia's too, a pure gem. He was a gentleman; he was a good friend and a compassionate one too. It wasn't unusual for him to display intimate gestures like hand-holding, hugs or kisses, since he had always done the same with me. Though, Kiara had always said it was only because he liked me. Then, there's Alessia; does he like *her*?

"Okay," Ked announced once Dylan had left, "pick a film from the shelves in the sitting room whilst I switch on the heating."

Alessia nodded, watching him disappear into what looked like a kitchen. She sighed, tying her hair back before hesitantly walking into the sitting room. She turned on the light, being instantly welcomed with a grey themed room, complimented with subtle whites. She smiled—like me, she could appreciate good interior.

Alessia found the shelves quickly, gaping at all the films Ked had. He had more than Dylan, she observed, eyes wide.

Ked came back into the room when she was holding two cases, and she turned to see him holding two mugs.

"I hope you like hot chocolate," he said, setting one down on either side of the sofa on small coffee tables. She flashed a small smile, nodding.

He gestured towards her hands as he turned on the DVD player. "You picked a film?" He asked, picking up the two remotes.

She looked down at the two films she was holding, pursing her lips. She handed her choice to Ked wordlessly, still afraid to say anything.

I knew from real life experience that Ked is one of the least judgemental people you could meet and, even if he was, he wouldn't be rude about it. He doesn't hold things against people; he likes to think the best about everyone. It's why he's so loved by everyone—sure, Ked holds a big place in our friendship group, but if he didn't have us, he'd be fine just hanging out with a new group every day.

Our friendship group had started out with just Dylan and I, and Ked was the third addition. I had met Ked in my drama lessons, and I remember vaguely Dylan being hostile towards him at first. Ked said that the above ceased to exist after Dylan realised that Ked was gay—he too believed Dylan liked me.

Ked invited Alessia to sit beside him on the sofa as he switched on the movie, placing bags of food between us on the sofa. Alessia sat rigidly, not moving.

Finally, she asked, "Is Olivia going to be okay?"

Ked looked up at her from where he had been opening a bag of popcorn. He smiled, holding up his phone to her, "Dylan is sending me updates."

Alessia nodded, turning back to the screen again.

"You want your phone?" Ked asked, placing his mug down after taking a sip. She nodded hesitantly, watching him reach for her blazer and pull out her phone, passing it to her.

"Thank you," she said timidly, watching as the opening credits displayed on the film. "You guys all sound like good friends," she said quietly, turning to see Ked grin and nod.

"We are." He said.

She smiled, nodding in response. Despite her facade, Alessia felt envious. She wanted a group of friends like that—unconditionally caring and loving, wanting only the same in return.

What Alessia wasn't aware of is that she isn't exactly *friend material*. She can't reciprocate a lot, and she often wants without giving. But, perhaps she'd change if she was actually given the opportunity to have friends.

As the film played on, Alessia finally found the courage to pick up a bag of popcorn of her own and start eating. When the film was finished, Ked and Alessia had finished all the food between them.

After pausing the credits, Ked stood up, announcing, "Right, let's get ready for bed."

After clearing away the empty wrappers and dirty mugs, Ked led Alessia to his cousin's bedroom, which he had tidied up, fresh sheets on the bed. Ked told Alessia that his cousin had a nightshift at work, and so it was okay to sleep in his bed tonight.

Alessia knew it was only down to Dylan, but she enjoyed Ked's company and his ability to be so accepting. They did not know each other, yet Ked was not hostile towards Alessia; he was welcoming.

When she was ready for bed, Alessia was suddenly, and quietly, joined by Ked. It was uncharacteristic for Ked. Usually he came bundling in, and even Alessia knew this about him. She frowned at him, waiting for him to begin speaking.

"Olivia's okay now, but Dylan's still concerned about her. He doesn't think she should go into school, but she's convinced she's okay." Ked explained, rubbing the side of his face—something he did when he was particularly stressed.

"I'm sure she'll be fine." Alessia said quietly, surprised by her sudden flux of good intentions.

Ked smiled, "Goodnight, Alessia, and wake up early enough so that we can get your school books from your house tomorrow morning." He said, before walking out and closing the door behind him.

Alessia sighed, getting into bed and settling down. She was exhausted.

She felt different tonight. Light, loved, and safe. She wondered if this is what it felt like to have people who cared about her.

But she knew that she would never actually find out; she knew that this would be the last of it. She just knew.

CHAPTER THIRTY-TWO

The following day, I returned to my throne inside of Alessia's mind, sensing her go limp, as if she didn't even feel like trying anymore. She had seen Dylan's devotion to me firsthand, and she had to be pushed aside to allow Dylan to care for me. She didn't feel like being second best, but she didn't know how to stop loving him.

I had met Lucas before school, and we shared a few intimate moments before school began. No one seemed to even notice that we had our hands linked, and that's when I noticed just how invisible Alessia is—even *with* Lucas.

When lunch rolled around, I took a deep breath, realising that Alessia had dance practise. And Olivia was in today. I wasn't sure how well Alessia would deal with her; I knew how this played out—I wouldn't be happy with my team, or with Alessia.

I walked into the hall as Olivia Clark, climbed the stairs as Olivia Clark, but as soon as the *real* Olivia laid eyes on me, I became Alessia Trent. I didn't want to be the one to clear up her mess.

The real Olivia Clark frowned over at her, watching her approach. She met her in the middle, a questioning look on her face. "Alessia, right?" She asked, eyes searching Alessia's for a second. Alessia nodded, crossing her arms over her chest defensively. "What are you doing up here?" Olivia asked, "we have dance rehearsals." She said.

Alessia nodded. "I know—I'm on the dance team now." Olivia's eyebrows shot up, and she glanced around her at her team.

"Is this true?" She asked Ashley, who was coincidentally nearby.

Ashley shrugged, "Ask Kiara." She said, before walking away and herding the girls together.

Olivia frowned, suddenly stumbling, confused as to what to do. She glanced over at Kiara, sighing.

Alessia noticed how Olivia was suddenly apologetic as she turned to face her. "I'm sorry, Alessia, but we're mid-competition right now. I'm sorry my teammates gave you false hope. Maybe next term?" She offered. I hated to disappoint people, it's probably where my obsessing over good grades comes from, and so I was genuinely looking out for Alessia, apologetic over the mistakes that had been made on my behalf. I was just trying to fix the situation, but Alessia was having none of it.

She pulled a face, "One of the girls gave me a CD with all the tracks on them, and I've been practising with every spare moment I've got," she told Olivia, "I'm sure if you helped me..."

I remembered this. Alessia was preying on my need to fix a situation, and I realised it.

I shook my head, "Sorry, Alessia, but I look forward to seeing you in the summer term." With that, Olivia turned around and strode off, saying something to Kiara quickly before beginning the practises.

Alessia wanted to rip the speakers from the walls and throw them at Olivia. I was beginning to realise that Alessia was somewhat impulsive. And so I flipped the control, taking my position back.

I took a deep breath, before turning around and descending the stairs with my head held high, as if that was supposed to happen, as if I was supposed to get turned away. Walk like you know where you're going, talk like you know what you're talking about. Fake it until you make it.

I got to Alessia's replacement locker down in the lonely depths of the school, exchanging her dance bag for her school bag, before pulling out her phone and texting Lucas.

When he didn't respond, I frowned. He had the read the message, yet was not typing. I shook it off, setting off to where we said we'd meet at lunch. When I got there, though, he wasn't sitting there, but on a nearby bench by himself.

"Hey," I said, dropping my bag down on the table and sitting beside him. "What are you doing here? I thought we were meeting by the statue?" I asked him, confused. Lucas wasn't looking at me, and I didn't know if he was even listening to me.

"Lucas..?" I asked, confused.

Finally, he looked up from where he was staring down at his lap, turning to look up at me. I saw instantly that his eyes were gleaming with tears, and I frowned, trying to reach out. He recoiled against my touch though, making me frown up at him.

"Is it true?" He asked, voice breaking.

I frowned. "...What?" I asked, trying to search his eyes using Alessia's.

He swallowed, "Did you go out with Dylan last night?" He asked, and my heart stopped, "And did you kiss him?"

Frozen, I could only stare at him as he waited for my response, each second making him appear more and more broken. I cleared my throat, looking away. Tears sprung to my eyes, and that's all Lucas needed.

He rose from the bench, taking his bag and walking away. I stared after him for a few moments, before I too rose, grabbing my bag and running after him.

"Lucas!" I yelled, sprinting, "Lucas, wait!" I caught up to him, stopping in front of him and halting his pace. He stopped in front of me, appearing annoyed but not looking at me.

Breath laboured, I opened and closed my mouth, trying to think of something to tell him. How do I tell the person who loves Alessia most that, whilst I promised I cared about him as Olivia Clark, Alessia Trent loves Dylan and kissed *him*? But I didn't. But I am also Alessia Trent.

I shook away the confusing flurry of thoughts, simply just asking, "Who told you?"

Lucas huffed, "Does it matter?"

"Maybe." I said quietly.

He shook his head, and I could see as the tears threatened to spill. "It does to me." With that, he side-stepped around Alessia, storming off once more.

But I wasn't having any of it.

I started running again, grabbing hold of his arm and preventing him from walking any farther.

"You have to understand...I didn't mean to, I wasn't myself." I told him, trying to put down into words what I have been trying to understand for months now. *Why, as Olivia Clark, am I living in Alessia Trent's body?*

Lucas scoffed, "Right," he said, "and I'm guessing you weren't yourself when you told me you loved me, either." He said, eyes shattered.

I swallowed. "Kind of..." I said, "But not in the same way," I told him quickly. "Something weird is going on, Lucas-"

"Yeah, me wasting any more time on you." He tried to leave after that, but I held on too tightly, throwing myself in front of Lucas.

"Please, *please* just listen to me." I begged, watching him contemplate this for a few moments. When his eyes softened, I began to speak. "I...haven't been myself recently. Sometimes I hate you, sometimes I don't. Sometimes I want to kiss Dylan, and sometimes I really don't. Sometimes I want to kill someone, and sometimes I love everyone. Lucas, I'm having a quarter-life crisis," he laughed, sniffing.

"I am so sorry, Lucas." I told him, mustering up all the persuasion I could.

Lucas' face relaxed, eyes entranced by Alessia's face and my words. He nodded, sighing. "This won't be easy," he told me, "but you're too pretty not to give a second chance."

I smiled, "I won't let you down." I told him, making promises Alessia Trent couldn't keep.

CHAPTER THIRTY-THREE

The next day was Friday and hence why Alessia's lessons were full of people talking about Matt's party, due to take place that night. Tops were exchanged in classes, rides were arranged, and drinking limits were calculated. But Alessia couldn't care less. She wasn't invited.

She was tracing circles in the side of her pencil case, mind far away from work, when someone joined her. Her partner was ill today, and so she had to start constructing their presentation on her own. Confused, she glanced over at the person, freezing when she saw Matt's face.

"My mum got a call last night; I'm due at the police station," he seethed through a smile, playing with her sheets.

Alessia frowned, "So? Someone caught you perving?" She asked, hoping he got what was coming for him. Especially after what he did to her.

Matt suddenly leaned in closer, making her jerk back, hitting her head against the wall. "Yeah, and you're the snitch." He hissed.

Trying to ignore the shooting pain in her head, Alessia scrunched up her face, saying, "I said nothing."

She was telling the truth—technically. Alessia Trent didn't say anything, but *I* did, whilst controlling her body. So if this moment really happened, if Matt is really 'due at the police station', someone else must've said something. Alessia didn't want to admit what happened to her, but *I* did—on *her behalf*. It's all very confusing. But, in real life, Alessia said nothing, so someone else must have.

Matt scowled, "Stop lying." He said, voice low and threatening.

She seemed to curl into herself, "I'm not." She whispered.

Matt considered this for a few moments, before drawing back and humming. He glanced around the classroom, before his eyes landed on someone. "No," he said suddenly, "you're right; you wouldn't say a thing because you wouldn't dare put yourself in that position." *Well, at least his ego is still intact.*

Alessia glanced over at who Matt was staring at. Olivia Clark. *Me.* Matt thought that *I* had said something.

"*Her?*" Alessia asked. Truth be told, it wouldn't be a bizarre accusation. But no, in reality, I said absolutely nothing. Though, Matt didn't seem to think so.

Alessia's mind began to wander over all the reasons that I would want to speak up and snitch on Matt. Then she realised.

She glanced between Matt and Olivia. "You...you did it to her *too?*" She asked, disgusted and surprised.

Matt rolled his eyes, "Don't act like that doesn't make you happy; you hate her."

Alessia was quiet for a few moments. "Is it that obvious?" She asked, voice low.

Matt nodded, hardly paying attention to her as he stared at Olivia—stared at *me*.

"She's Dylan's best friend; why would you risk that? He'll kill you if he finds out." Alessia said, her words ringing true. It was half the reason I couldn't tell Dylan. I didn't want him to believe Matt over me, but then I didn't want him to believe me and fall out with Matt. I couldn't win.

Matt laughed, "He's not going to find out, Less, because you're not going to tell anyone." He said, voice menacing.

She shrunk back, asking quietly, "Won't she say something, though?"

Matt laughed once more, "No," he said, "she has a reputation to uphold, and she knows Dylan will never believe her."

Despite Alessia's apparent hatred for me, she still threw Matt a disgusted look. "I can't believe you."

Matt hummed, licking his lips. "How about we work together?" He suddenly proposed.

"No way in hell," Alessia said, "my partner is ill, not exiled to Alaska." She said, making him pull a face.

"No, stupid bitch, I mean to take down Olivia." He said. I froze from where I sat on an imaginary bench in Alessia's mind.

Alessia moved slowly, considering this. "How?" She asked, making Matt smile.

"Well, you hate her, and I want this whole sexual assault thing to go away, so we just pin it on her and call it a day." Matt said, waiting for Alessia's response. "Come on," he said, "or I'll tell everyone about all those photos you sent me." He whispered.

Alessia stared at him, eyes wide. "I didn't send you any pictures." She said, voice shaking.

"Yeah, and who's everyone going to believe?" Matt asked, before dropping Alessia's sheets on the table in a mess. "I'll message you." He promised her, before leaving as the lesson finished.

When lunch came around, I took control of Alessia's body so that she wouldn't ruin her lunch date with Lucas. Lucas was such a sweet and kind boy; he didn't deserve to love someone who didn't feel even a slither of what he did.

Lucas had to leave early to change for PE next lesson, and apologised simply with a kiss, before joining his friends and walking into the sports hall. Alessia didn't have that privilege. She couldn't just hang out with her other friends; she *had* no other friends.

Feeling as though everyone was staring at me and judging me out on the field, I rose to my feet and decided to make my way back into school. I felt naked as I walked past all the huddles of friends, a lone fish amongst a sea of sharks. That's what Alessia's life often felt like.

After the horrid walk of shame, I made it inside and hurried straight to the toilets, thinking there would be no one in sight since it was still quite early. I was wrong. Kiara and her other group of friends were hanging out, fixing their hair and makeup.

Walking into the bathroom under their gazes, I definitely felt like a fish amongst sharks.

"Ah, Alessia," Kiera Daye, a fairly popular, rude girl, said tauntingly. "We were just talking about you." She said, making the other girls laugh.

"Yeah," Katy Oswalt chimed in, "Kiara was just filling us in about everything pathetic about you," she said, sneering.

"Tell her, Kiara." Lizzie Whilte goaded, poking Kiara with the end of her powder brush.

Kiara didn't turn, but glanced at Alessia through the mirror. I was confused to why Kiara was holding back, why she hadn't said anything yet, but then I remembered. Alessia's blackmail—the emergency contraceptives.

"Well," Kiara began, "I think she already knows." She said, making Katy laugh, but Lizzie was less than amused.

"*Come on*, Kiara, don't go soft on us." She complained, dropping her powder brush before placing her hands on her hips.

I noticed Molly Harte in the background, brushing her long blonde hair through, ignoring the other girls. She was the girl who had given Alessia the CD with the dance tracks burned on, and so perhaps she didn't want to make fun of Alessia. Or maybe she was waiting to pounce.

"I'm not going soft," Kiara assured them, fluffing her hair, "I'm just waiting for my moment." She said, checking her reflection in the mirror once more before spritzing herself down with the sweetest perfume in the world. Alessia *hated* it; whenever she smelt it, or a similar one, she always thought of Kiara, which made her think of her horrible secondary experience.

"Come on, girls, I'm meeting Johnny before German." She said, flicking her hair over her shoulder and leaving.

Lizzie and Katy exchanged glances, before Katy yelled, "We'll just meet you after school!"

Kiara didn't respond; I had a feeling she had just left, and didn't intend on waiting for her fiends anyway.

But now she was gone, she couldn't mediate the fight that was going to go down in her honour. Alessia trembled, and I too felt as fear rose in my throat—*Alessia's* throat.

Lizzie approached Alessia, a menacing look on her face as she crossed her arms over her chest, "what have you got over Kiara's head?" She asked, stepping closer to Alessia, making me shrink back. I still had control of Alessia's body, but I was more than willing to give it back if it meant escaping Katy and Lizzie's wrath.

"I *said*," Lizzie raised her voice, slamming Alessia's body into the bathroom wall, "*what* do you have over Kiara?"

And that was it. I evaporated, escaping Alessia's body in fear. Alessia noticed Katy guarding the bathroom door as Lizzie held Alessia up to the wall.

Alessia shrugged, "A few things."

Lizzie's hand moved, and there was suddenly a stinging sensation on Alessia's left cheek. Lizzie had slapped Alessia.

"Liz," Molly began, "Liz, let it go, we're going to be late." She said, anxiously wringing her hands inside out.

Katy pulled a face, "We have fifteen minutes, moron."

Alessia couldn't believe how some people treated other people, never mind their own *friends*. School is a very messed up place.

Lizzie drew closer to Alessia. "You leave Kiara the hell alone and sit back down in your spot on the food chain." She hissed, her face inches from Alessia's.

Alessia swallowed, not responding.

Katy laughed, "Well done, Less."

"Less friends, Less meaning, Less..." Lizzie drew off, raising her eyebrow at Alessia. Suddenly, she appeared inspired, "Less hair!" She exclaimed evilly. Alessia frowned at Lizzie, not understanding what she was talking about.

"Liz, no." Molly warned, stepping closer.

"Molly," Katy said, throwing scissors to Lizzie, "you say anymore, and it'll be your hair down the drain." She seethed, growing annoyed.

Her Life

And that's when Lizzie took the scissors to Alessia's hair.

She screamed, trying to push Lizzie away. But her obstruction only led to a painful slash on the back of her neck.

"Oh," Lizzie said, "Alessia, you're bleeding."

She laughed, chucking the scissors in the sink and promising Katy she'd buy her some more.

"Let's go," Lizzie announced, picking up her bag and marching out of the door.

"You too, Molly," Katy said, voice warning. Molly took one last glance at Alessia, before ruefully picking up her bag and leaving.

Alessia was alone again, with Less friends, Less meaning, and Less hair.

CHAPTER THIRTY-FOUR

Alessia's wound was bleeding too much for her to just ignore it and go to lesson. She did the best she could in the girls' toilets, and she knew the school nurse wouldn't be able to do much more. After handing back the control to her, Alessia had decided to just leave the school, taking on a guided tour down her secret path.

It was so obvious, yet I had never thought of it before.

When Alessia was out of school, she considered what to do next. She had always been okay on her own, but since Dylan had been so resourceful the last time she had injuries, she considered whether or not she could use his help again.

With a reluctant sigh, she decided against it, and began to speed through the forest. When she had checked the time for the fifth time in just five minutes, I began to feel suspicious. Was Alessia's bleeding wound really *that* important to her? If it were me, I would not be able to leave the bathroom, never mind the entire school, yet I've come to learn that Alessia and I are very different people.

When she got to her house, and in record time, she cracked open the door hesitantly, and I thought maybe that was it—she didn't want to get caught by her dad. But then she left her front door ajar, spiriting up the stairs and into her room.

I knew she was in a rush when she didn't lock her bedroom door; something even I had learnt was a necessity when I was Alessia Trent. She dropped to her floor, hastily pulling out the wooden box that contained her stashed drugs.

I then realised what was going on.

She quickly checked the notes in her phone before stashing a bag of pills into her hoodie pocket, which she had put on after discarding her blazer.

When Alessia left the house, she seemed to move faster than before—if at all possible. She got back to the forest in less than ten minutes, heaving as she leaned against the big grey stone I had seen on my first day as Alessia Trent. It was the stone that had '*Alessia was here*' carved into it.

That seemed like a whole world away now. As if I was a ghost in motion, slipping into a new word, a transverse body transcending across two realities, falling into a stream that filtered me into pitfalls in Alessia's body.

It was weird. I knew I was Olivia Clark, and not Alessia Trent, but my memories as Olivia Clark felt slippery in my grasp. They didn't feel tangible at all, as if they didn't even *exist*. I was beginning to lose myself in Alessia Trent's consciousness, no idea of how or why, or even if I would get back to the person I once was.

Someone cleared their throat, alerting both Alessia and I and making her turn around. A man dressed head to toe in formal wear nodded at her, and the two engaged in the quickest transaction of all time.

Alessia fingered the notes in her pocket, counting out £500, before thanking him, telling him, "May 12th." Before leaving.

It was the weirdest thing, almost like a ghost sighting—you can't prove it, but you're sure it happened.

It's almost how I felt about being Olivia Clark in Alessia Trent's body.

She got home soon enough, and was staring at her still bleeding gash on the back of her neck. I then realised that she had no choice but to come home; she had to sell her drugs, and get her money. It was the only way she *would* get money.

Now she had to figure out what to do with her wound.

She paced the short length of her bathroom about twenty times, before she heard her phone ringing. She tried to ignore it, thinking it was just Lucas pestering her as usual—which I didn't think was a bad thing. But, after another ring, she huffed, deciding to answer it.

She walked back into her room, freezing when she saw the contact name. It was *Dylan*. *Dylan* was calling her.

I felt as her heart assumed a lighter weight, floating in her body as she watched the phone ring for only a few seconds longer.

When she picked it up, Dylan asked, "Alessia? Is that you?"

She smiled, sitting down on her bed. "Yeah." She answered simply, reaching up to twirl her hair, then realising it was gone.

Dylan was saying something over the phone, but she was too busy moving slowly over to her full length mirror, peering at her reflection. Amongst the chaos of selling drugs and losing blood, Alessia had forgotten that she was Alessia Trent with Less hair. And that this is what she now looked like.

She let out a sob, trying to muffle it with her hand as she slapped it over her lips, but Dylan heard it.

"Alessia?" He asked, sounding concerned. "What is it? Where are you?"

She opened her mouth to reply, but was interrupted by another voice on the other side of the phone. On Dylan's side.

"Hey, are we going to maths?" It asked. And it was my voice—Olivia Clark's voice. Not only was it easy to recognise, since it was my *own voice*, but it held a distinctive note to Alessia. She could always tell it apart from other voices—it was just so light and cheerful. That's what she thought, anyway—*I* thought I was just talking normally.

The noises through the phone became muted after that, as if Dylan was pressing his phone against his chest to keep their words secret, yet Alessia could still make out what they were saying.

"Yeah, Liv, give me five seconds." He said, and Alessia waited for her response.

"Are you okay?" He asked, after a few moments of silence. "Olivia?" He asked, more concerned, and also more concerned than he would've ever been for Alessia, so she thought.

"I just..I just need a minute," she said, voice sounding jarred and shaky.

"Oli-"

"Tell Mr Packinson I'll be a few minutes late." Olivia said, before all became silent once more.

I vaguely remembered this day. With mock GCSE exam results coming in, the vandalism, the dance competition, and other small things, I was beginning to feel as though I was drowning. And, sometimes, I started to. My mum said it sounded like a panic attack when Dylan had explained it to her on my behalf, but I objected and said it was absolutely nothing.

And it was; there was absolutely no point in worrying—it was just exam stress. But Dylan always worried about me anyway. And Alessia knew that as much as I did.

"Ales-"

But before he could even finish her name, she hung up. She was scared to admit that it might not be worth trying to get Dylan, and so she simply avoided doing it.

After losing her only source for medical information, she treated her injury using Google—probably not the best doctor the U.K. has seen. Alas, Alessia seemed satisfied with her work, and the bleeding was silenced, which she took as a good sign.

Staring in the mirror at her neatly dressed wound, holding her hair up to see it, her lips turned upwards slightly. But when she dropped her hair and it didn't fall back down to her lower back, her smile fell.

Alessia had been bullied for as long as she could remember. The bullies had started with verbal bullets, and they slowly turned physical. Usually, they liked to insult her appearance and push her over. Now, they've *ruined* her appearance, and she couldn't find the banister to pull herself back up again.

Alessia had reached rock bottom. If not for the first time, then for the first time in a *very* long time.

CHAPTER THIRTY-FIVE

As Alessia Trent hit the cold stone floor, so did I, Olivia Clark. Alessia's emotions ran deep and ran fast, whirling me into a flurry of anguish. I could be as happy as could be, but with Alessia's sour mood, it wouldn't be enough.

As Alessia continued to spiral, so did her school life. All homework that I had left for her to do had either not made it in to the teacher, or came back with the worst results I had ever seen. Alessia had pushed me back and alienated Lucas, telling him to leave her alone—I guess there were worse things she could've said to him. The bullying got worse as Alessia began to submit, and her father continued to be unconditionally cruel. Her life was turning upside down, and I just wasn't strong enough to hold it still.

Dylan was the only constant, the only happy note to her life. She saw him, and everything floated away. He anchored her.

But he also anchored me, and it seemed more and more impossible to gain his attention by the day. As Prom neared, Alessia sat on her own wants and needs, and waited patiently for the inevitable—for Dylan to ask me, Olivia Clark, to prom.

The idea made her slow; it made her heart feel heavy. Yet, she couldn't ignore it. She couldn't ignore anything, and that's what made her weak—a target.

"Aw," Alessia broke out of her train of thoughts, seeing Lizzie standing in the reflection of the mirror Alessia's eyes had faded into. "Your hair has grown out nicely," she sneered, making Alessia angry. She kept a lid on it, though, trying to remain calm.

Lizzie huffed when Alessia didn't respond, joining her in the mirror and rubbing under her eyes, perfecting her makeup. "The least you could do is respond, you delinquent." She spat, pulling her brush out of her bag so that she could brush through her silk blonde hair. Alessia had always been jealous of blonde hair, and found herself admiring it in the reflection.

When Lizzie caught her staring, though, she sucked it right up. "I know, Less, I'm pretty." She said, smoothing out her hair as she smiled.

I had always thought that there was no problem in accepting and acknowledging your own beauty—whether it be an inner thing, or an outer thing—as long as you weren't too boastful about it. But Alessia was much opposed to the idea, thinking any kind of self-encouragement was vain and egoistical.

Maybe that was because she had never thought she was at all beautiful, or worth anyone's time. But maybe *that's* because that's all she's ever been told.

Alessia didn't respond to Lizzie again, making her more annoyed. She slammed her bag down on the side, whirling around to face Alessia.

"What is it with you and disrespecting kind people?" She asked, "first with me by being my ex's affair, then with your blackmails to Kiara, now, you're onto Dylan. *That's* disrespectful. Both to him, *and* to Olivia. And you know it. But you don't even care."

Alessia, sighed, trying to walk around Lizzie so she could use the toilet. Lizzie side-stepped, though, blocking Alessia.

After a few moments of staring at Alessia with a look of disgust, her arms across her chest and a smile formed on her lips. She seemed to have an idea. "*Oh*, I'm sorry; did you need to use the toilet?" She asked.

Alessia deflated, not even wanting to try. But she did anyway, "just move, Lizzie." She said weakly.

Lizzie's nostrils flared, "*This* is what I mean; *this* is disrespect. You didn't even say 'please'."

Alessia rolled her eyes, waiting for Lizzie to move.

"Fine," Lizzie said sweetly, making Alessia confused, "you can use the toilet," she said, though slowly sounding more and more insane. Alessia watched her carefully, trying to decipher her motives so that she could try to dodge the attack.

Suddenly, Lizzie grabbed onto Alessia by her shortened hair, dragging her over to the first cubicle. "You can use it for a dunking," Lizzie taunted, making Alessia's eyes go wide. Lizzie shoved Alessia into the cubicle, locking the door behind her.

This had happened many times to Alessia, and she had only escaped several. Over the years, her bullies had acquired protection methods—they had taken her bag, throwing it over to another cubicle; Alessia couldn't leave it behind. They had also bribed her by taking her phone and used violence. Their latest method was to lock the door. Simple, but effective.

Alessia shoved Lizzie with all the might she had, before using the toilet as a stepping stone up to the wall that divided the two cubicles. Alessia was ready to jump over, when and realised that she no longer had her bag.

She looked down at Lizzie, who was holding her bag in her fake tan ridden hands, a smirk on her face. "Looking for this?" She asked.

Alessia gritted her teeth, "Give it back, Lizzie." She said, warningly.

Lizzie shrugged, "Come get it."

Alessia knew better than to trust that Lizzie would just give it back, but she had no choice; she couldn't let Lizzie just keep her bag.

Regretfully, she climbed down from the wall, holding out her hand expectantly for her bag.

Lizzie's smirk grew. "I won't dunk you...if you let me into your phone." She said, flashing the object at Alessia.

Alessia clenched her jaw, "Just give it—"

"Do you *want* me to shove your face into a bowl of toilet water?" Lizzie taunted, spinning Alessia around so that she could see the bowl for herself.

She grimaced, sighing. "Fine. There's nothing interesting in there anyway." She said, taking the phone from Lizzie and tapping in the code. Lizzie stole it back instantly, dropping Alessia's bag to the floor.

Alessia picked her bag up hastily, pulling it onto her shoulder as she tried to see what Lizzie was doing on her phone.

"Nice," Lizzie said suddenly, "you've got Lucas *and* Dylan in your messages." She said, showing Alessia what she was referring to.

Alessia rolled her eyes, "Yes, I'm into *both* of them, you caught me." Lizzie, having detected the sarcasm in Alessia's voice, clenched her fists, growing angry.

She returned to Alessia's phone, and Alessia supposed she was scrolling through the texts. And then Lizzie grew angrier.

"I can't believe you," she said suddenly, showing Alessia what she was looking at, "first my boyfriend, now Dylan?"

Alessia stared at the picture that Lizzie had found in her camera roll, eyes wide. *Crap.*

The picture was from when Alessia first stayed the night at Dylan's. It was a picture of the two, the room dark and their heads rested against the headboard of Dylan's bed.

Lizzie's eyes suddenly flashed. "Wait until Olivia sees this." Lizzie taunted, smiling as she sent the picture over to her own phone.

She threw the phone at Alessia, who just managed to catch it before it fell into the toilet, before she unlocked the door and left. Alessia froze in shock, watching as Lizzie disappeared.

"*Lizzie*!" She shouted, panicked. "Lizzie, stop!" She yelled, seeing Lizzie disappear around the corner.

Alessia followed after her, receiving odd looks from students who saw her sprinting along corridors.

Finally, Alessia found Lizzie, out of breath in the girls' changing room. She held her phone out to the girls, and Alessia saw as Katy, Kiara, and few other girls stared at it.

Olivia wasn't present.

I never saw that photo.

But some of my friends had.

Catching Alessia as she crept forward, Katy said, "Well, well, well, Alessia, what do we have here?"

"Please just delete it." Alessia begged. Katy exchanged looks with the other girls, before they all began to laugh.

"Do whatever you want with it," Kiara said, picking up her bag and throwing it on her shoulder, "I was supposed to meet Olivia five minutes ago." With that, Kiara left, leaving the girls stunned.

"What is it with that girl?" Katy muttered, annoyed.

Lizzie pulled a face at Alessia, "It's *her*," she told Katy, an accusing tone to her voice, "she has something over her head."

Katy rolled her eyes, "Yeah, and now it's making her soft," the girls were silent for a while.

Finally, Lizzie spoke, "I guess we make our own decisions now."

Katy turned to her, eyes searching hers. "This is too big to make a decision of on our own," she said, glancing between the picture and Lizzie.

Lizzie scoffed, "We can do whatever we want; Olivia doesn't care about us, and the only one she does like is Kiara, the girl who can't be bothered to do anything these days."

"I think we should just delete it," Mollie said quietly, reaching up to take the phone from Lizzie.

Lizzie snatched her hand away, though, making Mollie jump.

She waited until Katy gave in, before smirking, walking over to Alessia. Alessia started to back away, seeing the menacing look on Lizzie's face.

"I'll delete this photo," Lizzie began, "but I want you to do it, *actually* do it."

Alessia frowned. "What?"

Lizzie rolled her eyes, "It's been some time since a scandal, and with Olivia distracted by that vandalism and all those police officers walking around, it'll be easy. I know you want to do it."

Alessia huffed, "For God's sake, Lizzie, I'm not a mind-"
"I want you to get with Dylan—and I want it to be mega."

CHAPTER THIRTY-SIX

Alessia wasn't stupid. She knew that she wouldn't be any safer with Lizzie's offer. Lizzie was proposing that she'd delete the photo, but only if Alessia gives more proof by *actually* getting with Dylan. It made no sense.

"We'll deflect any rumours until you're ready, and then it'll be the only thing talked about for what's left of our miserable year." Lizzie said, after Alessia had brought up the aforementioned issue.

"What you're saying is, you'll protect me until what? May? June? That's still not good enough." Alessia said, crossing her arms over her chest.

"Oh, loosen up, Less," Katy said, stepping forward, "we're bored, and you're bait. By the time we get to June, everyone will be gone anyway; you'll be safe."

"Yes, I'll be safe after everyone goes—but you want this to all blow up with everyone *there*. I'm sorry, but no." Alessia said, shaking her head at the girls.

"Then we share the picture." Lizzie said smugly.

Alessia sighed, "Do whatever you want with the picture." She said, turning to leave.

"Wait," Alessia recognised that the voice was someone new, a girl in the group who hadn't spoken yet. She turned, seeing Ashley walk over to Katy and Lizzie, where Alessia had just been stood.

"I'll put a word in for you to get you back on the dance team, *and* I'll get you Olivia's favourite perfume, *and* I'll get Olivia distracted for you—for the *whole* three months." She proposed, making Lizzie and Katy exchange glances.

Alessia pursed her lips, thinking about this for a couple moments. "Okay," she said, making Katy and Lizzie grin at each other. "But on my terms," Alessia continued, making the grins fall slightly. "You cover my back with Olivia and Kiara, but I want the whole school to know that it's Alessia and Dylan now; not Olivia and Dylan. Get Olivia completely out of the picture and you'll get your scandal."

Katy and Lizzie exchanged looks.

"Done," Katy said.

"And done." Lizzie put in, and Alessia watched as she tapped around on her phone before turning it around so that Alessia could see that the photo was gone.

And that was it. The girls only wanted something exciting, one last bomb to go off before they left the school. But Alessia wanted something bigger. She wanted love, and she wanted *me* gone.

That was fuel enough; the girls had just made a bet to drive a wedge between Dylan and I.

When Alessia got home from school, she walked into a cloud of smoke, realising her dad had friends round, before sprinting up the stairs in fear.

She slammed her door behind her, locking it and throwing her bag on the floor, letting her blazer follow in suit. She stood in the corner of her room for a few moments, just pondering what to do next. Then, Alessia walked over to her full-length mirror, peering at her reflection. She sighed at her short hair and mascara that bled down onto her under-eye bags.

When she was done criticising her appearance, she quickly changed into comfortable clothes, before pulling out her sketchpad from her under her bed. She sat upon her duvet, pulling out her pencils from her drawers before she flipped through her many sketches, finding the one of Dylan.

She had yet to finish it, even though she had been working on it for quite a while now. I noted that Alessia believed that drawing helped her to think. It was like sketch-therapy.

She pulled up the picture of Dylan that she had been sketching from, finishing his lips, drawing on his neck, and adding final touches and shades.

When she was done, Alessia had a plan.

The girls would get Olivia—me—away from Dylan, and so the only girl in Dylan's life would be Alessia. That made it a lot easier for Alessia, who was already nervous enough about vocally expressing her feelings.

Alessia planned to tell him at his house, in his room, on his bed. She would spend the night again, somehow. She would show him her drawing, tell him how she felt, and then kiss him.

With her feelings put so explicitly, Alessia hoped that Dylan would take this kiss more seriously than the first and second—of which he seemed to have forgotten about.

I disliked her plan. It made Dylan a pawn in a *very* wicked game. Then again, maybe Dylan was the prize, though that still didn't make me feel any better. The whole thing made me feel all kinds of weird; Alessia was basically planning an American high-school movie-type takedown. She would just dangle everything Dylan and I had in front of us as if we were just extras in her orchestrated production.

She smiled down at her sketch, proud of it, before deciding to start another. Instead of using Dylan's Instagram, like she had done for the first one, Alessia found mine. I watched through her eyes as my posts were displayed on her phone screen.

Whilst I felt as though I'd sunk to the bottom of a sea of sadness from seeing all that I had lost, Alessia felt both envious and infuriated by what she saw. She found me annoying, but she didn't know why. Deep, deep down, though, I think she did; she was just jealous.

I'll never know exactly what of, but Alessia is jealous of me, and always has been.

She found the perfect picture. It was a selfie I had taken of Dylan and I, and we looked so, *so* happy. As though we couldn't have foreseen how ruined our lives would become. As though *I* couldn't have foreseen that I would next see this photo through the eyes of someone else.

Alessia only cared for how pretty Dylan appeared in the photo she had chosen, instantly beginning her work. But as *I* stared down at the photo, I realised how much I had lost. My body, my mind, my life. And now Olivia Clark was nothing more to me than a myth, and Dylan a talisman of a good life—now just a dream.

Now, in her life, all I am to Dylan is Alessia Trent, the weird girl that no one seems to like.

I watched as Alessia poured herself over her drawing, finishing it when it was pitch black. She left her drawing on her bed to sneak downstairs to make some food, and when she came back, there he was. Dylan was on her bed, at last, but just a sketch. Not the *real* Dylan.

She smiled, biting into her pizza and gazing down at her drawing. She sighed, tracing the sketch with her index finger before closing the book and returning to my Instagram.

Alessia started by looking only for photos with Dylan in, but she soon found herself looking at ones of just me, or me with my friends. She was jealous of every detail, but she told herself that I annoyed her so that it wouldn't hurt as much.

She thought that my hair was somehow shinier and silkier than hers, although they were practically the same. She thought my chocolate brown eyes were much easier to look at than her striking green ones, and that my facial features were beautiful and petite. She thought that my figure was better than hers, that I was small, yet not lacking, whereas she was simply skin and bones. She thought that I was much more calm and collected; cool, whereas she was haphazard and awkward. Lastly, she thought Dylan loved me, and not her.

In my life, I would've never known the way Alessia thinks about me, but in her life, I do.

CHAPTER THIRTY-SEVEN

In the next week, study-leave for Alessia's exams begun, though Alessia spent more time plotting than studying. Before Alessia's year group had all disappeared for study-leave, Alessia had been tactfully getting closer and closer to Dylan, ready for the big finale.

She was thinking this Friday. Dylan had told her that he wasn't going to Matt's party, since Olivia and him had fallen out—of which was down to the girls and their plotting. After the argument, Dylan no longer felt like going to the party. Alessia would act as both the damsel in distress, and as an aid for Dylan on his very lonely Friday night.

In the current moment, Alessia was sat in the school library, though merely to get away from her dad. Her textbooks were scattered around her, but her sketchbook right in front of her—the centre of her attention.

"What are you drawing?" Someone asked suddenly, and Alessia turned to see Lucas stood behind her. She jumped, before glaring at him.

Lucas stared open-mouthed down at what Alessia was drawing, instantly figuring out that it was Dylan. He glanced between the drawing and Alessia.

I, of course, had been the one to promise loyalty to Lucas, and not Alessia. Therefore, it was times like these that made it hard to defend Alessia. Especially when there was proof of her affections for the wrong person right in front of her, on a table in the library.

I flipped the control instantly, taking back the reins. I had only done this a few times since I had last given up, and each time was to save her from another problem of her own doing. "Lucas, it's just a drawing," I explained to him.

He shook his head, "So is there one of me too?" He asked.

I paused, "Uh, at home." I told him. Alessia was pretty good at lying, but I wasn't. Lucas sensed this.

He sighed, "Right," he turned to leave, but I got up to chase after him.

"Lucas," I whispered, grabbing onto his arm and pulling him away from the working students.

"No, Alessia, this is the third time now," he said, running his hand through his hair, trying to use the ruse to distract from the fact that tears were springing to his eyes.

"I know-" I paused, "wait, *third* time?"

Lucas looked away, clenching his jaw. "I heard what you did at Matt's party." He said, making me frown.

"Sorry?" I asked him, confused.

He sniffed. "Making out with Matt."

I simply opened and closed my mouth, very aware of Lucas' eyes on me, waiting for me to say something.

I swallowed. "Even if that were true, I haven't been to one of Matt's parties in ages."

Lucas scoffed. "Sure, and the whole of Matt's friendship group is spreading immaculate lies about you?" He asked bitterly.

"*Yes!*" I replied, before realising that I should quieten down, "because that's what boys like Matt and his friends do. They don't care about anyone but themselves and they use and humiliate girls just for the fun of it."

"Yeah," he said, "maybe so, but even your love backed it up." He said, nodding over at Alessia's sketches, which were now a few metres away.

"'My love'?" I echoed. "*Dylan?*" I felt as Alessia's heart sank. Mine followed soon after. I shook my head, "Dylan wouldn't have lied."

Lucas scoffed, "Of course, Matt's friends are all jerks but Dylan is pure." He said, laughing without humour.

He then turned to leave.

Quickly, I grabbed onto his arm, spinning him around, "Yes," I told him, "Dylan is so pure, and so kind," when Lucas started frowning at me, I realised my eyes were beginning to water. I cleared my throat, "And I really care about you, Lucas, and I won't let these untrue rumours ruin this." I told him, pleadingly.

"Ruin what?" He asked, tugging his arm out of my grasp. "There's nothing here, Alessia."

My breath hitched. "There *is*." I said, though maybe I was just trying to convince myself and Alessia, rather than him.

"You, and whatever other twenty personalities you have, love Dylan, and that'll never change. Right now, I have too many exams to worry about to even give a second thought to this. If you really want me, if you want *this;* I'll be on the other side of the GCSEs." With that, Lucas turned around and left.

With a bitter taste in my throat, I realised I had well and truly made promises that Alessia Trent, sure enough, couldn't keep. I shouldn't have risked it. But for the promise of just one good day, of making Alessia's life *acutely* better, I did. I risked it.

I sighed, closing my eyes to calm down, letting the horrible feeling that was bursting inside of me settle. Opening my eyes, I turned around to where Alessia was once sitting, packing up her sketchbook and shoving it away into her bag, before doing some actual revision.

I was revising for history, which is a paper that Alessia is supposed to sit tomorrow morning, and so I had to make sure that I sat that paper for Alessia. I wasn't sure if Alessia would retain memories that I controlled. I wasn't sure about anything these days, especially feeling as though I had a past life, as if I was Olivia Clark. It's been so long now; it feels like a memory for many times ago, but somehow, somewhere, I know for certain that I was Olivia Clark before this life. Before *her* life.

Now, I'm Alessia Trent, and with nothing else proven to me, that's all I know right now. If I was Olivia Clark before, I have now been lost—I have sunk to the bottom of a pit in Alessia's soul, where it's likely that I'll remain.

I revised for an hour longer before packing up, sighing. I slung my bag over my shoulder, trudging over to the exit of the library. It was getting dark outside, and so it would probably be a risky mission getting back into my—Alessia's house.

But I didn't even get a chance to get far; outside of the library, I was confronted.

"Isn't you Alessa?" The voice slurred, falling into me.

I caught the person instinctively, frowning. "I am *Alessia*." I said, correcting them on the name but not on their first error. It was a boy, and he smiled up at me.

That's when I realised who it was.

Leon Junior.

As a recap, Leon was the first boy who had ever shown me—Olivia—attention. I fell for him like a stupid kid, and he broke my heart. Not only that, but he sold a story to the entire school that I was a slut, and that the only reason he broke up with me was because I 'wasn't good enough in bed'. He then proceeded to *change* the story, saying that I was 'frigid', and that he broke up with me because I 'wouldn't do anything in bed'.

It didn't matter that what he had said didn't make sense, or that he had no proof; people believed him. I hated him. He was the first person to ruin my days at school, making me the target of unwanted male attention, rude photoshop edits, and cruel text messages.

It soon died out. But I'd never forgive him.

Holding him now, I shook with hatred. But I was not Olivia Clark, I am Alessia Trent. And even if I *am* Olivia, I wear a permanent mask that just won't budge.

Leon hummed, smiling, "Let's do somethin'." He slurred once more, making me scoff in disgust and push him off me.

"Go home, Leon." I ordered, trying to walk away.

"Aw, man, you're just like that Olivia, man." He said, tripping and landing with his limbs tangled in a gate.

I stood, frozen, watching him pull his limbs away from the green painted gate.

"*Olivia?*" I asked.

He hummed again. "Yeah, that one. She's a bloody slut for Dylan, but no one else."

I pulled a face, my hatred bubbling. "You talk shit, Leon." I spat, watching him laugh, before slipping and hitting his head on the concrete brick wall. I stared at him, not sharing any sympathy as he groaned in pain. He deserved it.

"I don't talk nothing but truth, baby, and you know it." He said, recovering.

I clenched my jaw. "I'm leaving, Leon, stop talking to me now."

I turned around, ready to leave, when he began to speak again, "I'll be telling everyone about this," he slurred, and I heard him trip again.

I sighed, not turning around, "That you're harassing me in an alleyway?"

Leon didn't respond for a while, and I considered turning back around to see if he had died. That would sure be a score. Then I heard him say, "Sure."

I rolled my eyes, walking away quickly, for fear of him following me.

CHAPTER THIRTY-EIGHT

In the next week or so, Alessia had sat five papers, and she was not nearly done. I let her sit all of the subjects she had revised, whereas I would take control and sit the ones that *I* had revised for. It was as if we were divorced parents sharing a child. Ironic, since that was Olivia Clark's life.

Today was Alessia's first history paper, and I woke up feeling a mixture of things. I felt lost, but also ready to get down to school and give the paper my best shot.

I got ready hastily, throwing Alessia's hair into a bun before quickly leaving the house. When I got outside, though, I was welcomed by a new addition to our front door. An eviction notice.

I stared at it, my heart stopping.

'*EVICTION NOTICE*' it read, and, with a basket full of regret, I let my eyes scan the rest of the letter.

'*To Tenant: Mr H Trent*

You are required to leave this address by, or on, 3 September 2018.'

I glanced across all the boring details, over the signature of the landlord, and skipped to the end.

'*Dated: 3 June 2018*'

Well, shoot.

I read the notice a couple hundred times, before realising that my bottom lip was trembling.

It was then that I let out an ugly sob. I slapped my hand across my mouth, silencing the cries as they escaped. I fell to the floor, curling up and whimpering, tears falling from my eyes.

"Just let me go home," I begged nobody, my voice jarred by the sobs. "Let me live that life, as Olivia Clark, and not this life; not *her* life," I continued, hiccupping, "*please.*"

As expected, no one responded, and so after five or so minutes, I dragged myself up off the floor, swallowing and tearing the notice down. I shoved it into my school bag before trudging down the front drive, starting my walk to school.

When I finally got to school, I only had enough time to throw my bag into my locker and go to my exam.

"Alessia!" Someone called suddenly.

I turned slowly, recognising the voice. It was the head-teacher. But it wasn't him who made me freeze; it was the two police officers beside him.

Flashes of what Alessia had done to my locker came back to me, and I recalled that Alessia and I had been two distinct substances at that point. Now we melted into almost one.

The head-teacher approached me, "Do you have an exam, Alessia?" He asked, the officers lurking behind him.

"Yeah, I do," I told him, smiling.

"Ah, I was hoping to pull you aside for a quick interview. It's nothing serious, the police officers and I just want to talk to everyone in your registration class regarding the vandalism that took place last month." He explained, making me gulp.

I glanced at the officers, then back at the head-teacher. I nodded, smiling, "Okay, that should be fine." I told him.

He smiled also, "Okay," he said, "maybe we'll catch you after your exam," I responded with a smile and a nod, watching him mirror it. "Well, good luck, Alessia."

I thanked him, before spinning around and briskly walking down the corridor, using the excuse of hurrying to my exam to deter from the fact that I was actually running away from the officers. And why? Because Alessia Trent sometimes cannot be controlled. And it'll all come back to *me*. For, anything that happens to her respectively happens to me.

I shook the thoughts away, only knowing that I had to get to the exam hall and do well in this exam. Hopefully, if Alessia got good results, she would have a bright future. Perhaps that was just wishful thinking, though; it seems as though nothing I can do can change this destructive path that Alessia is headed down. Only *she* can, and she's stubborn as hell.

Sitting down in the exam hall, my hands began to tremble. I took off my blazer, hanging it on the back of my chair before taking ten too many gulps of water as the invigilators read out the rules. I began foot-tapping as I became too anxious, but that soon drew in some annoyed glances.

I closed my eyes and took a deep breath. I had been scared to do my own exams, sure, but this was a different kind of fear. A horrible feeling had sunk to the pit of my stomach, and was suddenly stirring.

I wanted to go back home. It was the underlying problem, yet it was the most impossible one. Well, not the *most* impossible—I *could* go back to my house, to Olivia Clark's house, though it wouldn't be mine anymore. That's because the biggest problem is that I am no longer Olivia Clark, and soon, Alessia Trent will no longer have a home herself.

I didn't even realise that the exam had started until an invigilator walked past me, pausing to glance back at me with confusion. I quickly flipped over the first page, trying to focus my mind; I tried to concentrate on the history that was on the school's curriculum, and not the one on my mind—*my* history.

I answered all the questions to the best of my ability, surprisingly, never really stopping for more than five minutes. When the exam was over, I closed my paper and sat back, clutching onto my pen so tight that I feared it would break.

It was one obstacle, and it had deterred my thoughts for just an hour and a half, but that was just an hour and a half. It was nothing against twenty-four, and it was certainly nothing against a week, a month...a year.

I had been trapped inside of Alessia's body, almost becoming her, for seven months now. That's just over half a year—would I reach a year?

No, I suddenly thought. That's impossible—isn't it? Tiny memories from Olivia Clark's life were still scattered around the place, but I managed to uncover just one. The last moment in her body.

That was early October—so surely I can't live in this body beyond October. But then, what beyond *that*?

I didn't remember what had happened to Olivia Clark. I didn't remember how I had got here. I also didn't remember if I had even had that information in the first place.

Perhaps I *am* Alessia Trent, but just having an existential crisis.

I was too distracted whilst walking down the corridor that I bumped into someone. Startled, it took me a while to register what had happened. I glanced up to see a police officer, the person I had bumped into.

My eyes widened, and I suddenly fell back into motion. I clamped a hand over my mouth, "I am so sorry!" I said, watching the officer's face relax, and a small smile unfold. And then, her eyebrows furrowed.

"Aren't you Alessia Trent?" She suddenly asked.

Despite my earlier misted thoughts, I replied with no hesitation, "yes."

She nodded, pursing her lips, "We'd like to interview you," she said, and I felt as Alessia's body froze. "You weren't available earlier, were you?" She asked, "But you are now."

I couldn't deny this. It would look too suspicious.

I swallowed my fear, "Yes, I'm free now." I told her. She smiled, before guiding me to a place that she had probably told me about, but I wasn't paying enough attention to recall if she had.

I recognised the route we were taking, though, and we were soon waiting outside of the head-teacher's office. I gulped, trying to keep my nerves from my face. It would give me—or, Alessia—away in a *second*.

She rapped at the door, waiting for it to open before she said, "We'd like to hold another interview,"

The head-teacher opened the door wider, glancing over to see me before smiling. "Of course," he said, "come on in."

The head-teacher was trying to assure me that it was a minor interview in a major scheme of events, but I was too worried to hear anything. Alessia wouldn't have had nerves like these, but Olivia sure did. And I still couldn't shake her; shake whatever kind of phantom life she had appeared from.

I was guided to a seat by the head-teacher, who then sat in the corner of his office. The two officers sat directly in front of me. One had a tape recorder, and one had a notebook.

"So, Miss Trent, correct?" The man asked, having pressed 'record' on the recorder.

I tried not to hesitate, but I felt my head twitch as I nodded.

I could've made a run for it—could've let Alessia pay for what she did. But I couldn't. I didn't trust Alessia; she'd probably dig herself a bigger hole than what it's worth.

So, here goes.

Here goes.

CHAPTER THIRTY-NINE

"Where were you at the time of the vandalism?" She asked.

I blanched. "And what time would that be?" I asked, trying to throw them off my fear.

She looked down at her notes, but it was the man that spoke, "Quarter past nine," he informed me.

I swallowed. *What were you doing, Olivia?* Well, *I* was doing nothing but unpacking my books for my first lesson of the day. But Alessia? She was *not* doing that.

I cleared my throat, "I was probably running down to the library; I had left some work down there and needed to collect it for first lesson."

Score. That would leave no room for an alibi, but then it would leave no room for them to check the attendance, or to ask a teacher if I was in the lesson. I was simply 'probably' running down some stairs.

"Did anyone see you?" The woman asked, "Another student? Or the librarian?"

I shrugged casually, "I was in a rush, I don't remember," I told her simply.

"We've looked at your attendance for that day," the man said, "you weren't present for lesson one, but you were for lesson two and onwards. Can you explain this?"

I sighed, looking away. *Damn it, Alessia. For God's sake-*

"I skipped," I lied, "I realised I was seriously, *seriously* behind. I hadn't done three pieces of homework, and I had missed many lessons. I took the lesson off, without the teacher's permission, to catch up."

I allowed the indecency of one action to cover up the truth. The head-teacher didn't look best pleased by my bunking, but it did cover up an even bigger problem. One he'd be *less* pleased about.

"And where did you go during this time?" The man asked.

I thought quickly, "The field," I told him, "I didn't want anyone to catch me."

It seemed to be making sense to them; I wasn't receiving any kind of suspicious glances, though I wasn't receiving much of anything. The police officers were keeping neutral faces—my only indication would come from the head-teacher. Though, I still took it as a score.

"Since you were walking around the halls at this time, did you happen to see any suspicious activity?" The woman asked, "Especially around your registration class?"

I shook my head, "Like I said, I went to the library, and then I went to the field. I wouldn't have had any reason to go back up to my registration class—not, of course, until I needed my folder for period four, which is when I realised it was blocked off." I explained.

Everything was quiet for a bit, and I sat anxiously, my thigh shaking as I bounced my leg up and down. The man read over his notepad carefully, before nodding to the woman.

"That's all, Miss Trent, thank you for your time."

I froze. That's it? I did it? Or, *did* I? This may have been the last nail in my coffin, or the first—they might start building a case on me right now.

"You're free to leave, Alessia."

The voice startled me. It had come from the head-teacher, and I glanced up at him to see him smiling down at him.

I smiled back, "Thank you, sir." I briefly left, though not too quickly. But when I was free, I rushed away, anticipation to get out of the school burning in my veins.

I soon reached the registration class, heading straight for Alessia's locker. When I got there, though, I came to a halt.

The door to Alessia's locker was dented in and hanging open. I frowned, glancing into the locker. Nothing seemed suspicious, especially when I found that Alessia's bag was in perfect condition. I slipped it onto my shoulder, running the pads of my fingers along the dent marks. I peered into her locker, seeing nothing wrong.

When I turned to leave, though, I was suddenly aware of something pressed against the back of the door. Curious, I closed the door so that I could get a better look, freezing when I saw what it was.

It was a photocopied, black and white, version of the eviction notice that I had found stuck to Alessia's front door this morning.

With a deep breath, I tore it down, my eyes watering. I screwed the paper up in my hand, throwing it into the bin. But then I saw one stuck above the bin, beneath the notice board. My nose flared, and I reached for that one also, tearing it down. When I was done, I turned around, and then I realised. The entire room was plastered in them.

The tears threatened to spill as my lip quivered, and I moved slowly over to one stuck to the bookshelf. I removed it gingerly, seeing that it was crystal clear—I was being evicted. Any normal person would've asked if I was okay, but no. None had. Loads of people would have seen it, since there have been exams this morning. My hands shook at the idea of that many people knowing about this notice.

News of Alessia's eviction had never gotten around to me–Olivia, and so it's likely that I wasn't in for this day, and maybe the day after. But a lot of people still were.

I heard laughing, before a boy in our registration class entered, a piece of paper in hand. Spotting Alessia, he grinned, "This true?" He jeered, displaying the sheet.

I gritted my teeth, marching over to him and ripping it out of his hands. "You're sick if you find that funny." I spat, throwing it into the bin, along with the others I had collected.

He scoffed. "Yeah, you're definitely an attention-seeker."

I turned to face him, eyes wide. "'Attention seeker'?" I echoed, "Not unfortunate or desperate for help, but attention seeking?"

He rolled his eyes. "I don't care for your sob story," he said, walking over to his locker, "I'm just putting my bag away."

Alessia was right. No one cared about her—and no one ever would. No matter how hard she tried, or didn't try.

The boy soon left, but others weren't far behind. They each entered, having their own mocks to throw at Alessia, before leaving.

It was Lizzie that entered next. "Nice," she said, showing Alessia the notice that she had now seen many, many times. "Maybe you'll be one of those people we donate stuff to when we have those charity days." She said, before bursting out into laughter at my expression.

"Wow, Less, you really *are* funny," she said, opening her locker, "though I'm not too sure that you're good enough for this mission with Dylan anymore—I don't think street dirt is his type." She sneered before leaving, cackling as she walked down the corridor.

It was then that the tears spilled, sobs wracking Alessia's body. I tore down all the notices, not knowing where the original was. I then ran out into the corridor, yanking each sheet down as furiously as the last.

I almost bumped into someone as I turned to start on the other side. "I'm sorry," they said and I glanced up, recognising the voice. It was Mollie. "I was..." she paused, and I took the time to look at what she was holding. "I was taking these down for you," she said, before shoving the stack she had collected into my hands.

I stared at them, before closing my fingers around them and holding them tightly. "Thank you," I whispered, refusing to raise my head and show her the damage that the bullies had caused.

"If it's any correlation, I know for a fact that it wasn't Lizzie or Katy; I was with them when we found them and they seemed surprised." She told me, eyes curious but gentle.

I flashed her a small smile, "You're a good person, Mollie, I don't know why you hang out with them."

She shrugged, thinking nothing of it, "It's only for a month longer."

I nodded, "Maybe, but a month is still a long time. To some people it's a breaking point, to others it's an engine towards success." With that philosophical seed, I slipped past her, moving towards the bin at the end of the corridor.

I was stuffing the sheets into the almost full bin when I felt someone standing behind me.

"I checked the Science and English corridors too," she told me, "did you want me to help you with the others?" She asked.

I turned to smile at her "That's okay, Mollie, I'm sure they'll be no more."

Mollie didn't look too convinced, but took off anyway.

I took a deep breath, heading for the next corridor. I was wrong, as expected. There were more copies—*loads* of them.

By the time I was finished, I had taken a grand tour of the school, with every piece of paper I tore down making me feel more and more drowned.

I want to go home. I want to go back to my life.

CHAPTER FORTY

I think I knew before I opened her front door.
    I walked into a cloud of smoke and immediately began coughing, trying to waft the smoke away from my face.
Having squeezed my eyes shut, I reopened them to see Alessia's dad in front of me. I froze. He glared at me. "Bunking off school?" He asked.
I shook my head, holding my breath, "No, I told you; I'm on an exam timetable."
He laughed, right in my face. His breath smelt of alcohol and cigarettes, and as though it had not been freshened in a while. "Lies, admit it."
I stayed silent. I was not a liar, so I wouldn't 'admit it'—but I knew he would only get angry if said otherwise. So I said nothing.
"Answer me!" He screamed, lunging at me, grabbing onto my hair and shoving me back against the wall.
Honestly, with the day I had just had at school, I was done with answering. I was done with everything.
When I didn't respond, he said, "Not only are you incompetent, but you're also costing me this house," he said, anger bubbling.
I stared at him, shocked, "*Me*?"
"Yes you, you selfish brat." He said, before gripping onto my hair and shoving my head back against the wall. It hurt, but it wasn't the worst he'd done.
I didn't respond, which seemed to infuriate him again.
"Nothing to add, hm? Maybe it's because you know I'm right." He growled, kicking me in my shins. I couldn't suppress the yelp that burst out in response. "Yes, that's right," he said, "and you're a mistake, too," he actually wasn't making much sense, then again, he never seemed too. "A very big mistake that's going to cost me this house—all for this ugly and worthless piece of *dirt*," he spat.
My eyes widened. I had seen Alessia's dad be very, very physically violent, but never verbal—not as much as this. I had to wonder whether or not her incorrect perceptions of herself and her self-worth stemmed from this, as opposed to the bullying. Though, perhaps it was just a deadly mixture of both—a poison.
"When the time comes, you're going out on the streets, and if you make any money from your corner job, you bring it to me. I'll get myself sorted, and you'll remain a piece of trash that I took out a little too late." I frowned up at him, eyes watering. How could he say such things to his daughter?
I knew that my family life wasn't exactly the image of perfection—if anything, it was the farthest from it—but even my dad didn't talk to me in this way. My dad may be short-tempered

and always nagging, but he always told me he loved me when he or I left, he always smiled when he saw me, and he always asked if I was okay at least once a day.

But this was not Alessia's dad.

Alessia's dad was cold; far removed. On a calm day, he would insult Alessia no more than ten times; on an angry day, he would hit her way more than ten times. He would express his hatred for her, but never seemed to give reasons why. Alessia had never done anything wrong, yet suddenly she was being thrown around like she meant nothing. But she *did*.

It's no wonder that she's so psychologically damaged—always searching for love in places that she won't receive it.

"Get out of my sight; you make my eyes bleed." He spat, kicking Alessia in the gut, making me double over in pain.

I tried to stop the groan that slipped out of my lips, but it was no use. And so, in crippling pain, I crawled up the stairs. I reached Alessia's room as fast I could, throwing my school bag onto the floor and locking the door as soon as possible.

Still groaning and grumbling, I stumbled over to Alessia's bed. I discarded her blazer and slipped into her bed with her phone in hand.

I spent the next half an hour in pain, enjoying my free time by wasting most of it on Instagram. And then I received a text message. In fact, I received *two* text messages—almost at the same time.

I opened the app, reading the name of the sender of the first message. Lucas. *Lucas?* I thought Lucas hated me after what Alessia had done and said. Instead, I was receiving text messages from him?

I read it quickly, eager to know what he had to say after days of silence.

'*I heard about the stuff that people were sticking around school today. Are you okay?*'

Everything that I had assessed about Lucas was true; he cared unconditionally about Alessia. Even though she could not care about him one single bit in return.

I smiled, responding quickly.

'*Kind of. Thank you for checking in.*'

I could have elaborated, but I didn't know by how much. What if he exposed Alessia's predicament after gaining more intel? *Wow, living Alessia's life has really made me lose my trust in people.*

I sent the text, leaving the chat to see who the other text was from. I paused, a light feeling overcoming me as I saw the contact name.

Dylan.

I missed my old life. I missed my home, my parents, my friends. And I missed Dylan. These small moments where he would reach out to Alessia were really the only time I got with him.

I was smiling before I even read the text message, but what I read made my smile widen.

'*Are you okay? I heard about all the sheets stuck around in school. Did you want to talk? Or go to the cinema? We could revise for biology?*'

It was simply a string of questions, yet I was grinning down at the message like a small child.

I tapped away a response quickly.

'*Honestly, not really, what they did made it hurt that much more. I'm thinking maybe revising takes priority? But the cinema is good too :)*'

A smiley face. *Does Alessia use smiley faces?* I sure do.

It was easier to be more honest and open with Dylan since I had a level of trust with him as Olivia Clark, and not only as Alessia Trent.

Dylan's reply came back instantly, as if he had been waiting for mine. Or maybe he was just sitting near his phone.

'I know. They're heartless. And yes, revising would probably be best, but then there is that new horror film?'

I was still grinning, despite talking about another horrible attack on Alessia.

'They are. And that's not very specific, but I'll meet you at the cinema at 7. Choose the film and I'll pay you back for the ticket. :)'

The next response was slow, and I soon got impatient, getting out of bed and changing out of my clothes. I had forgotten all about the injury to my stomach, and I soon regretted it as it flared up, the pain as fresh as when the punch was first thrown. I hissed in pain, bending over and clutching the painful spot. I rifled through Alessia's drawers, finding some painkillers and popping two into my mouth.

When I was pulling my t-shirt over my head, I heard the ping of a text message. Quickly, I slipped on my leggings before rushing over to my phone, seeing that it was a response from Dylan.

Beaming, I read it.

'You're lucky I like horror films, I just had to cancel plans to fit you in.'

Alessia pondered the idea that these plans could've been with Olivia, but did not seem to care if he had cancelled on her to be with Alessia. It actually made her feel delighted as her jealousy burned away.

I quickly responded.

'You didn't have to do that, but thank you. See you there :)'

Another ping. My heart leaped.

'For you. See you :)'

Whilst Alessia was flipping out, heart bursting with joy, I was just startled by his care for Alessia. I didn't doubt for one second that Dylan had a certain level of care for everyone—he was just that kind of person. He was a gentleman and a very good friend; I just found his level of care for Alessia confusing. I had never known that he was this close to Alessia. He never mentioned her, so maybe it wasn't that big of a deal, but it sure enough seemed like it was now.

I brushed that all away, realising that I was going out with Dylan. I was suddenly very excited, leaping up to pick out an outfit, despite the pain in my stomach.

If I were to stay here in Alessia's body for whatever is left of her life, I would sure cherish these little moments. The ones that reminded me of Olivia Clark and her life, a life that was better than this one.

CHAPTER FORTY-ONE

The next day, I let Alessia take control to sit her Biology exam. Yesterday evening was a dream from a sleep I've been drowning in for a long time.

Dylan had chosen that film he had wanted it see; it was vague, but very me. He bought the tickets, the drinks and the popcorn, and waited for me outside of the screen door. As ever, he was impossibly kind and caring, asking how I was before talking to me about the revision he's done for Biology. At my uncertainty, he went over a few things to fill in the gaps in my memory, and then promised that we would meet up before the exam this morning.

Alessia walked in now, seeing him just a few metres in front of her. When he sat down, he searched the incoming pupils for someone. His eyes landed on Alessia and he smiled. Alessia took her seat, though Dylan's eyes were still scouring the crowd. Alessia's eyes watched stonily as Olivia started for the aisle, seeing Dylan's face brighten.

Olivia shot him an uncertain look, and I could suddenly remember feeling all kinds of nervous for this exam back when I had her life. Olivia wasn't particularly good at Biology or maths, but she could sail comfortably through pretty much anything else. This was one of those subjects that she just didn't excel in, and both she and Dylan knew that. Dylan flashed a reassuring smile in her direction, eyes gleaming with full and total confidence in her.

When Olivia was my life, I had never noticed that gleam before, but I think Alessia usually recognised it in Dylan's eyes when Olivia was around. That, and also a dazed and dreamy look that normally crossed his face. I was slowly realising that Dylan probably *had* liked me—likes Olivia, just like everyone keeps saying.

When the exam begun, Alessia tried to rid her mind of thoughts about Olivia and Dylan, and got straight to work. She hailed through the questions, which I was stunned at. She lost concentration midway through the paper, though, glancing up to see Dylan working in a similar way to how she had just been. She admired him for a few seconds, before smiling, and then glancing away. Her eyes landed on Olivia, who was stationary, save from the pen she was tapping against her chin.

It was a habit of mine—of Olivia's—to tap my pen against my chin when I was particularly stuck. It got so bad during the exam period that I actually came out of the exam hall with red marks along my chin.

I let Alessia work as I thought back to that time. I remember coming out of the second Biology exam, which had been my hardest paper to date. Stressed, I had tapped viciously at my chin, leaving red marks on my skin, which Dylan had spotted when he found me outside. I remember the feeling of his thumb against my chin as he brushed over them gently, telling me that I had to stop with the pen tapping.

I lost myself in Alessia quickly, wanting to avoid the peril that was suffocating memories that didn't even seem like mine anymore. But when I looked up at the real Olivia Clark, I could practically envision myself in her body once more. It was weird, and very, very confusing.

Soon enough, the exam ended, and Alessia finished the paper with a flourish. Looking down at her work with the perspective of Olivia Clark, I could be pretty sure that Alessia would achieve an A, or maybe A* grade on this paper. It would be impossible for her not to—her answers were almost impeccable.

We were dismissed row by row, and Alessia watched as Olivia and Dylan shared a quick look when she rose. Next, it was my row, and I took back control, pushing back out of my chair and following the stream of people out of the door.

Someone tapped my shoulder when we reached the corridor. "How was it?" They asked. I turned to see Dylan smiling at me.

I laughed. "Good for you, I see." He looked down modestly, though too shared a laugh.

"It was a good paper." He said, raising his head as he suddenly started to search the crowd ahead of us.

I hummed in agreement, "It was. I was surprised by how much I knew." I said, watching him smile.

"I told you that you could do it." He said, making me blush.

I laughed awkwardly, it becoming my turn to duck my head. "Maybe." I admitted, hearing him chuckle.

When I looked up again, I saw his eyes frantically searching around in front of us. I held the door open for him, and he shared his gratitude before he continued to look around.

I cleared my throat, clutching onto my pencil case tightly. "Are you looking for Olivia?" I asked hesitantly. Feelings of envy sparked in Alessia, but I was much too curious to care.

Dylan smiled absentmindedly, "Yeah," he said, before glancing over to me, "sorry, she was just so nervous before this exam; I want to see how she did...and if she's okay."

Something in my heart grew wings and flew away.

"Have you asked her to Prom yet?" I asked, though I already knew the answer.

He beamed, but quickly turned his head so that I wouldn't see his cheeks flushing. "Yeah," was all he said, and I smiled.

"Took you some time, how did you ask her?" I asked.

"I was nervous, okay? And nothing special, really." Whilst I was secretly in love with his 'nervous' comment, Alessia wondered whether he kept the details to himself to save her pride. She was, after all, obsessed with him.

I nodded, catching the door to our registration class corridor, holding it open for him.

"Did she say yes?" I asked him, watching him stay back to hold the door open for the others that were behind us.

He smiled. "You make it sound like a marriage proposal," his eyes became distant at that, but not sad. I watched him with confusion. I could read Dylan, of course; he's been my best friend for years. But this look was odd.

"But yeah, she said yes." He told me. That smile never left his face.

I didn't ask him anymore questions, not even about the details of his Promposal. It was mainly because he seemed hesitant—and I already kind of knew how he had asked Olivia. Since I had once been her.

It was a Saturday, and Dylan and I were just having a casual day out—sometimes it was to the park, sometimes it was to the cinema, sometimes it was just at home. This time, it was at a theme park that I had wanted to go to for *ages*. It wasn't until the end of the day, though, that he had finally asked me. It was simple, really—he had bought me the gemstone necklace that I had been admiring, and casually asked me as he passed me the bag after the checkout.

Times were easier then—easier when I was Olivia Clark.

When we got to our registration class, it was empty. The rest of our class had either already gotten here, or were yet to come. Alessia's locker was still battered, but the teacher let her switch temporarily to one on the bottom.

"I'm sure Olivia is around here somewhere," I assured Dylan when I saw him anxiously checking his phone.

He smiled up at me, "Well, yeah, I promised her I'd give her a lift; I don't think she'll be leaving without one," we both laughed at that, but I sobered as I locked up my locker.

"I don't think that's the only reason she'd wait for you," I told him, rising from the floor and slipping my bag onto my back.

He frowned at me, slipping his phone into his blazer pocket. "Maybe." He said, before turning to his locker to pull out his own bag.

We were soon joined by people, but only a few. I tried to ignore the looks I was getting, that Dylan wasn't. I was simply waiting for him, yet they acted as if I was shovelling dirt into my mouth.

I was suddenly shoved, and I fell backwards, where I hit the radiator with a *bang*.

There was a moment of silence, and then people started to laugh.

"Who did that?" A voice suddenly demanded. I looked through the cracks in the crowd to see Dylan, face stern but eyes flashing. "Anyone?" He then asked, having gotten no responses.

A boy, Charlie Smither, scoffed. "The slut was probably just tryna bend over," he said, making everyone laugh, "weren't you?" He taunted, grabbing me by the hips suddenly.

And then, just as fast, a hand wrapped around one of his arms, ripping it and Charlie away from me.

"Don't touch her." It warned. I stared at Dylan, utterly confused and startled. I hadn't realised he even *knew* Alessia, never mind been this protective over her.

Another boy stepped forward, Jake Gardy, "Come on, Dylan, chill, it's not like she doesn't deserve it,"

Dylan's jaw clenched at that, but before he could say anything, another voice chimed in.

"How is life out on the corner, Alessia? That's the only way you'll stay in your house, right? If you trade your body for money?" It was Katy, and it made Alessia freeze. She was suddenly overcome with heavy emotion, just wanting to wrap herself up into her body and hide.

"*Enough*-" Dylan began, but he was cut off as he was shoved.

"Get out, Dylan, let us take out the trash," it was Charlie again, who grabbed me once more and threw my body into the lockers.

"Though, who'd want to wake up to something that ugly?"

Alessia had no idea who had said what, as she was suddenly sinking, and sinking into a place with no oxygen and with no light.

And then a fight broke out.

CHAPTER FORTY-TWO

I think I realised what was really going on when several punches came at Dylan. I watched in shock as Dylan threw himself into the boys, using all the power he could.
But they were too strong and too fast.
When he got slammed back into the wall, I started to scream.
"Stop it!" I yelled, jumping into action. The group that had once huddled around me to watch carelessly and heartlessly as I was bullied was quickly dispersing, not wanting to get caught. But if the boys didn't stop fighting soon, we would be.
"Stop!" I shouted again, watching Charlie hail a punch at Dylan. "Please!" But when I tried to stop him, he simply discarded me, shoving me over. I tripped and landed on the floor, where I hit my head. It was then that Dylan lost all control, as if he hadn't already.
I jumped up quickly, though, pressing a palm to his chest to stop him.
Suddenly, Alessia had taken over. Perhaps her fear was too strong, and I was getting lost under piles and piles of punches. The fight had reminded her of the physical abuse she endures at home from her dad, and she was shaking violently.
Dylan stopped, glancing down at her with a worried expression on his face.
Charlie and Jake suddenly backed away. "Come try us again when you have more fight in you."
Dylan and Alessia stood in silence for a while, both with laboured breath, and both looking at each other.
"You're bleeding." She told Dylan, reaching into her pocket and pulling out a packet of tissues. She hesitantly began to dab at his wounds, soaking up the blood.
"How's your head?" Dylan asked, taking the tissue from her hand.
She felt dizzy, so she knew that it wasn't good. She reached up, placing her palm to the back of her head. "Sore." She simply responded.
When he was kind of cleaned up, Dylan guided her out of the room, "Come on," he said, "let's go—I'll drop you home so that you can ice your head."
In the back of Alessia's mind, she could remember that Dylan was supposed to be giving Olivia a lift back to her house. But then, she didn't really care all that much.
When Dylan and Alessia walked out of the school's exit, though, Olivia was nowhere in sight.
I remembered this day. I had waited for Dylan for twenty minutes, but I didn't want to call or text him too much. I was upset after the test, knowing for definite that I had failed. I was feeling panicked, and simply couldn't wait any longer before the tears began to spill. I suppressed the sobs until I got home, which I had to walk for half an hour to, but I really needed Dylan in that moment.
But then, so did Alessia. I just didn't know that then.

The journey to Alessia's was silent, and Dylan would take his hand off the wheel every now and again to press the tissue to his nose, where blood was spilling out.

When Dylan had pulled up outside her house, he said, "You should ice your head as soon as possible and lie down—but don't sleep, not until you're certain you don't have a concussion. If you have any problems, let me know." He said, eyes filled with concern as he watched Alessia.

She nodded silently, glancing down at her clasped hands in her lap. When she spoke next, it was only in a whisper. "Thank you, Dylan," she said, "you didn't have to do that."

Dylan had no response, and Alessia gave him a small smile when she glanced up at him. And then she leaned in. She pressed a cautious kiss to his cheek, before pulling back and opening the passenger door to leave.

Alessia thought she had left Dylan stunned, and was proven right when she saw his car linger across from her drive longer that it needed to. She felt an emptiness when he left, as if she had sewn the pair of them together. She was getting attached, she realised, but it was hard not to.

Alessia unlocked her front door cautiously, but the house was silent. She relaxed slightly, closing and locking the door behind her as she crept in.

She ran for the stairs, dashing into her room and locking herself away. When she got there, I broke free, taking over her life once more. I exhaled. And then I started to cry.

I was confused, in pain, and scattered in fragments. I wasn't sure if I was Olivia Clark or Alessia Trent, or perhaps neither. Or even if I was alive—*was this just a dream? Just a trick?* Surely not. I didn't have to pinch myself to know that I was really here—I had mental and physical scars to prove that I was.

I took deep breaths, trying to rid myself of everything that burdened me. When that didn't quite work, I buried myself under the covers on my bed, even though they were thin since the temperatures never ceased to rise.

I held my limbs close to my body, shutting my eyes and inhaling and exhaling slowly. Living as a starring role in Alessia's life hurt; I couldn't imagine what living it firsthand, with no one to take control of your body when you're too in pain to go on, is like.

When I felt calmer, I unearthed Alessia's phone from where it had disappeared into her covers. But it was a mistake, of course. The bullies never left and there were already a never-ending stream of horrible messages piling up on Alessia's lock screen. It was no wonder that she hadn't just thrown it in a river and been done with it all.

I couldn't help but read them all. When I had first seen them, I had merely glanced over the beginnings of each insult. But I wanted to dig deeper; I wanted to understand Alessia and her life.

'Why do people like you? Oh wait, they don't HAHA'
'Fix your face darling xx'
'Ewww why do you look like that LOL'
'Wash maybe??'
'Your hair is absolutely disgusting. Dye it or chop it. Do something'
'Stop breathing'
'Heard you've been slutting around. Not surprised'
'Matt's spreading your nudes but no one wants to look at them because of how ugly you are OOPS'
'Fix ur face'
'Your figure is non-existent'

'Why do you look like an albino LOL the sun exists ffs!!!'
'Ugly and dumb'

There were so, *so* many more. Most were explicit and detailed ways in which Alessia should end her life.

I could never understand how someone could be so incessantly rude. How was it a universal idea that Alessia, or some other innocent person, deserves a life this hated? Who sparked the flame? And where does it end?

I refused to accept that Alessia's hatred for me came from this. I would have never started something so hateful, so loveless and soulless. It was beyond me. At least, that's what I thought. Alessia saw me in a completely different light.

She saw me as a mastermind. I controlled 'my girls', I gave them orders and they never let me down. But there was just one flaw in Alessia's understanding of me—Olivia Clark had never done such thing, I knew this for certain, and I couldn't control *everyone;* it wasn't just 'my girls' that hurt Alessia. Alessia knew this, but she still had some strange, undefined hatred for me, for Olivia Clark.

And that's how I fell asleep. Phone in hand, malicious words in my head, and anger and pain coursing through my body.

CHAPTER FORTY-THREE

The rest of the exam period went by in a blur. At times, I'd blink and there'd be a question paper in front of me. I'd try to answer the questions as much as I could, but, ultimately, the questions were not meant for me—they were meant for Alessia. Every time I woke up, I pondered just how far into Alessia's life I would make it—or if I would even go *back* to Olivia's, or another's, or if I'd just stay. The questions kept me awake at night, and I would wake with my bed and my thoughts disarray.

It was now summer break; I could easily catch up on sleep later on in the day if I wanted to. But if I did that, I left myself vulnerable to Alessia's dad.

Today, though, none of that mattered, and I wouldn't let it matter. My eyes ran over my Prom invite as I brushed a copper eyeshadow across my eyelids. I had to work Alessia's eye makeup a little differently to mine, since her eyes were a gleaming green, and mine a deep brown. Dylan would always call them a beautiful brown.

As I applied mascara, I swallowed, hesitant about tonight. Alessia did not have friends. Where would she sit at Prom? Who would she dance with? Her only chances were Lucas and Dylan; Lucas hates her, and Dylan couldn't spare more than a second thought for her if it meant giving up Olivia. The same also, apparently, applied to the journey there, since Dylan was driving Olivia. That left Alessia out in the cold, standing by the edge of the pavement.

That would be a problem that we would have to solve later.

I pulled Alessia's gorgeous violet dress up her legs, slipping my arms through it and fastening it at the back. It looked like a violet sky, lavender clouds hanging at the bottom and bright violet rays stringing across the top. Though, it didn't look nearly as dishevelled as you'd probably imagine from the prior description.

As I straightened Alessia's wild hair to resemble curls that were a little tame and voluminous, I watched Snapchat stories, seeing some girls already posting pictures of their dresses for tonight. Then there was Dylan's story. It was a picture that I remember as if it were taken just seconds ago. It was a close-up of Olivia's face, which was glittering with fresh makeup, though taken from the side. Her curls shielded her face slightly, but not enough that her face was completely invisible.

She was beautiful. That's what Alessia thought. Alessia suddenly felt extremely envious, yet not because she holds Dylan's heart, not this time. Alessia was envious of how Olivia looked, and she could only imagine how gorgeous her dress was.

I remember that dress. It was a maroon coloured gown with gold trimmings, one that cinched in at the waist but left room for a ting dosage of cleavage. It was elegant and classy, but teasing and flirty. It was everything I had wanted back then. But now it was just a dream.

I threw Alessia's phone across the room, watching it land smoothly on her bed. I took one last glance at Alessia before continuing to work on her hair. When every strand of hair was perfectly composed, I set the straighteners down and turned them off. I stared into the mirror.

This had once been something that had scared me. When I looked into the mirror, I did not see Olivia Clark, a friendly, popular, and pretty girl, but Alessia Trent, an empty, lonely and ugly girl. But none of that was true. Those were all beliefs concocted by the girl that I share this body with, this life with. Alessia Trent.

Olivia Clark was not always friendly, popular and pretty in everyone's opinion, and Alessia Trent was not always empty, lonely or ugly. Or perhaps not at all. But it's what Alessia thought, and it's what she's thought for a long time now.

I rose from her vanity chair, turning to walk to her floor length mirror. Again, I did not expect to see Olivia Clark, but Alessia Trent. I felt a dull ache when I met eyes that were not deep brown, yet it didn't startle me anymore. I really *had* sunk to the bottom.

I slipped some trainers on, and found a way to hitch my dress up enough that it wasn't obvious under the coat that I was going to wear. I would be travelling in style—public transport.

It was strange; as Olivia Clark, I had only ever dreamed about a limo or a fancy taxi. I wanted to feel pretty on my big day, and that included transport.

But as Alessia Trent, I felt lucky enough just to be holding the piece of card with my name on it—the invitation.

I packed a bag with Alessia's heels and other important things—like her *actual* clutch—before cautiously unlocking her door.

Hearing no sounds, I crept towards the stairs, checking again. When I got to the bottom, I realised that I was home alone.

That was another thing about Olivia Clark. She valued friends and family dearly, and it's not to say that Alessia didn't, but she didn't have any to value. Whilst a picture of me in my prom dress was my mum and dad's profile picture on Facebook for months, Alessia's father was one that could almost be non-existent. Whilst my friends celebrated me on their Snapchat stories, Alessia was a name that barely anyone remembered; it travelled like a whisper and halted when no one cared anymore.

I walked shamefully to the nearest bus stop, getting strange looks from those who passed me. I was lucky enough when the group of boys who were at the bus stop with me boarded the first bus that came, otherwise I feared that they would do or say something stupid.

I got on my bus with my head down, taking a seat at the back, again getting looks from those already seated. I tried to ramp up feelings of excitement within me on the journey, but I could only feel vacant as the feeling of loneliness trembled deep within me.

It took three buses and a one-stop ride on the train to finally get to venue, and when I was there, I was late by half an hour. I was guided by a party manager of sorts, who led me to the nearest toilets when I asked where they were.

In one of the cubicles, I quickly ripped off my coat and sprayed myself down with my perfume. I powdered my face and ran a brush though Alessia's hair. I slipped off my trainers and shoved them into my bag, bending down to fasten Alessia's purple heels onto her petite feet.

When I was done, I snuck out and found some sort of cloakroom, where I stuffed Alessia's bag and coat into a small corner.

Now ready, I exhaled deeply, running my clammy hands across the skirt of Alessia's gown. I could hear the music; I had been able to hear it since I got here. It flitted between pop and slow dance. When I finally entered the hall, it was playing an R&B song of sorts, and my steps seemed to mirror that of the beat of the song.

It was one of those songs that broke the dancing, and people dispersed, finding food and drink, or breaking into chatting clusters.

I let my eyes soak up the hall once more, just as they had done when I was Olivia Clark. Alessia was stunned by how a place could look so beautiful, but feel so daunting at once. She couldn't appreciate the glittering lights when judging eyes fell on her.

Alessia tried to stay to the walls, but as the song transitioned into a more of a slow-dance song, she found herself getting tangled up. She was soon pushed into someone.

Eyes wide, she finally realised that it was Dylan.

I remembered this moment as Olivia Clark. I had been dancing with Dylan, and everything had felt so velvet, carefree. Dylan kept telling me how beautiful I looked, and I had raised my head to glance up at him, telling him the same in response. Grinning, he had spun me. And then I got lost in the crowd. It seems that, as I fell into Matt's arms, Alessia had fallen into Dylan's.

Dylan beamed down at Alessia. "You made it." He said, eyebrows raised.

Alessia quickly relaxed, and I mentally stepped back to allow her this pure moment of gold. "I did," she said, "did you ever doubt me?"

Dylan's smile grew, if at all possible, but he didn't respond. Alessia relaxed in his embrace, pressing her face against his chest. It was a moment of bliss, one that she wished would last for the whole of eternity.

CHAPTER FORTY-FOUR

Eternity was only desired when you were in an oblivious bliss, which is what Alessia Trent was tangled up in.

Whilst she danced with Dylan, I was left trapped in Matt's arms. I was glad that Alessia could find joy in the same way that I often could—through Dylan, though I was not glad to be wrapped in a predator's embrace.

But Alessia didn't know this, and she didn't want to as she melted into Dylan's wondrous hazel eyes. Dylan held onto her tightly, guiding her through the dance and pulling her away from people that tripped into her. She felt safe—as I often did with Dylan.

"You look nice," Dylan said, making Alessia flush.

"Just '*nice*'?" She asked, watching Dylan laugh. She couldn't help but wonder if Dylan had paid me a better compliment, and she was right. And he didn't just do it once; he showered me with varying compliments all night.

"Well," Alessia said, admiring Dylan in a suit, "you look nice, too." It was now Dylan's time to flush. He averted her eyes, feeling awkward in his humble and modest way. He was used to dishing out the compliments, but not getting them back.

When the song changed, it was to yet another slow song, and Alessia felt her heart rejoice. She really liked Dylan, and she felt like she'd combust if she didn't tell him soon. Yet, she didn't want to. Alessia didn't feel confident enough that Dylan would like her back, not when she knew that his heart belonged to Olivia.

As Dylan spoke, Alessia felt her eyes giving her away; they were entranced, focusing on his eyes and lips. Alessia thought that maybe Dylan knew by now how she felt, especially as they had shared more than just one kiss. And—*oh*—they were good kisses. Alessia could almost remember how Dylan's lips felt on hers, and probably would have if she wasn't shoved to the side moments later.

Dylan was being greeted by many people at that moment, and when the dance started to shift slightly, Alessia watched as Olivia fell back into his arms once more.

Dylan's eyes filled with love, if that were at all possible, and his face brightened. Alessia felt her heart break. She thought that Dylan didn't care about her, and didn't even wait to see that he actually did as his eyes began to glance around the room, desperately looking for something. He was looking for *her*. But the tears were already spilling; she didn't have enough time to realise this.

She was now being stared at by a nearby table of people who had settled to eat. They shared whispers as they looked at her, and Alessia found herself biting the insides of her cheeks so that the tears wouldn't spill.

As Alessia rushed to the door, hoping for some fresh air, I realised, like most things, Alessia's Prom experience was in no way akin to mine. Despite the minor glitch, in which Matt promised to find me in my bed that night, my Prom night was spectacular. It was a night full of friends, memories, smiles and maybe even tears. But not the sad kind. Not this kind.

Alessia pushed open the clear door, stepping out into the warm evening of July the twelfth. She looked up to the sky, seeing swirling shades of pink and orange. The sunset was probably the only thing she'd want to remember from this night. It shimmered in the glance of her teary eyes, but it would still be something that she hoped would be engrained on her broken mind.

She took deep breaths, trying to mend herself before she would go back into the hall again. Just when she felt her tears dry up and hope return, a figure appeared in front of her.

The person hummed. It was Kiara. Alessia immediately straightened, tensing against the brick wall she was leaning against.

"You actually came," Kiara said, eyes wide as she placed her hands on her hips. "You can't imagine how surprised I am." She continued. Alessia said nothing, holding her breath and waiting for the horrible insult that Kiara was going to throw at her.

Instead, she reached out, fingers lightly touching a tendril of Alessia's hair. "Your hair looks pretty like this," she said, eyes full of wonder. Alessia frowned, watching her.

Kiara dropped the strand. "Why are you here, Alessia? You have no friends, no need to be here. So why?" She asked. Alessia gulped, watching Kiara. "Is it because of Dylan?" She asked.

Alessia had to admit, deep down, that Dylan was a very good reason why she was here tonight.

She swallowed, "I have as much of a right to be here as you do." She said.

Kiara laughed, holding her hands up in mock defence. "Watch the dig, I'm just curious."

Alessia watched her, waiting for her big move. But it never came. Alessia frowned, "Why aren't you hurting me? Or insulting me?" She asked accusingly.

Kiara cocked her head to the side, seemingly startled. "Do you want me to?"

Alessia shook her head, "Not particularly, but it's what you always do anyway."

Kiara smiled, nodding. "True, but maybe I'm trying to be nicer now," Alessia could hardly believe that, so waited for another motive. "I want to start college with a clean slate, that means clearing up...mess here first, so, I'd like to tell you that I'm sorry."

Alessia's eyes widened, her mouth agape. "Really?" She asked, at a loss for words.

Kiara nodded, smiling. "But first, I want to let it all out; give you an honest rundown of everything I think about you." Alessia frowned but didn't question it.

"You have pretty features," Kiara began, eyes on Alessia's face, "but thrown together in the way that they have been, they look haphazard. A mess." Alessia's smile fell. *Was this Kiara's big move?* "You're slim, which I guess is good, but you're just bones. No guy is ever going to like you because you're simply just a seventeen year old stuck in a ten-year old's body."

Kiara shrugged, reaching out to twirl some of Alessia's hair around her index finger. Alessia wanted to break away and smack her hand away from her face, but she didn't know what she would do after that. "Though maybe that's part of the reason that Dylan doesn't like you—Olivia is, after all, way prettier than you. And not to mention her personality; she's loving, friendly and caring. You're just...well, you're stupid, unpopular and...kind of one of those people that you never want on your team in PE because you'll just let us down."

Alessia could feel tears pricking at her eyes, but she wouldn't let them spill. She wouldn't show weakness under Kiara's harsh stare.

"Is that what your parents think about you? You're a disappointment? Because I can see it. And now you're all getting evicted; back off to troll land you go." Kiara leaned in, whispering, "no one as poor and as worthless as you should have ever been allowed to buy a gown so pretty anyway. You make the dress look ugly."

Prom went on behind them. No one noticed them. No one cared. That was the way that Alessia's life seemed to work.

"So," Kiara said, leaning backwards, "I am sorry, truly sorry that this," she spat, gesturing to Alessia's face and her body, "is what you've got to deal with for the rest of your lonely, lonely life." Suddenly, Kiara clapped her hands together, startling Alessia. "Well, that's it, I just thought I'd give you one last message—something to remember me by. Now, how about a picture? I think a picture would be great."

Kiara whipped her phone out suddenly, positioning herself against Alessia and pulling her roughly into the frame of the picture. Then she snapped it, let go of Alessia and grinned down at the end product.

"Beautiful," Kiara commented, "well, me, not you," she slipped her phone back into her clutch, frowning when she saw Alessia's face. "Oh," she said, placing her finger under Alessia's chin and raising it, "chin up, buttercup, you've still got two hours left to say the rest of your goodbyes; you can't ruin your makeup yet! Especially not when it makes you look a mere five percent better than your usual ten."

With that, Kiara shoved Alessia back into the wall before sauntering away.

Alessia clutched onto her chest, suddenly inhaling and exhaling way too fast for her to be able to catch up. She felt empty inside, as though Kiara had just torn away all that was possibly left inside of her and shattered it.

Alessia felt shattered.

And so did I.

I had never known Kiara to any more than loving, and protective of her friends; I could be nothing but ashamed of her at this moment. It was as if she was a devil dressed as an angel. Sure, I had seen Kiara fight my side of the battle, and *always* win. She would do anything for my happiness, but perhaps that was her undoing—and Alessia's.

Kiara could pretend that she was her own person all she liked, but it was just so obvious now how she wasn't. She was easily influenced by many things, and would drop everything for me anytime. Johnny also has this weird unspoken rule over her; she likes him, *a lot*, and she'd do anything for his approval. Even bully a girl to no ends. She'd do anything for me too, but I'd never ask this of her.

After that, Alessia dragged herself back inside, but to the cloakroom and not to the dance floor. She swapped her heels for trainers, pulled up her dress, and tucked herself into her coat.

Just before she left, she glanced into the hall once more. A slow dance was playing, and she didn't have to look for long before she saw Dylan and me dancing. When Dylan brushed a kiss against my—Olivia's—cheek, Alessia knew she was done here.

And not just done here, but done *everywhere*, at every time in every possible way.

For Alessia, enough was enough.

CHAPTER FORTY-FIVE

Alessia spent her summer break alone. Her only company was her father, who entertained himself more than he did her. Waking up with a start, she realised that she had been hailed to the floor, a regular occurrence throughout the heat and rest of the summer holidays.

She rose to her feet, walking over to her mirror to see how bad the damage was. And then she broke down into tears, wrapping her arms around her body—it was her routine healing process.

It was then that I took control, wiping her tears away and refraining from yelling in annoyance like I had done for the past six days now. I walked into her bathroom, nursed her cuts and scratches, before concluding that Alessia wouldn't need an ice-bag.

Leaning over her sink, I soon became bored. As Olivia Clark, my summer had been full of days out, nights out, and happiness and laughter. My family had gone on a week-long holiday before we were joined by Dylan's family for another week. It wasn't the first time that Dylan and I had been away with each other, but it was certainly the longest and coolest.

Becoming restless, I groaned, checking for signs of her father before leaving the room. I turned to the right, which led to a door that seemed untouched. I frowned, quickly becoming intrigued.

I slowly moved down the hall, eyes on the cream coloured door. When I reached it, I turned the brass door handle carefully, pushing the door open with just as much discretion. Once the door was open, I was greeted by a deep crimson carpet, pale pink walls, the same deep red on the bed, and beautifully varnished furniture. I couldn't understand it. I could tell that Alessia, nor her dad, visited this room often, but it still seemed like a shrine of sorts. Perhaps it was better likened to a sepulchre.

I wandered in curiously, spotting a picture frame on the side of the vanity. I picked up the picture, seeing three faces in the frame. One was Alessia's father, though as if from another life—another time. He was younger, a gleam in his eyes that was dead and gone now. He almost looked unrecognisable. In the middle, was a young girl, who looked vaguely like Alessia, and I could only assume that it was her as a young girl. Again, the joy in her eyes and face was unrecognisable, and I felt as though they'd both been through a time machine. Then there was a third face. I didn't recognise the woman, but as I stared at her, emotions stirred up within Alessia. It was her mum.

Alessia looked a lot like her mum, whose eyes were a brilliant emerald, nose a button and hair disarray in a curly mess. The only trait of her father's that I could see in Alessia was his dark hair and maybe his emptiness too.

Her Life

It could only be assumed that Alessia's mother had passed away, or perhaps left. It's probably the reason that Alessia and her father changed, becoming creatures with little happiness.

I set the frame down, gazing around the room again. There was a small table positioned on each side of the bed, one with a small framed picture of Alessia's dad, and another with a picture of her mum.

I choked up then, feeling Alessia's strong sense of loss and emotional emptiness. There was a void in Alessia's heart where her parents used to be, and she now attempted to fill it with Dylan.

I backed out of the room hastily, shutting the door before turning around and walking back to Alessia's room, where I shut and locked the door behind me.

Alessia's life was much more deserted than I had realised, and I soon let go of my control so that she could deal with it. But instead of shedding a few tears and then brushing it all under the rug, Alessia slipped on her trainers, before grabbing a bag and leaving.

She made her way to the bus stop with a brisk pace, hailing the bus that took the route to my house. I watched curiously. She had been doing this a lot lately, but I had yet to learn why.

Alessia got off the bus at the stop adjacent to my house, as usual, and walked down the road that my house stood on. She ducked down behind a bush, the typical position that she took when she watched and waited outside of my house.

At first, I thought it was just to keep tabs on Dylan, but Dylan wasn't always at my house, and surely she'd go to his if she was that obsessed. But no, she would sit here, sometimes for hours, just watching my house and waiting for me to suddenly appear.

And I did. Olivia Clark exited the house, chatting on the phone with someone. Alessia's eyes followed Olivia down the street before she began to pursue her. She lurked behind a wall as Olivia spoke on the phone, saying something about a park, and then about the bowling alley.

It was just a casual conversation, but Alessia was listening to her as if it were a top-secret conference. When a bus pulled up, Olivia's voice ceased, and that was when Alessia concluded her daily dose of Olivia.

It was a peculiar routine, and she did it almost every day. After crossing the road, Alessia jumped on the first bus that came and sat at the back, where she watched Snapchat and Instagram stories of the people who went to our school. It seemed that I wasn't the only one that she was keeping track of these days.

On the bus, Alessia thought back to Prom. It was something I often did, too. It wasn't a perfect night—my eye-makeup smudged halfway through, Matt sexually assaulted me again, and I sprained my ankle right at the very end—but it was very, very close. It was an enchanting memory, one I think I fixed in my brain to make it glisten and glitter more than it would've done before.

To Alessia, it was a nice way of decorating hell. It was like everything and everyone else she had known—negativity hidden behind a facade. She felt tears spring to her eyes when she recalled what Kiara had said to her that evening. It was all stuff that she had heard before, though maybe not said in person, or all at once with as much calm lustre as Kiara had delivered it with. It was like a lullaby but delivered from the tongue of a snake.

Alessia got off the bus soon enough, walking through the downpour with her head down. She surprised me when she didn't take the route to her house, but instead crossed the road and headed into the corner shop. Nells' corner shop.

Upon entering, she noticed that Nells was busy serving customers. She also recognised that Nells probably wouldn't expect to see her on a Saturday and so wouldn't greet her. Whilst Nells was occupied, Alessia busied herself by uselessly looking around the shop.

After roaming around the shop aimlessly for ten minutes, she noticed that Nells' line was down to just one person, and promptly picked up a random bar of chocolate. When she got to the front of the line, Nells was a little shocked. Alessia had anticipated this and watched as Nells stared at her with wide eyes. A grin soon grew on her face, yet Alessia could feel nothing but sadness, emptiness. Nells was a light in a very, very dark, and never-ending, tunnel for Alessia. But she almost just...wasn't enough.

"Lessie!" Nells exclaimed, sounding delighted, "It's so good to see you!" Alessia beamed at the older woman, handing her the bar of chocolate. "How are you?" She asked, "You got your grades back? What college are you going to? What will you study?" Nells' rambling made Alessia laugh as she fished around in her pocket for spare change for the chocolate.

"I'm...okay. My grades weren't too bad, but definitely not stellar. College..." Alessia trailed off, suddenly staring off into nothingness as if she were attempting to see into the future. She shook her head, brushing it off. "Might study the art of dying," Alessia said, and Nells took it as a joke, laughing loudly.

"You're very funny, Lessie; I'm glad you came by today," she said, taking Alessia's change and entering it into the till.

"Me too," Alessia agreed, smiling sadly. "Oh," she said abruptly, unzipping her bag and sifting through the side pocket, pulling out what felt like card. Nells watched as she produced an envelope, her name inscribed on the front in cursive. "This is for your birthday," Alessia revealed.

Nells' frown relaxed in seconds, her face brightening. "Oh, you didn't have to, Alessia!" She said, before opening it up and thanking the girl.

"But why so early?" Nells then asked, standing the card up beside the till, admiring it.

Alessia swallowed. "I wanted to make sure that you definitely got it." She said, watching as Nell smiled, before walking around to the other side of the countertop. Alessia knew that Nells should be using her walking stick, yet that she was too stubborn to, and watched as she hobbled over to her. And then Alessia was submerged in the biggest hug of her life—at least in a while.

Alessia didn't want to let go, but she knew she had to. She knew that she had to because she wanted to; she had never wanted something so desperately before this. She wanted to let go.

CHAPTER FORTY-SIX

The next day marked a week and a day until Alessia was supposed to start college. Instead of preparing for college—buying school supplies, researching course opportunities, buying a new bag, new clothes and figuring out how to style her hair for her first day, she was planning something much, much more sinister.

And I think I knew what it was before it happened.

She woke up later than usual and alarmed at that, too. She bolted upright, checking her room, her door and her lock. Her dad had not broken in and beat her in her sleep, but he had hammered a shower rail into the centre of her door. She stared at it, a numbness inside of her that soon exploded with emotion, and then settled down again. She couldn't decide which to be—vacant or overflowing.

She decided not to decide, and headed into her bathroom for a bath; just her usual Sunday morning routine. Once she was clean, she checked that the hallway was clear before running down the stairs and grabbing something quick to eat. She swiped something else, too—a knife.

I think I knew before it happened.

She ate her 'breakfast' whilst scrolling through an untold amount of Instagram accounts. She started with Katy, Lizzie and Matt, before working her way through Mollie and Lucas. Then she stumbled across Ked's, then onto Johnny, Kiara, Dylan. Finally, she sat and stared at mine, Olivia Clark's. Before long, she got fed up of studying my 'perfect face' and hurled her phone to the ground, fists clenched.

She checked the time—2 pm.

Alessia rose from her chair, throwing her unfinished food into her bin, before untying her dressing gown and letting it fall to the floor. Unexpectedly, she then turned to the mirror, staring at her reflection. She sighed—*what a shame*, she thought.

I think I knew before it happened.

As she pulled on her favourite jeans, she pointed out everything wrong with her appearance, most coinciding with Kiara's speech at Prom.

As she pulled on her favourite top, she wondered why it was that I—Olivia Clark—got everything good in the world. Perfect looks, perfect grades, perfect social life, and...Dylan. Alessia had tried to tell herself over and over again that it wasn't just about Dylan, that her hatred for me was just innate and caused by my actions, not her thoughts.

But then she began to wonder why she was defending herself so much. Maybe it was all her fault. Or maybe the world just works out this way. That's often how Alessia felt; the whole world was pushing against her relentlessly. Like a storm with no shelter. An epidemic illness with no cure. Like her life with no end.

I think I knew before it happened.

Time passed, and with every tick of Alessia's clock, a new thought processed. A new idea, a new method, a new thing to say. After thousands of ticks, Alessia sprang up from her bed and pulled out her favourite dark leather boots. She slipped on a black, thin jacket over her t-shirt; the temperatures were still high despite the dripping rain.

She didn't take anything else with her but unfolded the note that she had been working on all of last night, leaving it on her bedside table. Alessia then unlocked her door, checking for her dad before racing down the stairs when she assumed that the coast was clear.

She left her house in a hurry, but when she was finally outside, she froze. A new eviction notice had made it onto her front door; their stay had been extended, yet Alessia and her father would still be evicted in no less than two weeks unless they willingly left. She read the notice with a lump in her throat before reaching out and tracing the plated numbers on her door. They were once a gleaming brass against the glowing crimson of the door. Now, the brass was weathered and tarnished, and the red paint was chipped and covered with the same coat of grime. Untouched, unloved.

She sighed, trying to swallow away her tears as she locked her front door, sealing everything away. She then turned around on her gravel driveway, treading down the hill and onto the pavement.

As she walked, several thoughts darted into her mind all at once. She recollected memories of her mum and happy moments with her dad. The kaleidoscope of colourful memories soon broke away, and the realism of her nightmares returned. Her mum was gone, and her dad was unloving. She then thought about school; it provoked thoughts about Olivia Clark, and the boy that Alessia loved, Dylan.

It was a beautiful parade of memories, one that was shadowed by pain; cracking very gradually at the edges.

Reaching the bus stop, Alessia took a deep breath, closing her eyes and asserting herself. When the bus arrived, she boarded it with a feeling of dizziness, one that did not cease when she sat down—it got *worse*.

She didn't doubt herself; she was just overwhelmed with the number of thoughts and memories that her mind could conjure up all at once. Each was carefully selected, for either its pain or its pleasure, and shown in excellent saturation and light intensity.

As the bus drew close to the stop closest before my house and she pressed the bell, I think I knew before it happened.

She stepped off the bus, tucking her hair into her jacket before pulling up the hood, shadowing her face and her intentions. She walked breezily, as though she were completely fine. In truth, she was screaming inside.

That was when Alessia Trent spotted me—spotted Olivia Clark. Her eyes followed Olivia stonily as she trudged into the park, hands stuffed into her pockets as she sighed. Alessia frowned; what could have possibly upset Olivia? Was her hair not perfect enough? Was it that Dylan hadn't texted back after one second? Or had her mum not bought her twenty perfumes in time for college?

Just as I hadn't known anything about Alessia Trent and her life, Alessia was also oblivious to mine. She thought I was a flawless person with a flawless life. She was wrong, of course; the assumption was ludicrous.

Alessia followed me, ducking behind the pine trees, watching as I plonked down hopelessly onto a park bench. It was sheltered, and so not wet, but I don't think I would've cared if it was.

She watched as puffs of air escaped my lips, as though I were breathing heavily or angrily. At times, Alessia saw as I brushed at my face, and she wondered if I was crying, though didn't care if I actually was. After a while of sitting still and completely frozen, Alessia saw as I pulled out my phone. She thought that maybe I was texting Dylan, which only irritated her further.

She was right; I *was* texting Dylan.

Suddenly, a new set of emotions churned up inside of her, and I felt as her motives changed. Shocked, that's when I realised. I think I knew before it happened.

Alessia noted that I appeared to be almost sobbing now, though a soft laugh suddenly escaped me. That laugh annoyed her; it was so bright and full of charisma. Dylan loved it, and Alessia knew that—*that's* what she hated.

I almost couldn't watch anymore, feeling as something was being dredged up within me. But there was something so hauntingly beautiful about it all; these were the memories that had blurred and twisted when I became Alessia; when I had slipped into her life and out of mine. This was the one day that I just couldn't grasp onto, the one with bits and pieces that seemed to flee my hands every time I hooked onto one.

Alessia soon distracted me from these thoughts, shifting her standing position as she watched Olivia also alter her position, rapidly typing on her phone. She observed curiously as I—Olivia—tipped my head up to the sky. Frowning, she did the same, wondering what Olivia was looking for. There it all was again; the clouds covering the moon as if they were sheets of wool, strewn across the light and letting only tiny flickers through.

When Alessia focused back on me again, I was sat with my knees against my chest, a magpie across from me. Strong winds hit her at that moment, shaking the trees and making her wince.

I soon rose, a cloud of air escaping my lips as I walked along the path. Shivering, Alessia walked along with me to get a better view; she didn't want to lose me. That's when a twig snapped under her foot. At first, Alessia didn't care all that much, until another snapped, getting Olivia's attention. She turned quickly, frowning out into the distance. Instead of cowering back, Alessia grew impossibly more furious and impatient.

When Olivia turned, walking again, I realised just how much Alessia wanted to do this. I think I knew before it happened.

Alessia tore away from the trees, running towards Olivia at a speed so unfathomable; it was no wonder when Olivia jumped.

But I—Olivia—paused, peering at Alessia curiously, wondering what was going on. It was then that I just didn't know what to do—did I take my control back and not let the inevitable happen? Or did I-

"Aless-"

But it was too late. Alessia had struck out, fast and with so much power, shoving the knife into my lower chest. The girl in front of me—Olivia Clark, me, a life once lived—let out a strangled sound, eyes draining of life as she frowned at Alessia.

Then the frown fell, and so did her body.

Alessia unflinchingly stared down at the body that rested in front of her feet. She couldn't believe it, she couldn't believe that she had *actually* done it.

She took a deep breath. "This is it," she whispered, "two jarringly beautiful lives-" and then she did something that I had expected, yet hadn't at the same time.

I think I knew before it happened.

She stabbed herself. With the same knife that she had used on Olivia moments before, letting out a similar sound to that of Olivia's as she fell to her knees.

Before ripping out the knife, she whispered, and with tears in her eyes, "-gone."

And then it all went black.

CHAPTER FORTY-SEVEN

White.
 A bright white.
 A white so bright that I felt my retinas burning inside of my eye sockets.
Slowly and carefully, I let my eyes flutter open, though I squeezed them shut again when the harsh light burst in. Frowning, I tried once more, opening them to see nothing but a blurred white sky.

The more I concentrated and waited, the more it cleared and my vision became more focused. I soon realised that I wasn't looking up at a white sky, but a white ceiling. It was then that I started to hear all kinds of things, things I wasn't aware of at my first blink.

Beeping, frantic talking, doors opening and closing, heels clicking against floors—they were all noises that burst in just as suddenly as the white light had.

I titled my head slightly, trying to see what was going on. All I could remember was Alessia Trent. The darkness, the pain, the emptiness—the knife, and my death, and her death.

I was awake. Had that been a dream? I felt different; perhaps it was because I knew that this wasn't Alessia's room—especially not with all the commotion.

It was then that I thought about the possibility that I was in a hospital, that maybe Alessia was found, and here I am, *alive*. Or...maybe this was the afterlife.

All ideas were halted when I heard one singular word—a name.

"Olivia?"

I frowned—*Olivia*. It was a name I knew, and a name I knew well. I had once worn it and shouldered the weight of it, but then it all changed—then I became Alessia. I was Alessia and I had her life.

"Olivia, honey," I frowned, attempting to locate the voice. It was so distinctively familiar, and I was instinctively drawn to it. After a while of hopelessly looking, a face ghosted into my vision. I furrowed my eyebrows, trying to concentrate and make the image clearer.

When I did, it *was* someone familiar to me. She was my mum. She was Olivia Clark's mum.

In a moment of vulnerability, one that I knew would cause a massive disaster, I whispered, "mum?"

She was still Olivia Clark's mum, but I wasn't Olivia Clark, and so that word shouldn't have fallen from my lips.

But she did not look angry; she seemed relieved, tears spilling a thousand by a thousand. "Oh, honey," she said, brushing my hair back away from my face before tracing the lines of my cheekbones. "You're okay," she whispered.

I frowned. "What...what's going on?" I asked her, glancing around again, expecting to see the real Olivia Clark standing around somewhere.

But there it was—an emptiness of a different kind. I anticipated that I'd see Olivia Clark standing on the opposite side of my bed, with those ridiculous bows braided through her hair, that annoying laugh reverberating off the walls, and the too-happy gleam behind her eyes. But no, there was nothing.

It was like I hit a brick wall suddenly; I was expecting to hear things, *feel* things that just weren't there.

"You...you were injured, and you've been in a coma for just over a month. But you're here now, you're okay now."

I was extremely confused at that moment. A coma? The concept was absurd. Whilst I was trying to figure out what happened to Alessia and her hatred for me, Olivia Clark's mum was making up some facade about a coma.

"*What?*" I asked, turning to look up at her again.

"A coma, Olivia," she said, seeming to sympathise with my confusion, "do you remember what happened to you?" She asked carefully, glancing up at someone behind me. I turned to see a doctor stood beside a wall, holding a clipboard.

I pulled a face. "The fact that I got stabbed by Alessia Trent and now I'm living her life?"

That was the first time that I had pulled it all together like that.

My mum frowned. "You're not Alessia, honey, you're Olivia."

I froze. *What?*

"No, I'm not. I haven't been for seven months now," I glanced between my mum and the doctor, needing to see them confirm this; they didn't, they just exchanged concerned looks. "It's...it's September, right? That what it was yesterday, or...earlier. That's what it was when I-when Alessia stabbed Olivia, and then...herself."

I sounded confused—very, *very* confused. But I knew *exactly* what I was talking about. It was all true, right? It had all happened. I *know* it had.

The doctor suddenly spoke up, "Olivia, sometimes when people are in comas they dream...much like you would in normal sleep, just more extensive and perhaps more real." She explained.

I frowned between the pair of them. "You're wrong. It wasn't a dream; it was *real*. It was *all* real—the pain, the loneliness and the fear. You can't tell me that wasn't real," I sounded insane, "I'm Alessia Trent. I was Olivia Clark, now I'm Alessia Trent..." I broke off horribly, as though I had run out of breath, or ways to tell them that I was absolutely and completely right.

I *knew* that I was.

The doctor shook her head, "You're Olivia Clark, not Alessia Trent."

I shook my head, glancing between the doctor and Olivia's mum. "I don't believe you," I said, quickly growing agitated as I tried to push myself up on the bed.

"No, you need to be careful, Olivia," Olivia's mum said, ushering me back down.

"I want to see. I want you to show me."

The doctor and Olivia's mum traded troubled glances before they both agreed to walk me to the bathroom's mirror. My legs felt like they weren't even there, my feet touching on nothing. I was weak, but I couldn't understand why; I was fine just yesterday...or, whenever that last was.

When we got to the bathroom, I couldn't wait to get to the mirror and prove them wrong. But when I saw the girl staring back at me, I choked.

The loss of Alessia's hatred for Olivia suddenly made sense. I wasn't Alessia Trent anymore.

I was...I was Olivia Clark.

"Can I have a moment, please?" I asked.

My mum tightened her grip on my left arm, "I don't think that's a good idea, honey; you can barely stand as it is."

I shook my head. "I'll be fine," I promised her, breaking away from the doctors hold, "look, I'll just hold onto the sink." I did so, using my non-existent arm strength to keep me upright.

The doctor convinced my mum that a few moments alone would be fine, and then I suddenly *was* alone.

I stared into the mirror, at the eyes that stared at me back. It couldn't be real. Seven months—for seven months I have seen those bright emerald orbs. Now they were brown. And my hair, it was definitely dishevelled, but it was not curly. Then there was everything else—my nose, my lips, my body.

I am Olivia Clark.

I slapped my hand over my mouth as a sob almost escaped, my body trembling. I couldn't tell if I was relieved to be back, or at a loss.

I couldn't comprehend it. So, for a month I have been in a coma, dreaming about Alessia's life for seven months?

It was *impossible,* it can't have just been a dream; everything was so real. The...dream allowed me to see everything about Alessia's life; now I was just back here. I didn't understand it, and I had a sudden sense that I never would.

A knock to the door alarmed me, and I turned to see my worried mum peeking through the crack of the door.

I laughed, "Isn't this meant to be a moment to myself?" I asked, trying to put a brighter mood to play, though I was breaking inside.

She smiled sadly, "I couldn't help it; I was so worried, Olivia, but now you're here, now you're awake."

I beamed, though couldn't prevent the tears that were falling. "Do you believe me?" I asked and my mum frowned, despite that she probably knew what I was talking about.

She averted her eyes, "I believe that you had some sort of dream and that you think that you lived Alessia's life, but it just isn't possible." She said.

I turned away, feeling my lip tremble. "I swear it, mum, it was real, and I *know* it was."

I watched in the reflection of the mirror as she enveloped me from behind, running her fingers through my hair.

"I know," she whispered, "I know."

My mum could say nothing else—what else *could* she say? It can't be proven, and we both knew that.

I turned around, allowing her to pull me into her arms as I sobbed, remembering how desperately I had wanted this moment in those seven months.

Now, when I looked in the mirror, *I* looked back. I'm Olivia Clark.

CHAPTER FORTY-EIGHT

I had my first physiotherapy appointment later that day, and despite my mum's concerns, it seemed as though it may only take me a short while to get back up and running again. After all, the stab wound was to my chest, meaning that my limbs were fine; it just hurt to stretch sometimes.

I was back in my bed now, per my mum's instruction, and she promised me that my dinner would be coming soon.

"And so there were loads of letters, flowers, comments on your friends' Instagram for you. You should have seen them all, Olivia." My mum laughed, trying to catch me up on what I had missed.

In reality, I had only missed a month, which made it October 25th. But in my head, I had lost over half a year. I felt so out of tune and out of practice; it was as though I was discovering how to be myself again.

"Can't I still see them now?" I asked her, tuning back into whatever she was rambling on about at that moment.

She grimaced, pursing her lips, "I guess, just not yet, Livvy."

I sighed into my cushions—which were not as comfy as they sound. Suddenly, someone rapped at the door.

"*Ah*," my mum announced, "that must be your food." I frowned, glancing between my mum and the door.

She stood up, opening the door and saying, "Shaun." After a polite nod of her head, she smiled over at me before slipping out of the door. I frowned after her until I spotted who was at the door. *My dad.*

My dad closed the door behind him as I jolted upwards, exclaiming, "Dad!"

He laughed, setting a tray down on the table over my bed before pressing a kiss to my forehead. "Hi, Greeny." Greeny was nothing but a mocking nickname; something from my childhood that my dad liked to make fun of me for.

I beamed up at him as he took his seat, passing me some cutlery. I pushed myself up slightly before digging in.

"Aren't you going to eat something?" I asked him, halfway through my lasagne.

He smiled, shaking his head, "I already ate, Liv."

I nodded, continuing to eat, though frowned over at my dad as he fell into silence.

I groaned. "You've got that same look," I complained, wiping at my mouth with a napkin.

He raised an eyebrow, "What look?"

"The one that mum keeps giving me. The one that's as if her daughter has just turned to gold dust and will earn her millions." I described, making my dad laugh.

"Well, that would be nice too," After I threw him a sharp look, he continued, "you almost *died*, Olivia, I think we get the right to be a little emotional." He explained.

It was then my turn to fall quiet. "Mum said that there was loads of support for me whilst I was in the coma—what were you guys doing whilst I was...asleep?"

He smiled sorrowfully, "Crying, mostly," the look behind his eyes broke me. I realised then how deep the bags beneath his eyes were, and how much more stubble he had on his face than I had realised when I had first seen him. "We were so worried, Liv, so, *so* worried,"

I smiled, tears in my eyes, "I'm here now," I whispered, making him smile too.

He laughed, "Yes, yes you are. We were all practically dancing when we found out; you don't understand, Liv." I mirrored his grin, though soon wavered.

"*All*? I asked, "I presumed that it would only be you and mum?"

My dad furrowed his eyebrows, shaking his head, "Many people came to visit you, Olivia— your friends, your aunts and uncles, *even* Nanny Greta." I giggled. Nanny Greta was...*something*—out of her wits, really.

"My friends?" I echoed, watching my dad smile in response.

"Yes," he confirmed, "but there was one...someone who felt the need to stay here even overnight at times. He never left, Olivia."

I stared, swallowing, "What?" I asked almost inaudibly. I think I knew who he was talking about, what he was hinting at, before he even told me.

My dad nodded, "Yes, Dylan was almost more worried than *we* were at times."

My heart leapt, "Dylan..?" I had to make sure.

"Yes," he replied, grinning, "did you doubt that he would be here?"

I glanced away, speechless for a few seconds. "Is he still here?" I murmured, looking back up.

My dad nodded, "Of course, he rarely left at all."

I stared down at my food, though was suddenly miles away, thinking about Dylan.

"Anyway," My dad announced, standing up, "you finish your dinner, Greeny, then maybe open those presents before the nurses throw them away," I frowned over at him, though didn't have a chance to respond before he ruffled my hair and left.

When the door opened again, I was staring at the pile of letters and presents beside me, with an array of differently coloured balloons hovering below the ceiling.

"Ah," Someone said, "your presents," I turned to see my mum sitting beside me. "Do you want to open them? There should be one from Dylan somewhere..." she said, rifling through them and frowning when she couldn't find what she was searching for.

"Mum?"

"Yes, darling," She replied absentmindedly, still sifting through the various boxes and bags.

"Is Dylan here right now?" I asked. She suddenly stopped moving. "That's what dad said—is it true?"

She sighed, "Your dad shouldn't have told you that." She said, turning around.

"Why?" I frowned, "there's nothing wrong with him being here...with me seeing him."

"I know," My mum replied quickly, taking her seat beside me as she thought about what to say next, "I just think that maybe it's something we can tackle later; it's getting late now."

"But I want to see him, mum, I want to see Dylan and I want him to stop worrying about me," I said, hearing the potent sound of urgency in my voice.

My mum smiled sadly, just as my dad had earlier, "I don't think he'll ever stop worrying about you, Olivia."

I sighed, playing with my lasagne as I thought. I took a few bites before settling the cutlery back down. "*Please*, mum?" I asked, trying again, "there's no real reason why I can't, you're just worrying again."

My mum stared at my unwavering face for a few minutes before groaning. "*Fine*," she said, "but you should probably brush your hair first, and put on this cardigan on; it's cold out in the corridor. Did you wash earlier when I left you?"

I rolled my eyes at her overpowering concern. "Yes, mum, and if you want me to brush my hair then I'll need a brush."

Hair immaculate, cardigan wrapped around me and slippers on, I was ready to go. My mum walked with me, and she tapped my shoulder when she noticed him. I followed her gaze down a corridor, where Dylan was pacing, clearly talking on the phone with someone. We waited for Dylan to end the call, and then I silently persuaded my mum to leave. Once she was gone, I took several deep breaths before gingerly rounding the corner.

Dylan was not facing me, and he couldn't hear my footsteps. Seeing him again was almost like a dream, a vision; it was too unbelievable. I still couldn't fathom that I was Olivia Clark again—or *alive*, for that matter.

His hair was dishevelled, and I could see faint under-eye bags from where I stood. His outfit was admittedly not the best piece that he's drawn together, but despite it all, he was gorgeous—as Dylan had always been.

Getting closer, I told myself to say his name but suddenly forgot how to. Swallowing and asserting myself, I allowed my lips to move.

"Dylan?"

He looked up at those two syllables, eyes frantically scanning for something—he was looking for *me*.

When he saw me, his face glowed, and his eyes glimmered under the light. Tears. *He had tears in his eyes.*

"*Olivia.*" He responded, suddenly breathless. I continued to walk over to him, though too slowly to be moving at all.

As I moved, I thought about what I wanted to do, and what I wanted to say. Looking at him now, just as I had concluded through Alessia's eyes, it was so clear. Dylan likes me. He *really* likes me.

With that in mind, I didn't need to plan what to do next; I just *knew*. Reaching him, I placed my palms to either side of his face, checking for any signs of rejection on his face before I pressed my lips to his.

Slowly, but surely, his hands came up to my face too, fingers knotting into my hair as he drew me in closer.

It began cautiously, as though I was testing him—but when he kissed back, I could feel it. I could taste his desperation and love as much as I think he could taste mine.

Kissing Dylan was much alike to simply *being* with Dylan—but intensified. I felt safe, comfortable and ignited all at once. Pulling away, I saw that he felt a similar way.

He pressed his forehead against mine, holding it there with his fingers still buried in my hair.

"I've wanted to do that for ages," he whispered.

I smiled, "Why didn't you?" I asked, whispering too.

"I was so scared, Olivia. I thought maybe you wouldn't feel the same, that it would ruin our friendship." He said, suddenly exposing himself and ripping off the pretence.

My smile widened. "I *do* feel the same."

He sighed into me, pulling away from my forehead but then drawing me into a hug. I melted into him, savouring his embrace after so long.

"I missed you so much," he murmured, tightening his hold on me.

I felt as tears spilt from my eyes, and felt a similar wetness against my neck; Dylan was crying too.

"I missed you too," I whispered in return. It was then my turn to pull away, but his to kiss me.

And he did—he did kiss me. And it was everything I never knew I had wanted.

Until now.

CHAPTER FORTY-NINE

It was later that day that I began to hear whispers of Alessia. I was sleeping or, supposed to be; the doctor and my parents didn't suspect a thing. At first, they were talking about how pleased they were with my progress, but now they were talking about Alessia. I ached to ask questions, but I didn't want to give myself away.

Dylan had returned home after I had pestered him to get some sleep as I did so too, but he warned me that he'd probably be back. I felt light and warm just thinking about him now.

"You're sure? There's no chance?" My mum asked.

Confused, I focused more. "Definitely. There's no way we can take this any further without the suspect herself."

I shot up, eyes wide, "What's wrong with Alessia?" I asked frantically, searching my parents' wide-eyes.

The doctor stepped forward. "It's none of your concern right now; we're just focusing on you-"

"But I'm absolutely fine," I argued, "and Alessia...she stabbed herself right after; she's here too, isn't she?" My parents exchanged looks. "I knew she would be. I want to see her."

My mum sat beside me tentatively, placing a hand on my shoulder after brushing back my hair. "I don't think that's a good idea, Olivia, this girl tried to murder you."

"You still don't get it, do you?" I asked, raising my voice and making her flinch.

It was time for my dad to finally speak up. "Okay, Olivia, lower-"

"*None* of you get it. That girl was in endless amounts of pain! She was lonely and empty and hurting, really hurting. If you could only understa-"

"But she still attempted to kill you, Olivia!" My dad yelled, and I found myself flinching, just as my mum had done moments before.

Asserting myself, I quietly said, though loud enough for them to all hear. "I still want to see her."

At my persistence, the three were thrown into a quarrel, and I thought that perhaps they were all arguing the same thing. Losing hope, I slumped backwards.

"Olivia," my mum said, placing her hand over mine, "we've decided that you can have a few minutes with her," she said, making me shoot up once more, "she's not dangerous, not as weak as she is, but, Olivia..."

I swallowed, glancing between the three of them as I contemplated what my mum was trying to tell me.

"She isn't as good of a shape as you, Greeny." My dad said, picking up where my mum left off.

"Is she going to die?" I asked, voice shaking. In fact, my entire body was shaking.

"There's little we can do at this point." The doctor said, face unreadable. I guess she had perfected the look.

I looked away, feeling tears spring to my eyes. It wasn't fair. I had come out unscathed, yet Alessia loses her life. It wasn't fair, not at all.

"But, darling, she can still hear you now, but...we should be quick." I tried to stop the tears, but when I turned to nod at my mum, they were still free-falling.

My mum helped me out of my bed, and the doctor guided us all to Alessia's room. When I opened the door, my mum tried to follow me, but my dad placed a hand on her arm, murmuring something to her quietly.

Oblivious to this, and to the door shutting behind me, I walked into the room, staring at the bed.

It was the most surreal thing, to see Alessia Trent when I am not her; when I am not living her life.

I think I gasped; both at the mere sight of her and by how sick and exposed to wires she really looked.

I sat in the chair beside her bed, which looked untouched, and simply stared at her for a few moments. If I closed my eyes, I would be in her body again, and when I opened them, I'd be alive, Olivia Clark trapped inside Alessia Trent's body, but then she would be alive.

But would that then mean that I wouldn't be? I couldn't tell; the world works out in mysterious ways.

I cleared my throat. "Hi, Alessia, it's Olivia," nothing happened, as expected, so I took a moment to collect my thoughts. "You don't understand how, but I think I've walked in your shoes, Alessia Trent, and now I understand."

I sighed, closing my eyes, feeling the tears drying around them now, "I understand why you did what you did, and how you felt, and that...and that you liked Dylan—a lot. I was oblivious to all of it, Alessia. I didn't see your pain, and that I was perhaps a cause of it."

I opened my eyes, suddenly dazed, suddenly seeing intense flashbacks. It was as if I knew her by heart. "I've seen it all now, Alessia. You're a fighter, I promise you. But there was nothing you could do; you needed help, love and happiness. You could access none." I shook my head, feeling the tears. "But I could've helped you, Alessia, I could've and I-" I paused to let out an ugly sob.

Collecting myself, I wiped away my tears with my sleeve. "I didn't do anything. I watched as your whole world fell apart time and time again, not noticing the cracks or the fragments as they fell."

Cautiously, I reached out and clasped onto Alessia's hand. "I was a passerby, watching, not acting. I did nothing. But that was the problem. I'm not sure how much help I would've been, but you'd at least have one moment of bliss."

I shook my head. "I'm sorry," I said, wiping my tears away again once more, "what's done is done," my voice suddenly fell to a whisper, "I remember everything that they said to you, and none of it's true, Alessia, you're incredibly beautiful and smart and deserving of so, so much more."

I stared at her face, trying to remember the details of her face, matching them up to my time in her body, in her life.

"I know it's strange, but I've walked in your shoes, I've been in your life," I whispered, "I hope you find peace somewhere that isn't here-"

And then she flat-lined.

Her hand was still warm, but I dropped it suddenly, feeling as mine turned to ice. I stared at her, mouth agape.

I had seen this coming, but I almost couldn't believe that it was true. She was still there; she was still in front of me. But she was dead.

Alessia Trent is dead.

"Olivia," I jumped when someone crept up behind me, "we should go now," it was my mum, and she placed a hand on my shoulder.

I allowed her to guide me out of the room, not taking notice of anyone who awaited me outside.

Stepping out of the room, across the threshold between Alessia and myself, I suddenly burst into tears.

People were enveloping me in seconds, talking to me, asking questions. But I didn't know what to say; I didn't have anything to say.

Everything I had said was true. Alessia didn't deserve this—she just needed someone to understand and someone to care, and by the time *I* did, it was too late. She was already gone. She had already fallen and she was about to land. And she just did.

I should've seen it; we *all* should've seen it. I ignored every sign when I was in school—Alessia fearing me and my friends, Alessia running through school looking as though she was about to burst into tears, Alessia coming into registration with faint bruise marks on her face.

There were so many signs. But I just watched, and I did nothing else.

Perhaps that's why Alessia hated me—aside from being 'perfect'—I think she knew that I could see what was slowly happening to her, but I didn't do a thing.

We will never know what she knew or didn't know now. We will never know because she's gone.

CHAPTER FIFTY

I was left alone for the next few days after Alessia died, and didn't really care to identify those who *did* come to talk to me. Soon enough, I had been allowed to go home and had been here for two weeks now. But it just made it all so much worse. This was the place that I had longed to be for seven months—just as I had wanted my parents, my friends and Dylan. But now that I had it all back, knowing that Alessia would have none of those things, it suffocated me. I just didn't know how to explain it to any of them—they never believed that I had lived Alessia's life; I knew it for a fact.

There was someone beside me now, running a hand through my hair and murmuring soothing things to me. It relaxed me but didn't ease my regret or guilt. I was drowning in it.

I broke away from my dark trance as I felt kisses being brushed against my neck, and then I smelt the familiar aftershave. It was Dylan.

"We have to go soon," he whispered. I sighed, leaning back into him. We *would* have to go soon. I had been persistent about a funeral or just a simple memorial for Alessia. My parents had been hard to convince, but they soon realised that I was never going to shut up if they didn't.

Therefore, three weeks after Alessia had died, she was getting a funeral.

My family and I had found the guest list difficult; I had persisted that her dad wouldn't show up; I didn't want him there, but my mum sent a letter anyway. We also managed to find members of Alessia's family that I had never known existed before and sent the details out to them.

Aside from that, I sent one out to both Lucas and Mollie, the two people who had been the most compassionate towards Alessia during school. Dylan and I would also be attending—Dylan could pretend that he was going just to support me, but I knew that he was also upset about Alessia passing. I had caught him crying in my bathroom a few times. When I brought it up to him, he just told me that he was glad that it wasn't me.

Tuning back into the present moment, Dylan was trying to coax me off my bed, which I had been seated on for twenty minutes. I don't know how I got there, but I had finished getting ready long ago.

I rose with him and looked up at him as he held my hands. He pressed a kiss to my cheek, "I'm here," he said.

I let my eyes flutter shut as I savoured the moment. "I know," I whispered in response.

"Olivia!" My mum called to me suddenly, "Are you ready?"

I sighed into Dylan, remembering what he had just said.

Soon enough, Dylan and I were downstairs, watching as my parents rushed around for last bits and pieces—they had been spending an awfully large amount of time together lately.

In the car, I sat in silence, noticing how my mum played my favourite slower beat songs. She probably wanted to relax me, tempt me out of the shadows; it worked to some extent.

As soon as we arrived, my mum hurried in to set everything up, and my dad found the Mass booklets. Once I had one in my hand, I looked down at the front, feeling my heart lurch as I stared at the picture of Alessia.

In memory of
Alessia Trent
28/08/2000 - 10/10/2018

I allowed Dylan to guide me into the church and away from the frosty air, eyes on Alessia's as I walked. Entering the church, I looked up and away from the photo, seeing it blown up and framed in a beautiful rose gold frame. It sat beside a coffin, polished simply with brown varnish and complemented by gold accents.

My dad and Dylan guided me to my seat, right at the front, before asking me a thousand times if I was okay. I never responded, and was soon distracted as more people arrived. I barely recognised any, but I was guessing that the people who sat at the front row on the other side were Alessia's close relatives.

With my head still over my shoulder, I watched as Lucas, suited up with a dark blue tie—Alessia's favourite colour—arrived. When he saw me, he walked straight over to me.

I stood when he was close enough, and took one look at him before pulling him into my arms.

"I know how you felt about her," I whispered to him, feeling his arms circle around my body. "I'm sorry." When he drew back, he nodded and joined the row behind us, closely followed by Mollie, who I smiled at. I knew my parents didn't believe that I had lived as Alessia for a year, but there was a glint in Lucas' eyes that told me he hoped that it was true. We were now closer than he could comprehend.

When I sat back down between my dad and Dylan, Dylan leaned over to ask if I was okay.

I nodded, turning to smile up at him, "Just nervous for my speech." I told him and he squeezed my hand.

The Mass began promptly, starting with my mum shooing my dad over so that she could sit next to me.

Words were said, hymns were sung, and songs were played. Soon enough, it was my time to speak. I rose, feeling my nerves spike. I was a confident public speaker, having done quite a bit in school, but I was suddenly terrified.

I stepped up at to podium, setting my papers down onto the stand before clearing my throat.

"Three weeks ago, we lost a life that could have been saved." I began, before hesitantly glancing up at the crowd. "I don't like to live in regret, but this is something that I know will bring me much guilt; I could have done something, I *know* I could have. Alessia was struggling, and not once did I hold a hand out to her and let her hold it for a few minutes. I just left her out in the cold."

I turned the page, swallowing. "But I don't want to focus on this now, not today. *Today* we will celebrate Alessia and her life." I breathed, taking a prolonged survey of my spectators. "Alessia was a girl of love—she loved few, but loved them all intensely. She was bright, even if she didn't quite believe it herself. *And* she was something I could never be—she was strong and independent. She had a flickering light that she would not allow *anyone* to take, but it was that trait about her that was the strongest."

I rubbed my clammy hands against my dress, closing my eyes for a second and imagining that I was Alessia again. If that were so, she'd still be alive. It wouldn't be too late.

"She walked through fire day in and day out and continued to even if she was scathed and shattered. She was beautiful in every way, even if she didn't think she was—and her death was caused by damage done upon her soul. She's an irreplaceable light, and I won't let her death be in vain. Let her life, her *death*, be a lesson to us all—your words, unspoken or not, your actions, undone or not, *hurt people*. Look after people; try your hardest for them. Give everything you can, and nothing if it's that's all you can give. But *try*. *Please*, let this be the last Alessia Trent that we lose. Thank you."

I withdrew my papers from the stand, folding them up before turning around to Alessia's coffin. I walked up to it, kissed my fingertips before placing them against the wood. It was then that everyone else rose, walking up to her coffin to do similar things—say goodbye, kiss goodbye, or just *cry*. I didn't know what they were doing because I was soon rushing out of the church, bidding Alessia my last farewell before I threw open the doors.

When I was out in the cold November air, I looked up to the sky, perhaps thinking I'd see her there. I was clutching onto my papers as I shivered, as though losing them would break me even more.

"It was a beautiful speech," Someone said abruptly, and I turned to see Dylan beside me. He took off his suit jacket and draped it over my shoulders before pulling me into his side.

We stood there for a few moments, looking around at the venue, watching birds and clouds fly past.

Suddenly, Dylan placed a cold object into my hands. I looked down at them to see that I was holding a white glass object, and soon realised that it was crafted into the shape of an angel.

"It's another guardian angel," Dylan whispered before he placed a kiss against my neck.

It *was* a guardian angel, a little too late, but it was still there.

I forgive her for breaking my guardian angel and, in a dark twist of events, *I* didn't even end up being the one that needed it. I couldn't have helped Alessia when she was most desperate, but having been in her life, I now realise that all she needed was a guardian angel of her own. She just needed a friend, or small conversation, or someone to stand up for her.

It's too late for Alessia; her life is gone. But not for the next person.

I squeezed my eyes shut, encompassing the guardian angel in my palms and bringing it close to my chest.

It's not too late for the next person, for *their* life.

EPILOGUE

I breathed out, my breath showing like puffs of smoke in the cold December air. Shivering, I tugged at my coat, as if the futile action would heat me up twofold.

I reached the bench, sweeping rust-coloured leaves off the surface before sitting down. I laid a single white rose down on the wood beside me, knowing that a random kid was just going to come over later and take it or knock it off. It comforted me, though, so I did it.

I ran my finger over the plague as I let out a shaky breath.

'In memory of
Alessia Trent
28/08/2000 - 10/10/2018'

That's what the plaque read. After persuading the local council that Alessia was not a murderer, but a vulnerable girl who was being attacked in her *own* school, she got her own bench. I felt that she needed something like that, a token from me to say...to say that I'm sorry. It was *brutal* to be targeted in the ways that she was, and by faces so familiar, yet that discarded her so easily.

I closed my eyes. When I did that, I remembered. Having lived her life for seven months, it was easy to see things from inside *her* shoes; it was a beautiful nightmare. My mum had called it that a week after I had returned home and I had continued to call it that ever since. No one believed me—that I had lived as another person for seven months, but been in a coma for only one.

They were right, it *was* absurd. Yet I still believe it, and sometimes, I think my parents do too, and Dylan. He tells me that it's plausible, because of everything I know now, that I couldn't have known before—everything about Dylan and Alessia. He told me he'd believe only what made sense to him, and that's all I could possibly ask for.

I could never quite escape her, too, it's like she never *really* left. Except for seeing her face in most mirrors, I also hear her every now and then. *It's up to you now*, Olivia, she says. That's what she tells me.

My therapist wrote it off as PTSD from being stabbed when I had told her, but I wonder if perhaps it really *is* Alessia. I lived in her life for so long...maybe now she's living in *mine*.

But I didn't want to think like that, I didn't want to restrict my body to simply being a vessel. I *did* want mine and Alessia's story, though, to be a vessel of change. I wanted to show the world that words hurt, that you can't just hurt people and get away with it, that your actions have implications. I also wanted to remind people that just *watching* as someone repeatedly drowns can never be right; everyone must at least try to *help*. That's why Alessia was already gone by the time I realised—she just needed someone to see, to *actually* see.

"*Oh, Alessia*," I said, breathing out as I opened my eyes. "What should I do *now?*"

We were currently campaigning to sue the school for not supporting Alessia, but the case suddenly became tricky when we realised that Alessia had never *actually* asked for help whilst she was there. But still, the bullying was *so* clear, *so* evident—even *teachers* enjoyed mocking her from time to time.

We were also working to set up charities in Alessia's name; trying to raise funds for those affected by bullying or child abuse. It was difficult, but I just really wanted to do it. For Alessia, for *her* life.

We just wanted to raise awareness, to let everyone know Alessia's story. They *had* to know.

I would be attending some interviews once my therapist declared that I was fit for them, and I would use the publicity to spread the message. Our project was called 'Help The People' and was under the 'Alessia Trent Trust'. We just wanted to make a difference—I just wanted to be the difference that I couldn't be for Alessia.

I patted at my dry tears with my coat sleeve, before drawing it in closer to my body and crossing my arms over my chest. Letting my eyes wander, I saw as a group of primary school children played. At first, I enjoyed watching them play their imaginary games until I noticed a boy that had been left out.

I scanned the park for any signs of parents, but there were none, and so I continued to watch the boy with a frown on my face. Soon, another boy launched a ball, and I watched as it soared past me before glancing back to see the lonesome boy running in my direction.

I rose from the bench, trudging over to the kids' playground as the boy searched through the nettles and the bushes for the ball.

"Hey guys," I said, approaching them.

They threw me looks. "We aren't supposed to talk to strangers." A girl said pointedly, crossing her arms over her chest.

I smiled. "You're smart kids, then," I said, making her beam, "but what about being kind? Why can't that other boy join in?" I asked them, gesturing to the boy who was still concealed behind the trees.

A boy, carrying an abundance of sticks, shrugged, "He never does."

"Maybe you should invite him to play; he probably wants to," I suggested, frowning over at the boy who was still searching.

"He doesn't want us to talk to him, can you go now?" The boy who had been holding the sticks said, whilst shoving them into holes in the slide.

"I'll talk to him," I heard a meek voice say, and turned to see a small blonde girl holding a toy plane and, what looked like, a fairy doll.

I grinned at her, "I'm sure he'll thank you for it." I said, before deciding that I had overstayed my welcome.

I turned around to leave, seeing the boy rise to brush his hair back quickly before ducking back down again. As I approached the bench, I saw him rise again.

"Did you find your ball?" I asked him, standing beside the bench. He looked between me and the other kids who continued to play.

He nodded silently.

I smiled, "That's good."

He nodded again, but then furrowed his eyebrows at something besides me. "What's that?" He asked, causing me to turn.

I laughed, picking it up. "It's a white rose."

His frown deepened, inspecting it. "Why not a red one?"

I twiddled it between my index finger and my thumb, being mindful of the thorns. "It's a symbol of remembrance," I told him, gazing down at it. I could almost see Alessia's bright emerald eyes in the petals. *Almost.*

"*Remembrance?*" He asked, struggling with the word slightly, "Did you forget something?" He asked, making me chuckle.

"No," I informed him, suddenly becoming thoughtful as I glanced back over to the children who I had just been talking to. And there she was—the blonde girl holding the plane and the fairy; she was waiting for the boy.

I smiled, holding it out to him, "Why don't you give it to that girl? The blonde one." I proposed, watching him look confused for a few seconds.

"Bethany?" He asked, pondering this before taking it from my hands and peering at it one more. "Sure," he said, making me smile, "but what is she supposed to remember?" He asked.

I shook my head, "No, it means new beginnings too." I told him. He didn't even question it; he just grinned and turned around, running towards the playground.

They exchanged a few words, and then he handed it to her. She beamed at him before seizing him, and I watched peacefully as they hugged.

"I've got the ribbons and medals for tomorrow," A voice said behind me, making me jump slightly. The person placed a palm on my back, and I leaned back into him. "You watching anything interesting?" He asked.

I grinned, watching the boy and girl join in with the games, before turning to face Dylan. I encircled my arms around his neck, making him smile.

I shook my head, "No, but now I am." I kissed him, watching as he laughed when I pulled away.

"Cheesy." He commented, making me roll my eyes. He wrapped his arms around me and pulled me closer, and I let my head rest into the crook of his neck as I watched a flock of bird stream across the sky. They dipped and rose, each following the same precise movement.

Shortly after Dylan had explained that the aforementioned display in the sky was called a murmuration, we began to leave the park, and I started to ponder what life would be like now if Dylan had got here in time in October. If I had left in time; if I hadn't been stabbed.

But that was it, really, *wasn't it?* Alessia was set; Alessia was *done.* She'd thought about it every night, right under my nose. All the warning signs were there; even when I lived her life I still didn't see it.

Looking back now, it was so, *so* obvious. It was just there, blindingly obvious the entire time. But I chose to ignore it, thinking that I could fix Alessia.

Truth is, it's harder to fix things that are broken when half of the pieces are already lost, already scattered. Perhaps if I had tried earlier, the fragmented pieces would still be there. And then maybe *Alessia* would still be here.

But that's not how the world worked out. Alessia *isn't* here. And now I know, I had to live her life to know, that all I needed to do was notice her pain and help her.

All I had to do was *help her.*

All we need to do now is help *them.*

We *need* to help people, whether they're in pain or not, whether they ask for your help or not. We need to be kinder, more compassionate and empathetic.

And we can do it all in the name of Alessia Trent.

All in the name of, and to honour, *Her Life.*

Her Life

Chloe Pile

Hi all,

Firstly, I am sincerely sorry that you had to endure such emotional pain. Alessia will be treasured and remembered both in my created fictional world and in our minds.

But, for more than just 'Alessia Trent'.

I'm not here to scare you, warn you, or threaten you.

There are so many things we can do, and sometimes choosing to do nothing is worse than being the bully, or the problem.

If you're going to be anything when you grow up, be kind.

Let my small and meek story of Olivia, Alessia, and all those that accompanied them, be a display of that.

Now for some explanations.

Starting this story, I really always knew the end.

I am sorry to say that Alessia was always meant to die.

My journey to find inspiration for a new book led to me desperately stumbling across Wattpad. Soon enough, the seed of Her Life was embedded into my head.

I was inspired not only by stories here on Wattpad but by a film featuring my favourite person ever (Zoey Deutch - who is casted in this book as Olivia Clark). This film is Before I Fall.

Before I Fall is a published book by Lauren Oliver about a popular girl who has to live the day she dies over and over again.

She has to change her life in order to escape this cycle.

Now for some other things.

People Help The People by Birdy
The perfect sum-up of the concept and goal of this book.
Such a meaningful song.

Silhouette by Aquilo
Honestly, there is nothing better than this song.
It's the song that always makes me cry, yet I still can't grasp what all the lyrics truly mean (probably because I'm always sobbing).
I'm not going to try to explain it; it's unexplainable.
It's an emotion, not a definition.
You have to feel this song.

And, finally, for now at least, Bird by Billie Marten
This entire song is just Alessia Trent. It just is.
It's heartbreaking.

For a better grip of this story, I would recommend finding the playlist for it on Spotify.
I made it, of course.
You can find it by searching Her Life on Spotify.
It's in alphabetical order; there's no plot-line for it.

I thought about doing it in order of plot but it just didn't seem right for Her Life; *I think it works better as an ongoing, undefined and unspecified piece.*

You can't pick out one definitive song, or moment, it just carries on.

That's all for now.

Thank you to my readers, you are my biggest supporters and I hope the journey of Olivia Clark and Alessia Trent was one that you both enjoyed and can learn from. Remember that this story is fiction, yet the moral is all the same. Look after one another, and know that, although you can never truly be in someone else's shoes, you can still respect them in every way you can.

I would also like to give a quick thank you to my closest friends for all your continuous support on all my works, no matter whether or not you still have the time to read all my crazy and lengthy plotlines. Much love, Chloe and Annarie.

I guess a quick thank you to my other friends would be quite considerate too! Not all of you read my works, but your support, love and humour are invaluable nonetheless.

If you're interested in learning a little about me, I can give you a few quick facts!
1) I'm a Gemini
2) My full name is a grand total of 14 words long
3) This is my first published book!
4) My favourite colour is yellow
5) My favourite number is either 7 or 17

At the present time, you can find more of my works by my username __queenly__ on Wattpad, or by my website: https://moondustonbooks.wixsite.com/website.

I apologise if these details change but I do hope you'll be sticking around.

Thank you again for reading.

Remember to think about Her Life, *and their lives.*
'Help The People'

Goodbye from Alessia.
Goodbye from Olivia.
Finally, goodbye from me.

Thank you and goodbye, Her Life *readers.*
-Chloe

Her Life

Chloe Pile